I0547037

Love Comes Later

Mohanalakshmi Rajakumar

Best Indie Book, Romance, 2013
New Talent Award Finalist, Romance Festival, 2012
Best Novel Finalist, eFestival of Words, 2013

LOVE COMES LATER

ISBN-10: 061591683X
ISBN-13: 978-0-615-91683-5

Cover Design by Marsya Karmila
Photography by Omima Abdulla and Njad Al Misned
Interior Layout/Design by Indie Designz

Love Comes Later is a work of fiction. Names, characters, places and
incidents are products of the author's imagination, or the author has
used them fictitiously.

Other books by Mohanalakshmi Rajakumar. Available for sale on Amazon.com

An Unlikely Goddess

The Dohmestics

From Dunes to Dior

Mommy But Still Me

So, You Want to Sell a Million Copies?

Coloured and Other Stories

Saving Peace

For Hind, Lolwa, Asma, Mariam, Maryah, Nouf, Shefa, Maryam, Noof, Fatima, Hamad, Saad, Mohammed, Tariq and Saleh

A glossary of cultural terms and Arabic phrases
can be found at the end of the text.

Prologue

Abdulla's mind wasn't on Fatima, nor on his uncles or cousins. Not even when he drove through the wrought iron entry gate, oblivious to the sprawl of family cars parked haphazardly in the shared courtyard, did he give them a thought. Despite the holy season, his mind was still hard at work. Mentally he clicked through a final checklist for tomorrow's meetings. *I can squeeze in a few more hours if Fatima is nauseous and sleeps in tomorrow*, he thought, rubbing his chin. Instead of the stubble he had anticipated, his whiskers were turning soft. A trim was yet another thing he didn't have time for these days, though longer beards were out of fashion according to his younger brother Saad, who had been trying to grow one for years. Beard length. Just another change to keep up with.

Change was all around him, Abdulla thought. The cousins getting older, he himself soon to become a father. Abdulla felt the rise of his country's profile most immediately in the ballooning volume of requests by foreign governments for new trade agreements. By the day, it seemed, Qatar's international status was growing, which meant more discussions, more meetings.

He slid the car into a gap in the growing shadow between his father's and grandfather's houses. It would have to serve as a parking space. The Range Rover door clicked shut behind him as he walked briskly toward his father's house, BlackBerry in hand, scrolling through his messages. Only then did the sound of wailing reach him, women in pain or grief, emanating from his Uncle Ahmed's house across the courtyard. He jerked the hands-free device out of his ear and quickened his pace, jogging not toward the *majlis* where the rest of the men were gathering, but into the main living area of Uncle Ahmed's, straight toward those unearthly sounds.

The sight of Aunt Wadha stopped him short. Disheveled, her *shayla* slipping as she howled, she was smacking herself on the forehead. Then came his mother, reaching her arms out to him with a tender, pitying look he hadn't seen since his pet rabbits from the *souq* died. But it was Hessa, his other aunt – Fatima's mother, his own mother-in-law – who sent him into a panic. Ashen-faced, her lips bleeding, she was clutching the evil eye necklace he had bought Fatima on their honeymoon. At the sight of it, the delicate gold cord in Hessa's hands instead of around his wife's neck, Abdulla felt his knees buckle and the BlackBerry slip from his hand.

"What has happened?" he said. He looked from one stricken face to another.

Numbly, he saw his female cousins were there. At the sight of him, the older ones, glamorous Noor and bookish Hind, both now adult women in their own right, whom he hadn't seen in years, jerked their *shaylas* from their shoulders to cover their hair and went into the adjoining room. In his haste, he hadn't said *"Darb!"* to let them know he was entering the room.

"Abdulla, Abdulla..." his mother began, but she was thrust aside by Aunt Hessa. "Fatima," Hessa screamed, staring wildly at him. "Fatima!"

Rather than fall onto the floor in front of the women, Abdulla slumped heavily into the nearest overstuffed armchair. *Fatima...*

They left behind gangly nine-year-old Luluwa, Fatima's sister, who resisted when they tried to take her with them. His father, gray-faced and tired, entered. Abdulla slouched and waited, the growing dread like something chewing at his insides. His father began to talk, but on hearing "accident" and "the intersection at Al Waab" he remembered the Hukoomi traffic service SMS. Then he heard "Ahmed," and a shiver of horror ran up his back. The driver had been Ahmed, his uncle and father-in-law.

Later that night in the morgue, in the minutes or hours (he couldn't keep track) while he waited to receive her body, Abdulla flicked his Zippo lighter open and struck it alight. Holding it just so, he burned a small patch on his wrist just below his watchstrap. Even this couldn't contain his rage at the truck driver who came through without a scratch, at his uncle, or at himself.

The morgue was antiseptic, mercilessly public. The police advised against seeing her, insisting that he wouldn't be able to erase the memory of a face marked with innumerable shards of glass.

Surrounded by family and hospital staff, he couldn't hold her, talk to her, or stroke her slightly rounding stomach, the burial site of their unborn child. Any goodbyes he had hoped to say would have to be suppressed.

He would mourn the baby in secret. He hadn't wanted to tell relatives about the pregnancy too soon in case of a miscarriage. Now it could never happen: the need to visibly accept God's will in front of them would prevent him from crying it out— this woe upon woe that was too much to bear.

Fatima's body was washed and wrapped, and the prayers said before burial. His little wife with the round face and knowing eyes he'd grown up next to in the family compound, and the baby he would never see crawl, sleep or walk, were hidden from him now for all eternity. The secret she was carrying was wrapped with her in a gauzy white *kaffan*, her grave cloth, when he was finally allowed to see them. The child would have been named after Abdulla's grandfather if a boy, his grandmother if a girl, whose gender would now remain a mystery.

At the burial site, as was customary, he fell in line behind his father and uncles. Ahmed, the father, carried his daughter's slight form.

They placed her on her right side.

3

Men came to lay the concrete slabs that sealed the grave, so her frame would not rise up as it decomposed in the earth. Abdulla regretted not having been able to stroke the softness of her chin or the imperceptibly rounding curve of her belly. *I am burying my wife and our unborn child,* he thought, the taste of blood filling his mouth from the force with which he bit his cheek to stem the tears. Their secret would have to be lost within her lifeless womb. News of a *double* tragedy would spread with the sand under doors and into the ears of their larger circle of acquaintances. Someone would call someone to read the Qur'an over him. Someone would search out someone else for a bottle of *Zamzam* water from Mecca.

None of it would stop the acid from gnawing through his heart. In swirls of conjecture and pity, his newly-assigned role as the widowed and grieving almost-father, would replace his role as the eldest grandchild in a fertile and happy extended family. His birth order had focused their marital intents on him. Caught between duty and tradition, he did the only thing he could do. He tried to forget that he had been too busy to drive Fatima that day, the day he lost a wife and a child because of his own selfishness. He had thought they had years ahead, decades, when they would have time to spend together. A chubby infant growing into a child who went to school, for whose school holidays they would have to wait to travel abroad, and eventually another child, maybe several more. Now none of this would ever be.

He should have died with them. But he kept on breathing— as if he had a right to air.

They returned from the funeral to gather at the home of the grieving parents for the 'azaa, the receiving of condolences. Abdulla rode in the back seat of the Land Cruiser, his father at the wheel, his cousins and brothers messaging friends on various applications. For him there was no sharing of grief. This was his burden to bear alone.

He was the last to climb out of the car, but the first to see Luluwa hunched on the marble steps of Uncle Ahmed's entryway. The lines around her mouth, pulling it downward, aging her face, drew his attention; the stooped shoulders spoke of a burden heavier than grief for her sister. His mother saw it at the same time and hurried over to the girl, concerned.

"*Yalla,* what is it?" she said, pulling her up. Luluwa shook her head.

"Go inside, *habibti,*" said Abdulla's mother, but Luluwa shook free and drew back, panic in her wide eyes. Abdulla's mother turned her face back to the men. Then they heard the shouting.

"When? When did this all start?" Hessa's voice screamed, raw and startling, from inside the open door. "Leave this house."

The family halted in their tracks, exchanging uncertain glances. Ahmed emerged, looking shaken but defiant, a weekender bag in one hand. Abdulla's father, the eldest of the brothers, stepped forward and took him by the arm.

"Everyone is upset," he whispered harshly. He was trying to lead him back inside, as his wife had done a moment ago with Luluwa, when Hessa burst forward into view, her face aflame with indignation.

"Tell them," she spat at her husband. "Tell them now, so when you don't come back here everyone will know why."

The words made no sense to Abdulla. His first thought was to speak up and still the voices. He had already forgiven Ahmed in his mind. The accident hadn't been his fault. "There's no reason to throw him out," he called out, half-climbing the steps. "It was my fault, not his. I should have been driving them."

Hessa turned towards him and laughed in a way that made the hairs on the back of his neck stand on end. "Who needs to throw him out when he's leaving?" she said. "Leaving his daughter to a house with no man to look after her. She might as well have died with her sister."

"*Yuba,* no," Luluwa cried, moving toward her father, but her mother grabbed a fistful of her abaya and spun the girl around by the shoulders.

Abdulla's mind whirred to compute what they were witnessing. A sudden white-hot rage stiffened his spine. His gaze narrowed on Ahmed. *So the rumors were true*, he thought.

"He doesn't want me and so he doesn't want you," Hessa hissed, nose to nose with her daughter.

The family froze in the entryway as understanding sluiced them like rainwater. Ahmed stood for a moment in the glare of their stares. He shifted the weekender bag into his opposite hand.

Saoud, the middle brother, stepped forward to question Ahmed, the baby of the family, but Hessa wasn't finished yet.

"Go," she screamed at her husband. "You'll never set foot in any house with me in it ever again." She collapsed onto the floor, her *abaya* billowing up around her like a mushroom, obscuring her face.

Saoud moved quickly to stand in front of his brother as his wife helped Hessa up. "Think of your daughter," she added pointedly. "The one that's still alive."

Abdulla brought Luluwa forward. Her face was tear-streaked and her body trembling so hard it was causing his hand to shake. "Keep her, if you want," Ahmed said, his glance flickering over Luluwa's bent head. "My new wife will give me many sons." He sidestepped Mohammed and Saoud, continuing on down the stairs towards his car.

The look Hessa gave Luluwa was filled with loathing. She dissolved into another flood of tears.

The girl darted inside. Abdulla followed as his parents tried to deal with the aftermath of his uncle's leaving. His aunt looked as though she might faint. His cousins' faces were ashen. Mohammed and Saoud murmured in low voices about the best way to deal with their brother's child. She couldn't live in a house with boys; one of those boys, her cousins, might one day be her husband.

He followed Luluwa's wailings, sounds without any force, the bleating of a cat, like one of any number roaming the streets of the city. Without a male family member to look after her, she would be as abandoned as those animals. And, in the eyes of their society, as susceptible to straying. He found her on the sofa, typing away on her laptop, and hoped she wasn't posting their family's mess on the internet. Wedged next to her hip was an opaque paper bag stamped with their grandfather's name, the white tops of a few pill bottles visible.

Abdulla came and sat on the sofa next to her, unsure of what to do next. He was assaulted by her screensaver, a photo of Fatima and

Luluwa on the evening of the wedding reception. He hadn't yet arrived with the male relatives; the bride and the rest of the women were still celebrating without *hijab*. His wife's eyes stared back at him even as her sister's now poured tears that showed no sign of stopping.

With trembling hands Luluwa wrenched open the bag of medicine and dug around for pills. She let the laptop slip and he caught it before it hit the floor. As he righted it, the heading of the minimized Google tab caught his attention: suicide. For one moment he allowed himself to admit that the idea she was apparently contemplating had begun to dance at the edge of his own mind.

"Don't," he said. "What will we do if both of you are gone?" He put the laptop aside and, as if calming a wild colt, reached out slowly, deliberately, to take the bottle from her shaking hands. With little effort he wrenched it from her, and with it any remaining shred of strength. She dissolved into incoherent sobs, a raging reminder of what it meant to be alive, to be the one left behind.

Abdulla folded her into his arms, this slip of a girl who used to hide his car keys so that her weekend visits with her sister and brother-in-law wouldn't have to end, this girl who had already lost so much, a sister and now a father and mother. Instead of shriveling into himself, as he had felt like doing from the moment he saw his family in mourning, Abdulla's heart went out to Luluwa. He murmured reassurances, trying to reverse the mirror of his own loss that he saw reflected in her eyes.

"We can do this," he said. "She would want us to." She pulled away to look at him.

"Together," he said. From deep in his own grief he recognized the despair that would haunt him for years, and made a pledge to keep the decay he felt growing inside him from tainting someone so young. He would bear the guilt. It was his alone to bear.

He would speak to his father. If nothing else, perhaps Luluwa might gain a new brother, and he a little sister. Small comfort, but tied together in the knowledge of the loved one they had lost, a bond that might see them through what was to come.

Chapter 1

Maghreb adhan sounds out from the neighborhood mosques as the last rays of sunlight creep toward the horizon, turning day into dusk. In his mind's eye Abdulla sees the men in the family washing their hands and feet then lining up, kneeling, glancing to the right then the left, their voices united in reciting God's praises. He missed the call to prayer during his time in London. The warm familiarity of it calmed him then, even more so during Ramadan, the season of fasting.

But now it is Ramadan again and he has been home for three years, a widower for almost as long. It is nearly three days into the holiest month of the year, and prayer is the farthest thing from his mind, though he goes through the motions when the family convenes. He does his best to dodge them even during this season of togetherness. The Thursday night ritual inspires nothing but a desire to avoid being in their midst. His heart has grown cold under the weight of their repeated condolences, which attempt to ease the hurt of Fatima's abbreviated life. How can the loss of his unborn child be the will of God? Yet he won't blaspheme publicly by telling his family that he isn't sure this is a god he can keep worshiping.

These are Abdulla's darkest moments, just after he has been staring again at his dead baby's sonogram, with its frayed edges, a bisecting line across the infant's forehead. He has done this more or less nightly for three years. When he has finished, he completes the ritual by slipping the sonogram into its hiding place in the crevice between his BlackBerry and its leather case.

He checks his eyes in the mirror again, wishing there weren't so many veins visible from lack of sleep. Taking a deep breath, he pulls on his white embroidered *gahfieh*, a close-fitting skullcap. Next, a white *ghutra*, folded so that it hangs evenly on either side. The circular coiled black *'agal* on top, and he flips the ends of the *ghutra* over the crown of his head so they hang down on his shoulders. He does all of this as though he were going to join his father and uncles in the *majlis*, though he knows he can't bring himself to leave the bachelor quarters. Living in his boyhood room again is both comforting and numbing. It reminds him of his carefree life in the days before his brief marriage, but it also reminds him how the end came.

"*Yalla, wagt akil al 'ashaa, ya Abdulla!* Go eat dinner. They're about to sit down," Luluwa says, interrupting his thoughts and the well-trodden road they bend toward. She props herself in the doorway with childish abandon, the odd angles of youth still evident in her sharp features. She is twelve now, and blossoming underneath her characteristic gangliness are hints of the beautiful woman she will become. As much as she would like him to see her as such, he rejects the devotion he sees in her eyes. He knows the depth of his own selfishness, though to her he is the world.

The sight of his little cousin both eases and complicates the ache in his heart. She is, after all, Fatima's sister. Yet from the moment his grandfather took her into his house in the shadow of her mother leaving, Luluwa's childhood has been full of painful memories of the sister she has lost and the parents who rejected her. She has been hanging around Abdulla's house, and Abdulla himself when she can find him. She is now, without question, his little sister, and because of this he accepts her nagging. Abdulla can't help but love her, even if he often wishes she would leave him alone. Despite himself, he smiles at the sound of her heel tapping on the marble floor. He keeps his back to her, takes a deep breath, and continues arranging the edges of his *ghutra*, pulling the '*agal* forward slightly. Maybe she will get the hint and go.

If Fatima hadn't married me, she'd be alive, Abdulla thinks for the millionth time. *And Luluwa would still have her sister.*

But instead of leaving him in monastic peace, Luluwa saunters in and jumps onto the bed, bouncing up and down on her knees. He can see her from the corner of his eye, which means if she looks closely she'll be able to spot the telltale signs of his ever-persistent grief. She is wearing the same black leggings and t-shirt he saw her wear at least three days ago, but now she sports hot pink, silver-tipped stilettos.

"That t-shirt again?" he asks, hoping to distract her with the opening volley.

"This is Alexander McQueen," she retorts. "He designed Kate Middleton's wedding dress."

"He's dead," Abdulla says drily, deciding not to mention the fact that McQueen hanged himself.

"His label then," Luluwa waves. "Noor says he's— McQueen— is amazing." Abdulla keeps adjusting his ghutra with his back to her, willing the tears to dry. "'*Ammi* Mohammed will send someone to come get you. You don't want that."

Even though she is young, she's right. He doesn't want his father in here.

"Is that why you're here, O self-appointed messenger?"

She shakes her head while typing a message into her iPhone, silver but not adorned with crystals like those of other girls her age.

"I came to warn you," she says. "Noor says tonight the uncles are going to make, like, a big announcement. Like someone is getting engaged."

Their eyes meet in the mirror, and for a second he sees someone else, older, plumper, asking how they will spend their weekend, through a similar screen of lashes. Then she giggles, and Fatima's face recedes. It is just Luluwa, his dead wife's teenage sister.

A pair of silver-toned cuff links completes his preparations. He's ready. There is no avoiding it. Luluwa is right. He is running out of time, in more ways than one. His time as a grieving widower has extended far beyond what's considered "normal." His father has grown tired of his requests to maintain a low profile. He really should make an appearance.

"Alright," Abdulla grunts, trying to mask the raw edge in his voice. He tosses a baseball cap from the dresser at Luluwa, who deftly ducks it. "I'm going."

Luluwa sits up, thrilled she has made a difference. She puts the cap on her head and gives him a thumbs-up. Even in his amusement Abdulla can't help noticing the evil eye necklace, once his gift to Fatima, now belonging to Luluwa. The very top of it peeks out of her t-shirt, reminding him of happier times. Looking down, he notices her feet.

"What's with the shoes?" he says, making a sour face.

Luluwa ignores the question, determined to keep him on track. "*Yalla*, they're like, here," she says, waving her arms around as though hordes of cousins were at the door. "Haven't you heard anything I'm saying? They want to know which of our men is ready. In their roundabout way, of course."

He reclaims his cap by pulling it off her head and parking it on his doorknob. Then he ruffles her hair until it hangs in her face. Again he notices the familiar glint of the only thing Fatima ever asked him for during their three-month marriage.

"The necklace doesn't match either," he says. But Luluwa ignores him, as she has done the entire three years he's tried to trick her into giving it up. Her fingers fly protectively to her neck as she tucks back her sister's engagement present. As a special favor, she asked him for it from Fatima's personal effects. Now there is no way she is about to part with it herself.

"Look at your clothes," Abdulla says, laughing. "Haven't your cousins tamed the tomboy out of you yet? If you are going to be a girl, you should know what matches."

"You can't, like, imagine how bad it is," Luluwa pouts. "*Wallah*, they're so uninteresting. Like, please stop watching so much American television."

But Abdulla knows what she means. Apparently their female cousins think marriage and bad TV are the best ways to domesticate a girl.

"And when the subject turns to boys, it's as if you five are like, the only guys on the planet," she continues.

"Five?" he protests. Abdulla does not want to be included in any list of eligible men, especially the single men in the family.

"Well, be honest. Would you fancy any of them, even one of them?" She flips onto her stomach as Abdulla pretends to pause and consider.

"Hind thinks she's getting married, so they've all gone silly crazy. Even Noor—"

Luluwa breaks off to draw her arms to her chest in a swoon. Abdulla wags his head. "As far as I'm concerned, there's nobody suitable in this house," he says. "Father knows. Let him tell them that."

"This time they brought the baby," Luluwa is saying. "You know, Hassan's boy. He's become a real cutie."

"I'm not getting married again," he says, not hearing her. "Like, ever."

He shuts the door before she can show him the baby photos, his latest third cousin, on her iPhone. He presses his forehead against it for a second, trying to gather enough strength to go forward instead of beating the usual retreat back inside his cave to lose himself in the embrace of sleep.

On the walk towards the *majlis*, he flexes his shoulders as though getting ready for his daily run. Once inside, he leaves his sandals in the pile with all the others before entering the room reserved for the men of the family and their guests. This weekend even the oldest men of his family have gathered. There are at least four generations seated, sprawled and standing among the blue gilt-edged furniture.

"Every day there's something in the paper about it," his Uncle Saoud is saying. "So many applications for men marrying outside our community."

With a sinking feeling, Abdulla sees his father and other uncle nod in agreement. This isn't a new phenomenon, but the marriage issue for locals is a subject Uncle Saoud doesn't have the luxury of avoiding in his position as head of the Council on Marrying Foreigners.

"Settling your girls in a good home has never been harder," Saoud says.

Abdulla mentally kicks himself for choosing this moment to enter. But there's nothing to do but continue now that they've seen him.

"*Al salaam alaikum*," Abdulla says. He begins greeting them, starting with a kiss on top of his grandfather Jassim's head, with its wisps of grey hair escaping from under his *ghutra*, showing the respect and affection due from the oldest grandson. He greets his uncles and cousins with a handshake and the nose-to-nose bump reserved for closest family and friends.

"Are you in the fish market?" his father calls out from across the room, casting a cold eye on his eldest son's attire and the Adam's apple revealed by the opening in his *thobe*. Abdulla buttons the starched collar to his *thobe* without replying. The greetings end with a kiss on top of his father's wiry black curls. Abdulla turns, hoping to get in about thirty minutes with his youngest brother at the PlayStation in the corner and make a swift getaway. But his father's hands steer him instead into the opposite corner, where his uncles are drinking *gahwa*, Arabic coffee.

"You are overdue to make an announcement," his father says quietly in English.

"*Yuba*, let's not talk about this now," Abdulla replies in Arabic, as several of the youngest boys, his cousins—their parentage he can't quite remember—jump from one chair to another. Luluwa was right. They are out for blood tonight.

"In my day you'd be serving the *gahwa* to your elders," his grandfather Jassim booms, ending in a gut-wrenching cough that hushes conversation across the room. He dispatches one of the boys for Anita, the housemaid, to take the children back to the women, but not before he has ruffled their hair and slipped a few ten-riyal notes into the pockets of their *thobes* to show them he isn't really angry.

"Grow up and work hard," he rumbles at them. "If I still had my boat, I would take you out on the sea."

"And I would go with you, *Yaddi*," Abdulla's youngest brother says, "all the way to India!"

Jassim smiles and pinches the boy's cheek, then hides a grimace when the teen crushes him in a fierce embrace. The boys tumble out, leaving only the marriageable or married men behind.

Abdulla's father breaks the silence. "Your grandfather grows tired of waiting," he warns in a low growl, the rumble of an argument in the making. Surrender is the only option to bypass the coming storm of words.

But Abdulla is determined to maintain his marital resistance by sticking to a non-violent strategy of silence. Whatever his father says, he will swallow his anger along with mouthfuls of tea, knowing he is only doing what any Arab father would do for his eldest son: make him a husband and father, and therefore a man. Yet Abdulla has been through it once, and it didn't end well for anyone, least of all the wife to whom he was supposed to be such a blessing.

If only he could, he would go back through time and space to London and become again the bachelor he was three years ago, a wandering student in the bricked arcades of Covent Garden, idling with the street entertainers. Back then his biggest worry was contemplating how many of Ben's Cookies he could eat and how long he had to wait before going out for dinner at Mr. Chow's.

"*Ya waldi*," his Uncle Saoud says. "You know you are like my own son." He is the first to speak now, just as he was first to kick-start the previous engagement. Abdulla can barely see his lips in the curly strands of his beard. "What has happened is over. Forget all of it and start again. Afresh. New."

Abdulla tries to keep from flinching at his father's vigorous nod. All the men in his family are suddenly behaving like female matchmakers. And this on top of his mother's pointed mutterings whenever she lays eyes on him, as she oversees the gardener tending her jasmine plants when Abdulla walks out to his car in the morning, or late in the evening when he comes into the main house and she is watching Turkish soap operas dubbed into Arabic.

"Let's speak of this tomorrow, *insha'Allah,*" Abdulla offers in an even tone. This line worked for the first few months after he returned from England. The family gave him wide latitude, so he kept using it, desperate to buy more time. *Insha'Allah*, God willing. Though as far as he is concerned, God has little to do with this or much of anything else important.

There is no mirth in his favorite uncle's eyes tonight. Abdulla is momentarily overwhelmed by a memory of being in this position three years ago. Whether it is déjà vu or not, Abdulla can't tell. Three years earlier, a different Abdulla sat in this same room, in this same chair, brought like a misbehaving youth before his uncles so they could muscle him into doing his duty. Strategically his father trapped him then, as they have done now, in the *majlis*, where the family hierarchy cannot be escaped by excuses of football matches and waiting dignitaries. Abdulla feels bullied. The whole wretched process is drawing him nearer to hating all of them, not least because of their utter lack of sensitivity about Fatima. He is torn between rage and nausea, his forehead beading in sweat as he tries to adjust his *ghutra* for distraction.

"I'm still considering women," Abdulla says, clearing his throat. He used to take his younger brothers and cousins to Villaggio Mall so they could skulk around attractive girls. He hopes this counts. Anything, lies even, might be better than the right here, right now, of a formal sitting room in Qatar, his father's hand heavy on his shoulder, the eyes of his uncles and cousins peeling back the layers of his soul. But no, he is here, his father's slight shove to the middle of his back directing Abdulla to sit in the armchair to the right of Saoud. Unable to avoid what is coming, Abdulla sits, pinching the bridge of his nose, waving away Narin, the family's driver, who is coming towards him with a tray laden with more red tea.

"Because marriage," Abdulla continues, "is part of being a Muslim man, I know that. And when the time comes…" He falters, never a good liar.

The older men exchange glances.

"Aisha," his father says, twisting the jade beads of a *misbah* between his right thumb and forefinger.

"Nouf," Uncle Saoud cuts in.

"I don't want a wife who will spend all my money on Gucci or Prada."

"Allah knows it would take more than a few years for someone to do that," his father grunts. "You don't spend your money on anything else."

"What about Amal?" pipes up Khalid, his thirteen-year-old cousin, thrusting himself into the game of planning the rest of Abdulla's life.

"I told you boys to go and eat," shouts Jassim.

Uncle Saoud dismisses Khalid with a wave, but not before shooting Abdulla a considering look.

"You don't even know any girls," Abdulla says, giving the boy a light punch in the arm to keep him from feeling bad about being rejected from their small circle. "Get out of here."

"What about Amal?" Khalid repeats.

"No, no, no." Abdulla shakes his head. "No one from Al Khor or Wakra who wants to spend all day Friday visiting her family, gossiping with her ten sisters, me in the *majlis* drinking endless cups of tea listening to someone's plans for a new satellite dish in their winter desert tent."

"Haya?" says Khalid again, but this time as a parting shot from a safe distance across the room.

Saoud raises a fist as though intending to come after his youngest child if he doesn't exit. "Out. This is for adults."

The boy disappears.

"Even worse," Abdulla goes on bitterly. "A pious family where all the women wear *niqab* and the men travel to Dubai for their fun. Hypocrites."

"Enough, now you're like the women," his father says. He pounds a fist on the chair near Abdulla's elbow.

Abdulla sits very still.

Uncle Saoud indicates with a jerk of his head that Saad, Abdulla's younger brother, and the cousins should leave them.

Narin the driver is back, offering a new round, this time of coffee. Saoud grasps a *finjal*, a palm-sized coffee cup. Abdulla takes one next, gulping down half of it in one swallow.

His father, his uncles, again, the same room, the same conversation, only three years later. *Will they never be satisfied?* Abdulla wonders as he wordlessly sips coffee, waiting for their next foray.

Uncle Saoud takes him by the arm, leaning in, his touch familiar and close, something Abdulla missed during all his years in England. "It's been nearly three years, Abdulla," Uncle Ahmed says, joining them, patting his nephew's arm. Abdulla understands that Ahmed, as Fatima's father, carries more emotional weight than anyone else. If he urges Abdulla to remarry, they feel, it will seal the deal.

Abdulla is surrounded now, Saoud on the right and Ahmed on the left. He can't leave without causing offense. He grits his teeth and tries to resist the urge to deliver a punch worthy of a rugby brawl. It's clear to him that his father sent Uncle Ahmed over as backup.

"Fatima is still mourned," Abdulla murmurs, "if only by me" — the last under his breath, as Ahmed grasps his fingers in his own meaty grip. Saoud relaxes into his seat, letting his younger brother have a go. "I don't let go of wives as easily as some," he adds, under his breath, shooting a glance at Ahmed.

"Stop it," his father grunts, looking at the others until he's sure the slight has not been overheard. They are still conferring on potential brides. Of course it is easy for Uncle Ahmed to call for another marriage; it didn't take him long to take a second wife when he felt that itch men often joke about in the majlis.

"*Allah yerhamha*," his uncles say, calling for mercy on Fatima's soul. "She was taken from us, our daughter."

And my child, my unborn child, Abdulla thinks, *whose gender I didn't even know. Only God knew and apparently he thought it was a good secret.*

"Your grandfather has taken in Ahmed's daughter as the last girl of the house. But the rest of us are here among the living, Abdulla. You must do your duty by your family. Marry another girl and get this done." Ahmed's voice, firm but rising, is causing some of his cousins to turn in interest.

As though they don't know what's going on over here, Abdulla thinks. *Hate to tell you, but you're next.* He eyes them malevolently, some as young as twenty-two, who are no doubt trading stories of their exploits, male or female. Before he was married he used to listen, a silent witness to their raucous tales of girls. It didn't matter how holy the rest of their thoughts or actions were.

Three years ago, during a Ramadan *iftar*, Ahmed was asking: "What about Fatima?"

Abdulla had hesitated, so his father answered for him. "Fatima is a lovely girl," he said, blindsiding his son. Without an acceptable excuse or reason for delay, Abdulla felt the noose tighten. The reasoning seemed inescapable. He had to get married, so why not this girl from a good family—his own family. Fatima, the mischievous cousin who, when they were younger, had put sand in his favorite dessert when he wouldn't let her play his video games? He wasn't able to resist the tide. In a matter of weeks, it was done. He was married to Fatima, his first cousin, younger by one year, and they were given a brand- new apartment on The Pearl, just near the Ritz-Carlton.

As it happened, this girl-woman Fatima had her own plans and ambitions, of which he knew nothing in the years when puberty separated them. She was more than competent in her first job, as public relations officer for the National Bank, and he began to view her with admiration. Perhaps he had been lucky after all. They settled into the kind of easy camaraderie that eluded most of Abdulla's friends in their own arranged marriages.

But all that is gone. Today it is his Uncle Saoud's voice, not from the length of the room but right in his ear.

"Consider your other cousin, Hind. She went to a foreign school like you. You will be a good match," Saoud is saying.

Abdulla forces a smile, the only way to free his fingers from his uncle's vise-like grip. He knows he shouldn't complain. They are more modern than others, these men of his family. They do try to fashion matches that will make the couple happy, as opposed to simply seeking more money for the family or higher social allegiances.

"We'll set up a visit next week," his father says to Saoud, who nods solemnly, trying not to show his delight.

Abdulla married once because it was the right thing to do, and because the family wanted to see a grandchild. But after what happened, it is not as easy as they would wish for him to go down that path again.

"I'll pay for everything," Ahmed offers. The men look at him, and the regret on his face about his daughter's unexpected death is clear.

Sometimes, from the awkward way his uncle behaves when he's around, Abdulla wonders if Ahmed feels as guilty as he does himself about what happened.

"*Alai al talaq, mahad ydfa,*" his father replies, issuing something that is part cough and part laugh. *If anyone else pays, I'll divorce my wife.* The groom pays for everything; they all know that.

Abdulla resists snorting at the age-old saying, an empty threat indicating escalation between men arguing over a bill. The saying is usually applied to paying for dinner, but now apparently extends to familial manipulation.

"Your obligation to him is settled," Uncle Saoud says to Ahmed with a big sigh, clapping them both on the shoulder as though they have all won prizes in an endurance horse race. "His mother will come and visit our girl."

What a farce! The houses are in the same family compound, only a few hundred meters away from each other. Abdulla hasn't seen his cousins since the night of Fatima's death, except as shadows behind tinted car windows. Before that, he can vaguely remember their girlish faces in the years before he went abroad to the London School of Economics.

In a familiar routine observed for as long as Abdulla can remember, one taking place in *majlises* all over the country at likely the same hour, if not moment, the men are trickling into the dining room, where a table is so laden with food that there is hardly anywhere to put one's dinner plate.

Uncle Saoud is right. Resistance is futile. Though they joke about it in proverbs, divorce is always an option, Abdulla thinks. *Either that or running away.* Instead of voicing these ideas aloud, which he knows would only erupt the *majlis* into vociferous arguments, he leaves it for the others to work out. The pressure in the room has evaporated now, and his father and uncles seemed to have lost all interest in him, having discussed the details of his future. Their full attention has turned to filling their bellies. Unnoticed, he creeps back to his room, waving off Anita when she chases after him to see if he wants something to eat.

In the end, what they want is only what they all want, no difference between his family and his government: for single Qatari boys and girls to become men and women in marriage to other Qataris. The stability of society, they call it, ignoring the nearly fifty percent divorce rate and the many instances in which girls leave their husbands the morning after the wedding to return to their fathers' homes.

He can't think of anything he would want to do less.

Oh, wait—yes, he can.

There is one thing.

Get married.

Again.

Chapter 2

Luluwa washes her hands with soap and dries them on the powder-white towel. She takes the stairs two at a time, her legs eating up the staircase in half the time it would take if she were more measured, like her aunties. It's Thursday night, so she can't be bothered to waste any more time doing anything other than being with her grandfather. Reaching the top of the stairs she hovers in the doorway, waiting for him to notice her and call her inside.

The rest of the family wants to move his room downstairs, somewhere more accessible, but *Yadd* Jassim isn't having it.

"*Hayach*," she finally hears his sandpaper voice say, and she bounds inside at the invitation. The cool interior is slightly murky, since Anita has drawn the shades. Now, at nighttime, just a bedside lamp lights his weathered face and body, propped up in bed. At his age he doesn't have to fast during Ramadan but she suspects he has been doing so, like many religious people not taking advantage of the exceptions in their faith. He gestures to her, and Luluwa presses a kiss to his forehead before plopping herself into the bamboo chair beside the bed.

"How are you, *ya benti?*"

She smiles, because in the absence of her father, her grandfather, with only sons, has been showing her the care he always wanted to lavish on a daughter. Luluwa pulls her legs up under her and wraps her arms around them, conscious to avoid exclaiming at how frail he looks. The chair groans, its wicker bottom nearly worn through from her increasing weight and more frequent visits.

"What's the news?"

Luluwa rattles off the family's daily hidden details—Khalid's pranks, Noor's latest gadget, Hind's report card, Aunt Maryam's new car. This time there's a lot to report because it has been a week since her grandfather has had enough energy for their catch-up. *Yadd* Jassim listens to it all without criticizing her for being a busybody, sticking her nose into other people's business, or blatant eavesdropping. He halts her verbal torrent to laugh, raise an eyebrow, or ask an occasional question for more details.

"And Abdulla?"

Now it is her turn to pause. Luluwa sighs. She has avoided telling her grandfather what he already knows—what the whole family knows—in case it would worry him. His eldest grandson is an incurable workaholic.

"I don't know how to get through to him," she says, trailing off, chewing the end of a rope of her hair that has curled between her arm and leg.

Jassim shakes his head.

"I know, I know, it's not my job," Luluwa grumbles. She flips shaggy bangs out of her eyes. "I was going to say he reminds me of another workaholic," her grandfather admits with a slow grin.

"Who?"

No one in the rest of the family could be accused of taking work as seriously as Abdulla. Jassim points a gnarled knuckle at his own scrawny chest, causing Luluwa to raise her eyebrows in surprise.

"But you were a *tawash, Yaddi,* a negotiator. Didn't you hire someone to do the pearl diving for you?"

He coughs, beckoning her to hand him the glass of water on the end table. Taking a big gulp, he relaxes again against the frame.

"It wasn't that simple, *habibti,*" he says, closing his eyes and letting his head drop back. "The competition was fierce amongst the traders. It was always a race to get back and forth before anyone else."

Luluwa holds her own breath until his begins to slow, loving the moments ahead best of all. Jassim will forget she is even there and resume telling her the stories of his merchant days, when he was one of the few Arabs ferrying precious pearls to India, and gold out of Mumbai for the Qatari market.

No matter how many times she hears these stories, there is always something new, a detail Jassim remembers, or a person on *al-lanj*, the ship, who wasn't introduced in a previous version. During one such session Luluwa connected the purposeful choice of her name, "pearl" in Arabic, with the growth of her family's wealth, hard won by Jassim's relentless expeditions.

"So you see, they all wanted me to stay in Doha," he says, his voice faint, barely a whisper. "They said it was enough. We had enough to start buying land."

Luluwa chews on the ends of her hair, hoping they are finally getting to the year in which Jassim disappeared from Qatar to regions unknown, without the usual messages from the divers or crew.

"But you wanted to go," she prompts when the silence begins to lengthen, fearing he has fallen asleep.

"I wanted to go back," he admits, sinking down onto the pillows. "To see her again?"

He nods, as if the motion is made painful by the memory. "We married in secret. She was…"

"Pregnant?" she blurts, as if guessing at the next development in this evening's Ramadan special.

"With my baby."

"She was Indian," Luluwa murmurs, showing mild surprise despite her best efforts to appear sophisticated.

Her heart constricts and she fights the urge to pounce on her grandfather's bed in glee. She knew, she just knew, there was a thrilling personal story in addition to all the talk about travel on the high seas. The twinkle in Yadd Jassim's eye has no place in the tradition-bound society he comes from and still lives in now. He has always gone his own way. Even allowing Luluwa, child of scandal, to remain living on the compound is a testament to his willingness to break molds.

"What was her name, *Yaddi*?"

But he is out of her reach now, enjoying the rare gift of sleep, one that comes to him less and less easily as his illness grows worse. Luluwa smacks herself in the head for forgetting how frail he is. She wishes she could reach out and touch the stubby eyelashes that cast small shadows on his papery skin. She turns out the bedside lamp and tiptoes out of the room, wondering when she will finally hear about her grandfather's first love. The story keeps turning in her mind, even after they have broken their fast.

She eats with Abdulla's parents and brothers, as she has done for nearly three years, as though she were one of the originals. They pass plates for *machboos, harees and thareed*, the Prophet's favorite dish, made especially during Ramadan, and there's tamarind juice, also served only during the season. While normally she would toss back these delicacies, today she's deep in thought.

"Not feeling well?" Aunt Maryam asks. Luluwa shakes her head.

"I'm fine, '*Ameti*."

"Where's Abdulla?" Uncle Mohammed asks the table at large. No one answers.

Luluwa had seen Abdulla slip away to his room as soon as the men rose from sunset prayer.

"He didn't fast today," Saad says.

"Telling my secrets?" Abdulla appears in the dining room as Maryam dishes out another helping of French fries onto Saad's plate.

"Migraines, still?" Maryam says. Abdulla nods.

"Well, I always fast," Luluwa declares. "Even if I don't feel well and even if it's allowed. I never make up days."

"You don't always," Saad retorts.

In their back and forth the two are like biological siblings, the proximity of their ages making them nearly twins.

"You're a girl, so no, you don't."

"I do—"

"Luluwa, eat," Maryam says, as Abdulla slides into his seat at the table.

Luluwa reddens, only just realizing what Saad means. Her period. She has to make up any days she's not fasting when she's on her period. This is the first Ramadan this has applied to her and the idea is still new.

"I think I saw you at McDonald's before *maghreb*," Abdulla says casually in Saad's direction.

The boy's protests fade away under the inquisitive gaze of his parents.

Maryam elbows Mohammed.

"Were you eating?" he growls.

"No, *Yuba*," Saad squeaks.

"What were you doing at McDonald's?" Maryam snaps. Saad ducks his head.

"I was waiting for sunset," he says.

Luluwa passes the plate of French fries to Abdulla, who gives her a wink. No matter how much he pushes her away, she knows he still loves her, and her heart soars.

Chapter 3

Abdulla draws his fingers off the keyboard, adjusting white Bose earphones. He begins the piece again, for the hundredth time since waking up at *fajr*, the dawn call to prayer, unable to go back to sleep. Not that he actually got up to pray. Since the accident, he's rarely been able to bring himself to his prayer mat, much less the family mosque. His family keeps their opinions of his lack of faithfulness to themselves. Over the past years they've had bigger issues to worry about than his prayer life.

"Your cousin Hind is in the paper," his mother now texts, alternating with email attachments of the articles on her graduating class, as though he didn't know the reason for her sudden interest.

It's Friday, and the weekends are mostly his when there is nothing pressing at work, so he carries on with his music, not even bothering to shower. The keys silence the echoes of other weekends spent lazily in bed, contemplating a rounding stomach, names for a being they had not yet met. His back bends over the keyboard; again and again he plays, pausing only to search for another video online to challenge himself. On the weekend, cocooned in his own world, he doesn't have to talk, make pleasantries, and pretend life is normal.

But before long he hears sounds coming from the rest of the household. The women are back from their orchestrated errands. In between sets, he hears the car doors and the side entrance to the house opening and shutting. Click, click, click, he hears his mother's heels, likely accompanied by those of his aunties, Ahmed's wife and anyone else who wanted to go shopping so that the bride can be put on parade when she returns from the honeymoon and is visited by her friends and female relatives. A ridiculous exercise, since they have all known Hind since she was born.

"Abdulla!"

Luluwa must have been one of the click-clacks he heard moments earlier, because she now appears at his shoulder, examining the sheet music.

"*Bollywood Hits,*" she says, wrinkling her nose as she reads the page.

He shrugs.

"*Yadd* Jassim still talks about his time in that city as a trader. I thought I'd practice and play for him."

She runs an oval fingernail over the white keys with a tentative smile. "He would like that."

Black leggings emphasize Luluwa's gangliness, but today a red silk tunic falls at mid-thigh instead of a designer t-shirt. Today, in honor of the occasion perhaps, she is wearing a *shayla*, though it is slipping towards the back of her head. Already she's discarded her *abaya*, the outer garment worn by the rest of the women outside of the family compound. Partly because her own father may not have corrected her and their grandfather rarely leaves the house any more, Luluwa has the most leeway of any female he knows. His mother, who has taken on responsibility for Luluwa, is certainly no restrainer of character, having raised only boys. And Abdulla's father is always off breaking ground on yet another building, especially in the up-and-coming West Bay area, and can't be bothered with feminine affairs.

At Luluwa's impatient rap on the cover of his keyboard Abdulla slips off his headphones.

She folds her arms and regards him without blinking.

"I've been at the door calling you," she says reproachfully. Then, plunking hard on the highest notes: "Aren't you going to take me out to practice?"

"*Assif, habibti,*" he apologizes, since he would if she were really his younger sister and not his dead wife's. "I don't think I have time for a driving lesson today."

She narrows her eyes at him. He plays on. "It's only once a week," she says.

He grits his teeth at how sad she sounds, but the thought of her on the roads, in a country where traffic accidents are the number one cause of death, does nothing for his mood most weeks. He can't bring himself to tell her this, however, as the anniversary of Fatima's death is only weeks away.

Since she has come to live in their house, he has seen the same sleepless nights in the circles under the translucent skin around her eyes that fail to show on his own darker skin. She is still a child to him, her skinny arms and legs reminding him of the young goats on the family farm near the desert.

"Don't you even want to know what our cousin, the prospective bride, said when we saw her?" Luluwa's arms are akimbo, but this time she stamps her foot like their nanny Anita used to when the boys were scattering in all directions at City Center Mall.

Abdulla turns back to the keyboard, ready to put the discarded earphones back on.

"Why were you there?" he murmurs. "Traitor."

"Somebody had to go see if she was at all willing," she says, flipping the piano lid closed to stop him from playing.

He snatches his hands away just in time. And takes the earphones off again.

"Was she?" he asks, swiveling around to face her.

"You should get Anita in here to clean this," Luluwa says, wrinkling her nose again at the grease-stained pizza boxes piled up in the corner. "Is that what you eat?"

She protests when he takes her by the elbow, escorting her to the door.

"I want you to be happy," she says. "It isn't good for you to be alone like this."

Without meaning to, he pinches her shoulder. She flails back at him ineffectually, thumbs tucked inside her fingers.

"That's the way to get your thumbs broken," he says at the threshold, taking her fist in his and forcing her thumb across her knuckles.

"Noor and I agree. Hind's not right for you," Luluwa says, as he throws some mock punches at her. "She's too—"

"Luluwa! Your trainer is here." Khalid, his youngest cousin, shoots by to the garden on his scooter.

"Slow down," they yell at him simultaneously, but Khalid is already off to the passageway between their house and their grandfather's.

"You have a trainer?" Abdulla says, forgetting Luluwa was about to share an oracular revelation with him. "What kind?"

She makes a muscle with her biceps. "They think I'm too skinny. If I lift weights with her, then I may put on some muscle." She makes another face.

He tries to feel sympathy but can manage only relief. At least the family is meddling in other people's lives as well, not just his own. Maybe this will distract them. "Luluwa!"

She pounds him on the arm one last time, squinting up at him. "She's not the one," Luluwa says, putting her fingers on the scar tissue just below his watch. She presses the scar. When he doesn't respond, she whispers, "My sister would want you to be happy."

Abdulla pretends not to hear, and turns away. He looks at his wrist and remembers. Just after the funeral, before the visiting hours began, Luluwa was the only person who noticed blood running in a red streak down his sleeve. She and Anita bound up his wrist and then tucked the bandage back under the sleeve of a fresh *thobe*.

"I'm not going to marry her anyway," Abdulla mutters, as though they were kids and she was trying to interest him in a toy but he didn't want to play. "I'm never marrying again."

He sits back on the bench and starts practicing again on the

Bach theme he had been learning to play for Fatima's birthday.

"She wouldn't make you laugh," Luluwa says, chewing on the end of a piece of hair.

Abdulla grunts. He knows what she means. The lines around his mouth that used to bracket his broad smile are now more often than not turned downward.

For a moment, they hear the sound of their grandfather's cough.

"He's dying," Luluwa says softly, all traces of their childish shenanigans gone.

An image of their grandfather Jassim almost flashes in the air between them, his face from behind the wrought iron of the upstairs railing. He has barely come downstairs in more than a week. Abdulla searches his memory for the last time he saw his grandfather outside his house. It was that night in the majlis just over a week ago now, when the fateful decision was made regarding Abdulla's future. The old man didn't seem ailing then, just fragile. He didn't get up to say hello, but that was his right. It was the younger men's duty to come and greet him.

Abdulla feels a twist low in his gut. His grandfather has been the silent pillar of their family. He was Luluwa's champion on the day of the accident. The body had to be buried at the next prayer; wild with grief, Ahmed dissolved his marriage and revealed his intent to marry another, and Hessa, racked with shame, fled to stay with her eldest brother. Luluwa, rejected by both, was cast aside. But she couldn't be left alone, even for an evening, and Jassim knew it. He acted without hesitation, immediately ordering the transfer of her belongings from Uncle Ahmed's empty house into his own. This is the role his grandfather has played in the community as well. In the old days he would sit and listen to the complaints of the servants, the disputes of neighbors. He made loans when necessary, and sent food when the need was urgent. He fought for Abdulla's right to go to Sandhurst at a young age and then stay on in England for university. Father to three sons, Jassim had yet to see his immortality crumble on the carpet around his feet.

"He won't be with us long," she insists.

"I've heard all this before," Abdulla says, swallowing hard. He knows she is right.

With a shake of her head, and a pained look, Luluwa turns away. Part teenager, the slope of her back is that of a maturing young woman. He knows marriage would help ease the devotion he sees shining in her eyes, prevent it from turning into a type of love that he not only fears but dreads because he will have to deny her, this fragile girl who has come to represent everything good in his life since Fatima's death. His heart will never feel the reverberations of love again.

Abdulla returns his attention to the keyboard and tries to drown out the sound of his cousin's voice and her ominous predictions. If she is right, and Jassim is dying, there is no force that can possibly keep him single. After three years the right to grieve has lost its force, and lack of interest won't be tolerated. Now the family will prevail, on the undeniable premise that Jassim should see his first grandchild before leaving this world.

Let one of the girls from the other houses have the honor, with one of my brothers, Abdulla thinks bitterly, pounding on the keys the way his youngest brother Saad does when he thinks no one is looking.

Luluwa may not like Hind, but her opinion is not the one that carries the most weight. That prerogative belongs to his mother, Maryam, the woman responsible for training her daughter-in- law to manage the household and care for her husband's aging parents until they die.

Fatima got off easy in this regard because everyone was in such a rush. When she asked for her own house as part of the contract, the family instantly agreed, not wanting to scare her away with the idea of living on the family compound.

This time, the family will likely try to keep them close to keep an eye on things. His next wife, Hind or whoever they decide on in the end, will not be so lucky. The month is crawling by, even with the shortened work hours for fasting, but Abdulla is relishing the season in a way he hasn't done for several years. As long as it's Ramadan, no one can talk in earnest about arranging the engagement or the wedding. He welcomes any excuse for the delay.

Chapter 4

Abdulla suppresses a yawn, though no one is likely to notice, since most of the others at the table are on their mobile phones. People are returning to their desks after the week off for Eid. He can see jet lag in the bleary eyes and stooped shoulders of many of his counterparts. The ad hoc nature of conducting business at home never ceases to amuse him — texting, surfing the internet or chatting to a neighbor are all acceptable behaviors at most meetings.

"Al salaam alaikum," Uncle Ahmed says, striding into the room. Those assembled return the greeting as Ahmed takes his seat at the head, leaning forward onto the massive conference table. Around the room, the several members of the Marketing Subcommittee Taskforce, minor trade officials, glance at each other then back at Ahmed, the chairman of the taskforce. Those otherwise occupied finish their other business quickly.

Ahmed thumps the table once and resumes his former position. "Sports," he says, nodding, "are how we can make ourselves distinctive from the rest."

The assembled group is supposed to advise higher-ups on key messages for international media. Most of them are from Abdulla's department, but there are a few other men he knows only by sight, up-and-coming deputy ministers. *Wall-to-wall thobes*, Abdulla thinks. He can't keep up with the new appointments. He can't keep his mind on anything but the end of his freedom, which is about to be signed into reality. He looks at his watch. Perhaps time could just stop.

"Keep your phone on," Uncle Ahmed told him before the meeting. "Watch for the message."

The phone is in front of him now, alongside the bottles of sparkling and still water, notepads, pencils and built-in microphones that crowd the table. Sooner or later it will vibrate, and Abdulla will have to read the commencement of his sentence. Sweating, he takes a bottle from the empty place next to him, guzzling more mineral water.

"Let us keep our eyes on London and the Olympics next summer," someone pipes up. There is a nodding of heads and a murmur of agreement. After all, since the stunning award of the World Cup to Qatar, who can dispute the power of the sports world to catapult a small nation to instant headlines?

"We'll send a delegation to learn from them," Uncle Ahmed says. He's rubbing his chin, which shows only the slightest shadow of a beard. Gone is the full, curly one he has sported for most of Abdulla's life. Missing in the close shave is his distinctive white patch. Now, his exposed chin reveals a younger, more virile-looking Ahmed. Marriage, or remarriage, seems to be agreeing with someone.

"We'll learn what they know, then put our brand of desert hospitality on it. We can be even better than London."

Another round of murmurs. A popular trip for sure, Abdulla knows, given how much people still love "Londoning" even though the colonial era is supposed to be long over. Were it not for the impending *milcha*, Abdulla might have considered volunteering, at least to put himself out of his father's reach for a few weeks. But the time frame is so far in the future—next summer, months and months away, and by then, who knows? He will be married by then. *London?* He wonders, half- whimsically, if he'll ever see London again.

"We need to bring up our own teams in advance of the Cup," someone is saying, echoing Chairman Ahmed, who wags his head up and down with such enthusiasm his *ghutra* wobbles.

Abdulla swallows, his breath constricted by his starched collar. He drinks more and more water as the discussion swirls around him. *The world's fattest nation, planning to integrate sports into society?* he thinks. *Why not get rid of McDonald's first?*

"You want to say something?" Uncle Ahmed's eyebrows draw together, a ripple of creases rising on his forehead.

In the growing silence, all eyes turn in the direction of the chairman's gaze. Abdulla raises his shoulders to shrug but the glowing red light at the base of the microphone in front of him makes him realize he has spoken his criticism out loud. He clears his throat. A few of the young dignitaries near him *(why hasn't he bothered to learn their names?)* look as though they might agree, though they avoid making eye contact when he sweeps the table in search of a reply.

"Eating habits," he manages. "If we are serious about sports, we need to do something about eating more healthily."

Not a perfect recovery, but it'll do. Ahmed nods, the lines around his eyebrows and forehead relaxing. The conversation addresses this unexpected vein as people debate the feasibility of making non-fast food attractive to teenagers.

"No one wants to eat traditionally," one of the other managers says.

Abdulla knows everyone is thinking the same thing. The speaker's girth is evidence that poor eating habits are not a problem that plagues only the young.

"But if you're at Whole Foods in South Kensington, it's packed with people shopping for fresh edibles," Abdulla says, drawn into the conversation despite himself.

Ahmed and a few others are nodding again. Abdulla can't remember a meeting when they've been able to speak so frankly.

"Realistically, we'd have to bring something like that here to compete against Carrefour's produce," the portly manager says, bringing up the contrasting point of view.

"I'll look into it." Abdulla surprises himself, and his uncle, by volunteering.

Ahmed looks down the table, his gaze lingering on his nephew, and Abdulla resists the urge to take the offer back. The eyebrows on his uncle's furrowed brow are shapelier than Abdulla remembers. Is the new wife making his fifty-something uncle into a metrosexual? The conversation continues to flow around him, now on how to go about creating incentives for young people to get involved in team sports. In the ensuing discussion no one mentions girls, even though there are plans for the women. Abdulla rearranges his *ghutra* and thinks of Luluwa and how much she loves playing football in the league at her international school. But he's already introduced enough controversy into a meeting that, like an increasing number of the ones that fill his diary, are perfunctory rather than purposeful.

His phone buzzes. Ahmed stops in mid-sentence and looks sharply at him.

Abdulla unlocks it to find exactly what he is expecting: *The sheikh is coming tonight for your milcha. Be home by maghreb.*

Summoned home before the sunset prayer to see the mulla who will marry him. So it begins. Again.

Abdulla pinches the bridge of his nose in what he hopes the rest of the table thinks is a gesture of concentration. Fatima used to call this mannerism his old-lady maneuver. "It's better than saying something mean," he would protest, but that only made her laugh at his restraint.

The meeting is breaking up, so he rises quickly and heads for the door. Ahmed tries to catch his eye, but several attendees engage him in post-meeting talk, allowing Abdulla to make a quick exit.

There is no need to stay, Abdulla thinks, striding down the hall. But there is something unsettling in Ahmed's look, an urgency in his eyes. Abdulla has not seen that look since the day of Fatima's death. It's almost as if Ahmed wants a last look at the man who is his son-in-law. The last living vestige of the life Fatima lived, however briefly, and might be living still. *If only she had lived. If only.* Abdulla shakes the thought out of his head. After all, Ahmed will see him again in just a few hours. But it will be after the ceremony that seals

Abdulla's fate as a remarried man. Maybe that's it—the next Abdulla Ahmed will see will be a new Abdulla. Maybe Ahmed knows he will never see this Abdulla again and wishes to say goodbye, with a look at least.

The thought doesn't slow Abdulla a step. If anything, it speeds him up. He makes a mental list of all the tasks he needs to do to make an initial exploration of setting up a food chain franchise. In recent years, starting a business has become all the rage—cupcakes among the women, and restaurants among the men. He had barely gotten settled into married life before the accident ruptured his sense of order. A sense of the unknown, accompanied, he admits, by the first stirrings of excitement he has felt in years, balances the dread he feels at the task awaiting him at home.

Chapter 5

"*Insha'Allah kheir,*" the sheikh says, as he hands over the contract bearing Hind's signature.

Abdulla takes it with his right hand, trying to show deference to the man, as is his due. But it's all so familiar—the lined face chanting suras from the Qur'an, his uncles looking on, his father wiping sweat from his forehead in what Abdulla can only read as relief. He is led by Hind's father, Uncle Saoud, from the *majlis* through their shared courtyard towards the room where he will have dinner with Hind—his cousin, who is more or less a stranger. On this night they are engaged, legally married in the eyes of God.

Neither he nor Saoud speaks, as if by tacit agreement in their silence that they are resolved to see this through. They enter the house by the main door. There are screens shielding the hallway and beyond, the rest of the house where the women are gathering for their feast to celebrate the marriage of the first daughter. He follows Saoud into the formal sitting room, the rectangular space lined with brass-armed cream sofas. There is a table with two chairs, like in the movies, placed in one corner, a flower arrangement of an explosion of multicolored roses in the center.

It's tall enough for them to hide behind rather than talk to each other, he thinks, over the dinner that will be served to them here, away from the rest of the celebrating women, the men eating in the *majlis*. Simple, he requested, for this second engagement.

"Your mother sent this over," Saoud is saying. There is a square red leather box with a brass clasp and a smaller red box on top with identical gold patterning on the edges. The necklace and ring, gifts from the groom to the bride. Gifts he chose himself the first time. For Fatima.

"Abdulla, I know you won't mind but there's something you should know. Hind—"

"Yes, Baba?" Hind answers from the foyer.

At that moment the owner of the voice materializes, a woman who bears no resemblance to the girl Abdulla remembers. She is almost as tall as he is, although that could be because of heels, and, unlike many girls her age, thin. Wearing a long-sleeved white dress, a silver embellishment at the waist, as she moves towards them her right leg keeps appearing in a slit several inches long.

"Hind," Saoud says. He looks from one to the other and then, as the families have agreed, leaves them alone.

Abdulla realizes Hind is sizing him up, unlike Fatima, who sat on the sofa and glanced up from under her lashes as he put the necklace around her neck while her mother and sister hovered. Despite her direct gaze, so different from the blush that warmed Fatima's cheeks the entire two hours he spent with her, he notices Hind's sleeves fluttering slightly. She is trembling.

He clears his throat and crosses to the boxes.

"These are for you," he says. He opens the first one, turning back to her to reveal a square diamond flanked by two smaller ones set in a band of even smaller stones winking up from the red cushion. Of course his mother's taste isn't what he would have chosen. That other ring so long ago had been only of gold, now melted down into a lump he keeps in the drawer by his bedside.

He hands over the ring box as she comes nearer. If they are fake lashes, they are very, very good. She takes the ring box as he opens the one with the necklace. He pulls out a multi-tier pearl choker, the row closest to the neck edged with diamonds. The ring box dangles from her hand, the ring still in it. They face each other. She is clenching her hands together.

"It's normal to be nervous," he says.

"Are you?"

"Well," he says.

There's nothing else to say that wouldn't be a lie, so an awkward silence grows between them. He certainly can't give voice to what he's thinking. *I've done this before.* He turns to pick up the necklace, absorbed in the movement, missing the pained expression that flickers across her face. It is his turn for trembling hands now at the sight of her shoulder blades in the deep V of the dress, or maybe it's the mounting sense of betrayal of Fatima's memory, he can't tell.

"Dinner is served." Noor bursts from behind the screen, a few of the Filipino catering staff behind her bearing an array of meal-related items.

They spring apart. Abdulla tosses the necklace back into its box.

"How's it going in here?" Luluwa slides into the room on the heels of the last server, narrowing her eyes at him. Her hair is twisted up, the lids of her eyes ringed with deep black liner, and there is glitter across her collarbone, drawing the eye to the strapless sweetheart neckline. The bell of her gown has fabric twisted in rows up towards her waist.

He tries to hide his relief by feigning irritation.

"Wow," Noor is saying at the sight of the ring, which is still in Hind's hand. "Put it on!"

Her sister complies, and Noor admires it from several angles. Luluwa comes closer, giving it a good squint before wandering over to the box containing the necklace. Making sure neither of her cousins is looking, she pulls a face then shoots Abdulla a look, which he returns with a shrug. She picks up the necklace, so unlike anything he would ever choose, and she lets it dangle in one hand, pointing in question.

Busy, he mouths as uniformed servers go back and forth carrying several plates, a bowl, glasses and cutlery. Their table for two is filled with samples of what the ladies are eating in the other room.

"Photographer, before eating," Noor says. "You're both wearing white."

"I'll go," Luluwa says. She returns with a short woman holding a camera in one hand and a detachable flash in the other.

"Sit, sit."

Aunt Wadha is now in the room, as is his mother and even, incredibly, Aunt Hessa, Fatima's mother. It's her presence that turns the blood in his veins cold. She is a shadow of herself, even in her finery, the metallic green of her dress casting a sallow light onto her face. Abdulla sits in the wingback armchair, his hands folded, as Hind is posed beside him on an identical chair, the necklace secured by his mother. The flash pops repeatedly as they are put in a variety of poses, on the sofa, standing, and then sitting again. They never touch, the smiles frozen on their faces.

Now that they are legally married he can call, text and go out with her, in the presence of another relative, until the reception, after which they will live together as man and wife. As Hessa hovers at the edge of the room while Wadha fusses over Hind, Abdulla remembers the scene as she surely does. Fatima in brown, a color he wouldn't have thought could be pretty, but that somehow on her was transformed. The sash around her waist and trailing down the side in one of the poses the photographer used, Abdulla's hand entwined with hers, the gold band standing out against the smooth background.

"You're not going to stay all night, are you?" his mother whispers when everyone else is focused on the bride's portraits. "She wants to have fun with her friends."

The photographer is zeroing in on the henna patterns snaking up Hind's fingers and hands, disappearing into the sleeves of her gown. Noor is arranging Hind's hair for a close-up.

"I'll let you ladies have your fun," he says.

"Aren't you hungry?" Hind is half off the sofa, as if she means to come after him. Her mother presses her back, making a *tsking* sound, indicating the photographer should continue.

Abdulla pauses in the doorway, the tableau of his cousins, aunts and mother behind him.

"I've got to get back to the office," he says. He leaves, walking away in strides that press his *thobe* against his ankles.

"She has set a condition," Luluwa says, coming out of the door after him, almost running to keep up.

"How much will the divorce cost me?" he replies, without slowing down. "Fifty or a hundred thousand?"

Luluwa grabs him by the sleeve, drawing him back underneath one of the lime trees planted by their grandfather.

"You look like a cupcake," he says. "Who picked this out?" In truth she is a vision, even if an overdressed one, dolled up by their aunts for the ladies' dinner in case anyone is bride- shopping.

"This isn't a game," she says. Her earnest eyes search him but he looks away, flicking an imaginary piece of lint from his sleeve. "She told the sheikh her condition is to be away for a year to finish her master's. And when she comes back, she wants to work."

It's his turn to clasp her hand, latching on to it, hoping she hasn't suspected, unlike anyone else, that this fact alone made him agree—a condition of temporary separation, one that no one else would want him to focus on. The news from the sheikh has become a beacon of hope, suddenly the most interesting angle about his wife-in-name-only. Hind will be away for a year.

"I know, Lulu," he says. "He had to tell me first."

"In the UK," Luluwa says, though he hasn't asked the question. Luluwa squirms in his lingering grip, and he releases her and takes a deep breath.

"Stop snooping," he says. "You shouldn't be involved in these things for adults."

His mind whirs as fast as it can go, as he turns away from Luluwa and back towards his room. Hind will live in the UK, alone, an unchaperoned Qatari girl, though this last part is irrelevant to him. If he puts off the reception until after her return, it means at least thirteen months or more they can continue as before.

"She'll be back eventually," Luluwa calls after him. "Your wife will come back."

He pretends not to hear. Another year will buy more time, maybe a way out of this madness. He married once because it was the right thing to do and because the family wanted to see a grandchild. A mistake he will do everything in his power to prevent from happening again.

Chapter 6

Noor is on the loose. Hind can tell from the staccato sound of heels on the marble staircase. In the hours since the *milcha* everyone in the house has been preparing for the ladies' celebration, and the only way her sister could be more excited is if she were the bride herself. Hind keeps zipping up the suitcase even as Noor, without knocking, throws open the closed door to her room. One more on a growing list of irritating things she will not miss. A list she has been harboring in her mind, unwilling to write down in case it jinxes the freedom that is so tantalizingly near. *Her last night in Doha. For a quite a while.*

"Dinner," Noor says. "The real dinner this time. When you actually eat."

Hind offers a shadow of a smile to placate her, even as the zipper resists. She puts one manicured hand on top and tries to squeeze the edges together.

"A few more minutes," she says. "I'm almost done."

"Some quick change," Noor grumbles as she trails around the room, which is full of the wilted remnants of a day spent preparing bridal finery: the white gown from meeting the groom tossed in the corner; the backup option; shoes strewn on either side of the bathroom door; rhinestone clasps, also discards, bright against the cream rug; the dresser top littered with an array of cosmetics and perfumes abandoned at various stages of use.

"People are used to it," Hind says. "They expect the bride to keep them waiting."

Everything around them says Hind is experiencing one of the biggest events of her life, everything but the absence of any shred of glee in her heart. Hind reopens the suitcase and scans the contents, assessing what can be dumped.

"Because you're changing," Noor retorts. "Not because you're packing."

Hind ignores her sister's pout. There is a stack of sweaters, jeans, and boots for the coming winter, since she will be dealing with seasons now, not just the steady palette of boiling, hot or tepid sunny days. A mega-bottle of honey her grandmother has sent up, the prayer rug her mother has thrown in, a laptop and charger, toiletries, and books she has started and can't wait to finish when she has more privacy. Not to mention a stack of *gahwa* coffee cups that are sure to break the moment someone at Doha Airport tosses the bag onto a belt.

"He's kind of hot," Noor says. "Right?"

Hind saw Abdulla's profile as he walked across the compound to their grandfather's house. The perch she and Noor used to toss water balloons from as children, and the safety of her tinted bathroom window, allowed her to watch as men filed into the *majlis*. He was thinner than she remembered, with angular features, broad shoulders, a spotless white *thobe*, no doubt starched by Anita for the occasion. But nothing that said mine, nothing distinguishing him from the rest of the men in the compound, the rest of the men in the country—in the world, for that matter. And that didn't change when they were face to face. Though, she can't argue with Noor's assessment. The years have whittled away any tendency towards the plumpness she sees in other men his age. Such bright, searching eyes, and well-defined lips—it must be proximity, but she doesn't remember him being *that* interesting.

But instead of giving any of this away, she shrugs at Noor's expectant look and pulls out the honey, encased in a glass bottle that is also a likely candidate for being pulverized en route to London. She sets the *gahwa* cups on the rumpled bedspread beside the nectar of the gods, discovering a profusion of plastic bags of coffee powder only her mother could have stashed in, then carton after carton of condensed milk. She tosses them out, one after the other, a few of the bags and cartons sliding off the duvet and onto the floor.

"What is *Ummi* thinking?" Hind says, all but shouting. "One of these bursts open and everything is ruined."

"Yeah, she could have got the cans, those hold up." Hind halts her excavating to glare at her sister. "They have milk in London," she says.

"Who cares about milk?" Noor retorts. "You are about to go to your engagement dinner."

Hind sticks her hand back in the bag and fishes out an insulated *dallah*, used to pour Arabic coffee.

"What do you think he's thinking?"

"Second time to the show," Hind replies. "Doubt he's thinking anything."

In the growing silence she looks up. Noor is pressed against the padded headboard, legs crossed at the ankle, texting, tweeting, or something that requires her face to be inches from the phone.

"Luluwa says he is nervous."

"You're not talking about this to her?"

Hind abandons the suitcase for a second and snatches the phone out of her sister's hand. Noor's blank look might as well have been a question mark rising in a cartoon bubble over her head.

"No one is going to get excited about second-hand goods," Hind says, tossing the phone out of reach onto the bed. "I'm the second wife."

"You've got to be kidding," Noor says. She smacks herself in the forehead. "Really?"

"He was married to our cousin, but maybe you don't remember because you were a pre-teen."

Noor comes across the bed towards Hind on her knees, pulling up the vermillion skirt of her gown. She picks up her phone, brandishing it like a baton.

"Married to Fatima for three months! The first wife is dead," she says. "*Allah yerhamha,*" she adds, invoking a blessing on the deceased.

"Second-hand is second-best," Hind says. Divested of its stowaways, the suitcase zips up without a hitch. "There's no point in pretending otherwise."

"He's not going to see you that way." Noor's eyes filled with admiration. "You're smart, and stylish—"

"Not *me*," Hind says. "I'm the virgin after all. *Him.* He's someone else's man. Not mine."

"You're crazy," Noor says. "He's older, lived abroad, will let you drive, see your friends."

She is ticking off each of his attributes on her fingers. "Probably only wants three kids instead of five. Letting you study abroad…"

Here she pauses for a second and glances at Hind over her outstretched fingers. "And what's with the sudden condition anyway? You never said anything about even applying for a master's."

"How noble of him," Hind says. "I'll be a professional baby maker. Do you think people list that on resumes?"

"Something's wrong with you."

"Me? I'm the one—"

"A few more things from your mother."

Their father lingers in the doorway as if a spell prevents him from crossing the threshold. Noor takes the ceramic *midkhan* and plastic containers of spreadable cheese he is holding.

"You don't need to bring these up, *Yuba,*" Noor says. "I'll come get them."

"Or the maid could put them in my bag when I'm not looking," Hind snarls.

Her father's gaze takes in the disheveled room, flicking over the pile of discarded items at the foot of the bed then back to rest on the two of them. "Your mother wants to make sure you're comfortable," he says. "And she wants you downstairs to greet your aunts."

Seeing the deep lines under his eyes, Hind resists the urge to shrug like a teenager.

"Allow her this," he says. He glances around again at the chaos, his empty hands dangling at his sides. Just when she thinks he'll leave, he comes into the room and straight towards her. "I didn't know you wanted to study," he says, then puts an arm around her shoulders. "You did well to ask. It's your right."

She holds still, tempted to relax in his touch, even if the praise is for something she detests.

"The two of you will do well together," he says to Hind, squeezing her arm.

"This is what I'm saying," Noor says.

Their father clears his throat. He smiles at them both, eyes traveling the room once again, lingering on a sepia photo Hind has tucked in the corner of the mirror on her dresser. A photo of all the girl cousins when they were still young enough to play in the family pool. Then he leaves.

"I'm telling you, this is a great deal," Noor is saying.

"Your opinion has been duly noted," Hind mutters, but only to herself. Noor is only saying what everyone else is thinking, the reasons her parents chose Abdulla.

Hind tosses the newly-arrived items on the floor, where they sink into the other things in the discarded pile. The pale pink incense burner with lace pattern work matching the wallpaper in her room lands with a clunk. Broken, or at the very least chipped. Her mother probably searched all the shops in the city for it. But it's not as if Hind is going to burn *bukhoor* in the UK.

"Let's gooooo," Noor says, all but stamping her feet.

Hind flicks a glance at the mirror, her breath coming out in a whoosh, only now admitting the small shred of hope she had that maybe, just maybe, they'd be able to work something out together. Instead she still feels the sting of their failed attempt at a meal together.

She considers her appearance. Ice blue, the dress she has chosen for the party to mark her becoming a married woman. The rhinestone-encrusted empire waist emphasizing her bust, only a cover-up for the growing hollowness inside; the mermaid silhouette enhancing her legs, making them appear even longer by hiding her feet; the pearl and diamond choker restricting her ability to breathe; the several-carat engagement ring burning a circle on her finger. *What a waste*, she thinks. But the suitcase behind her reflection reminds her that freedom is nearer than ever, even if it comes at the price of this farce.

Chapter 7

Dev, the Sri Lankan worker, brings in a chocolate basket so wide his arms can barely stretch across it. Abdulla waves him away but the man insists, a huge grin on his face.

"Sir, Hamad had a baby."

Abdulla grunts in reply, a response he knows is much like his father's when hearing trivial information. Though his father would be delighted at the news that Abdulla's secretary Hamad, a man he's never met, is doing his duty by his family and procreating. And by society. *Ergo* his country.

"The wife had the baby, Dev," Abdulla says.

Dev hoists the basket onto Abdulla's desk as an office messenger wanders in to get Abdulla's signature on a sheaf of papers. Abdulla indicates that the boy should leave the papers on the table, and sees his covert looks at the chocolate basket. He twists off one square piece and tosses it at the messenger, who clasps the chocolate to his chest like it is worth the gold foil it came wrapped in. There is a flash between the two workers, and for a second Abdulla thinks he detects envy on Dev's face. But it is quickly replaced by that simpering smile worn by all the tea boys and messengers who work in the department.

They leave him to the silence of his office, and for a second Abdulla has an urge to call them back rather than face the round of well-wishers he knows will soon descend on his lackadaisical secretary, the back of whose head he can see from the corner of his desk. Hamad won't do any work today; it will be spent showing off photos of the baby, as well as drinking cups of tea with each visitor.

As if he were at home in his majlis, Abdulla thinks. There will be a lot of this since, as Abdulla has gleaned from the grapevine, the baby is a much-anticipated boy. He pulls the sheaf of papers toward him—all authorizations for business-related travel, most of it to London, a few trips to Germany, one to Switzerland. He signs, indicating where Hamad should come after him to stamp the various documents. Without a stamp the requests would be returned, as there'd be no proof that the trip had been approved, which means they would be trashed and each applicant would have to start the process all over again.

Abdulla is unsure whether any of the applicants' needs to go abroad are genuine, but knows he'd be very unpopular if he didn't sign. A yearly trip to London with per diem is expected for most of the ministry's employees. The male employees, that is, he reminds himself as he finishes, putting the lid back on his pen. They are the only ones funded to travel.

No wonder Hind kept her request to study secret until the last moment. Now she is away, away from him and the pressure to schedule the reception, after which they will live together. After her return—he tries not to wish away the year that has been granted to him—she will join the other female employees of his section in a separate part of the building, the women's area. He'll have to call or go over in order to see her, or any of them.

"Alf mabrook!" one of Hamad's well-wishers exclaims in congratulation.

"Yetrabba fi 'izzak," someone else says.

Despite his best efforts, Abdulla still feels his heart clench at these words, knowing that his own unborn baby will never "be brought up in his father's glory," as the saying goes, while Hamad's might.

"*Allah ybarek feek,*" Hamad replies, returning their blessings. There are three guys in the anteroom crowded around Hamad's desk. *Like a bunch of women,* Abdulla thinks to himself.

His heart twists at the thought of the photo tucked in his phone case. The edges are fraying; sooner or later it will split in half and the only image he has of his unborn child will also be lost to him.

He turns back to the contracts a few international suppliers have sent in response to his request for franchise agreements. The rumors about the oil wealth of the Gulf are clearly reflected in the inflated quotations. He immerses himself in the increasingly familiar world of contracts, relishing the need to decode their intricate, indirect language.

"Sheikh Abdulla," one of the visitors calls out. "Join us this weekend! We're going to the camp."

"Thanks, but I've got some meetings arranged," Abdulla says. He is still waiting for a few grocers to get back to him, but the guys don't need to know nothing is confirmed.

Hamad shakes his head as if to avert their attention, but his visitors carry on.

"Hamad here will need someone during his wife's *nifas*, the forty days she is recovering," another says as he grasps Hamad by the shoulder.

Some of the men chuckle, but Abdulla blanches at the reference to the escorts they hire for such occasions.

"Does no one have any work to do today?" Abdulla mutters as he hands the completed dossier back to Hamad. He gives the group one look before he exits, car keys jingling in the pocket of his *thobe*.

"He'll never come," Abdulla overhears Hamad say in a hushed tone.

"Into boys?" someone asks.

Another man, one who cared about these kinds of rumors, would have gone back, double-time, and either thrashed him for the insult or taken up the invitation, to remove any such doubt. But Abdulla does neither. He keeps walking through the carpeted hallways of the Diwan towards the rear exit. Let them think he is gay. In their gender-segregated society it isn't uncommon for people to have such relationships—yet another thing no one wants to talk about.

When he does have those urges it is often late at night, and he deals with them in the same manner as young, single men all over Qatar. By himself.

Chapter 8

Hind throws her mobile across the hotel room in frustration. She returns to Craigslist, hoping there's a new post. Today's visit to a property, the latest in a series of failed attempts through estate agents – who divine from the minute they hear her name that she is from the Gulf and therefore made of money, and only show her places well above her student price range – has her despairing of ever settling into this, her best year ever. With the start of classes in a few days, she has yet to settle the most basic of questions about her new life.

An email alert from the laptop brings more questions from her mother and sister. The preparations for the wedding continue in her absence, the presence of the bride unnecessary, much as it was for the engagement. Ideas for centerpieces, photos of dresses and suggestions for favors trickle in, as the money her father gave her for the first term trickles out. She can't ask for more money and raise further questions about the feasibility of her being out on her own, though he would probably give her whatever she wanted. As it is, the family is trying to tighten the noose and get her to stay with one of their relatives.

"If she wants to be an overeducated wife, fine, but without any family escort, ill-advised." Her aunts issue dire warnings, but her father waves the worries aside whenever his wife parrots them at the dinner table.

"He's agreed," he says, meaning her husband. Hind shudders again at the thought of Abdulla, more or less a stranger, having so much influence over her life. If there is a silver lining, it is that in much the same way he slipped out of their engagement dinner, he is staying in the shadows now that they have permission to talk and text as much as they like. She doesn't know whether to be grateful or resentful of his inattention. If she were in Doha, Noor would surely take issue with their negligence of the privileges of the engaged, and push them to spend time together. At the thought of more awkward gatherings, Hind realizes what a blessing being in London is. Ten times what she originally envisaged.

She tries not to count the texts, phone calls and emails from home as anything other than the price of freedom, the penalty for lusting after an advanced degree that no one sees the point of since her engagement to Abdulla. Instead, she perseveres with the estate agents, learning to Google them for client comments, before finding one earnest British-Algerian woman who seems to take pleasure in their shared Arab identity, her tight curls bouncing in delight as Hind replies to her questions in Arabic.

"*Ahlan, ahlan,*" Assia says, welcoming Hind into her office. Hind is grateful for the woman's effusiveness. This is the first person she's spoken to after a weekend spent alone, and in Arabic at that. Assia takes Hind on an exhausting set of tours that are as depressing as the previous ones, only this time because of how little space her father's generous allowance gets her. This, plus the modest salary the government gives her for studying, money she had hoped to save up for she doesn't know what, all go into the apartment they finally locate in a building in South Kensington.

Hind manages to sign a lease and unpack five suitcases before the orientation day for new graduate students at the university; outfitting the rest of the apartment will have to wait.

When she arrives for orientation, bang on time, which would have been considered early in Doha, she is the last student there. So much for trying to avoid the stereotype of being "on Arab time." The British are so punctual. Everyone else in the auditorium lobby is checking and rechecking the status of their book orders, unused pens and pencils, or clocks on their cell phones.

She pushes her bangs off her forehead, wondering if she has time to head to the bathroom and touch up her makeup, when her phone rings, breaking out in the loud tones of Rihanna's "Rude Boy," a joke she allowed herself after the disappointing meeting with Abdulla. In the hallway it peals out, announcing her status as a non-intellectual. She silences the ringer, glancing at the caller ID. Another phone call from her mother wondering what she's up to, will she come home during the winter break, wouldn't she rather stay with some cousins from her mother's side who are also studying in North London. One of the aunties is actually there getting some medical treatment—does she want to live in her extra room?

"If I wanted to live under the eyes of your sisters or my cousins," Hind answers in increasingly loud Arabic, "I would have stayed in Qatar!" She grinds her teeth, knowing her mother can't see her. *For now I have a year in London,* she reminds herself, mentally steeling herself against the idea that the tentacles of domesticity are reaching across the ocean for her. *A year,* she keeps repeating, as if the words are some kind of prayer.

Her shoulders are still shaking with what's left of her fury as everyone else files into the auditorium, the doors of which have opened behind her. She stands still for a while, trying to will away the negativity, as Oprah always tells her viewers. Instead of feeling grounded, a sob rises in her chest. She hiccups but soldiers on, not wanting to miss a moment of what she's paid for with her future.

"Tissue?" an Indian girl with a disconcerting American accent asks, as Hind slides into the empty seat beside her. Black lashes so long they surely aren't real frame eyes full of unasked for sympathy. "My parents are the same way," the girl says, patting Hind's shoulder.

Hind returns her intrusive kindness with a shuttered glance. "You've been screaming on the phone for the last twenty minutes, sweetie. Anyone who got here early heard it all." The girl offers a sympathetic smile, exposing white, even teeth.

Hind accepts the tissue, dabbing at her eyes with one hand while the other worries a strand of pearls. "Thank you for the tissue."

The girl smiles again, giving Hind's shoulder a squeeze. This is the first time anyone has touched her since she moved to London. Even so, her instinct is to move away from, not toward, this over-friendly person.

"I'm Sangita," the girl whispers. The tutor drones on in the front of the room about when they will get their class assignments. "Where are you from?" Hind asks, taking in the girl's accent and silver halter top, which are at odds with her golden skin and long, black hair.

"India," Sangita winks. "By way of America. The Brits aren't used to that!"

Neither, Hind has to admit, is she.

At the department lunch a few hours later, Sangita seeks her out again.

"Where are you living?"

"South Ken," Hind says, and then allows herself a moment of pride. "I just signed."

Sangita gives her a high five and Hind, feeling slightly teenager-ish but still proud, follows through.

"Mine isn't going half as well," Sangita says without being asked. Comfortable with self-disclosure, she tells Hind more in their first twenty minutes than Hind has ever revealed to many of her family members in Doha. Sangita refuses to take money from her parents because this would mean they could come and stay whenever they wanted.

"I'm looking at places in North London," she says, taking a bite of the department-provided fish and chips.

"That's forty minutes away," Hind says. Sangita shrugs. "Price of freedom," she replies.

This is a sentiment Hind understands, so she doesn't continue with the brimming questions she has about safety in North London. Besides, from the confident way her disheveled acquaintance moves, Hind surmises that she can handle herself, or if nothing else yell loudly for help.

As the first day ends, Hind trudges back to her empty apartment, missing her sister Noor in a way she never would have believed possible, even though many tried to warn her. Sitting on the bar stool at her kitchen counter drinking tea, she doesn't know why, but in the center of London, living her dream, she feels loneliness growing in the silence of the apartment she has fought so hard to live in, unchaperoned.

The evening news darkens her mood even further. The grainy footage of a mall fire in Qatar is on AlJazeera's English channel. Hind watches, phone in hand to the live Twitter stream, computer open at her feet, as children are lifted through the roof of Villaggio Mall, plumes of smoke blackening the blue sky. Tears roll down her cheeks as her family call her periodically through the night.

Thirteen children, four teachers and two firefighters are all dead from toxic smoke because no one could get to the activity center inside the mall where they were trapped. The recriminations start; the government mobilizes a press conference. Hind watches it from the Skype camera Noor has trained on Qatar TV in the family's living room.

She has never felt so far away from home.

She receives a text. All of her relatives are on BlackBerry Messenger or WhatsApp. *Saw the fire. Terrible. Call me if you want me to come over. Sang.*

Hind wipes fresh tears away, startled by the Indian girl's thoughtfulness.

A *"Thanks"* is all she manages to send back.

The scale of the tragedy is unlike anything Hind or anyone in Qatar has ever seen. She goes to bed knowing that the idyllic world she left behind in Doha no longer exists, unsure if she is prepared to face the new one.

Chapter 9

Hind fills the hours as best as she can, not with shopping, as her family does on its summer vacations to London, but with reading the hundreds of assigned pages for her courses in theory, literature and statistics.

She takes first one and then a second bus to campus, past Harrods and the other haunts of their summer visits, and then walks several blocks to campus. This is no cab ride to Oxford Street.

No matter how much she reads, underlines and marks up the pages, the words won't come to her when she's actually in class. Despite the best training at an American university in Qatar, she is at a loss in the graduate seminars in England, hoping no one else can see how much she struggles to keep up.

Danny, a fellow student in their cohort, volunteers to moderate the first class discussion.

"Yes, but why did Edward Said become such a luminary?" Hind is put off by the question and by him, his stained teeth and tattered sweater, his calculated sloppiness. These Brits.

With a slight shock, she realizes Danny's owlish gaze, along with everyone else's, is trained fully on her.

"Orientalism is so obvious," Hind stammers, "if only to the Orientals."

No one looks satisfied, but her throat is dry and her mind empty of any other words. Instead of sinking down into her chair or running from the room (her immediate impulses), she sits up straighter, trying to pull something out of the tangled jumble of words on the page in front of her.

"People are products of their culture," the girl Sangita cuts in, filling the awkward gap, "so they can't see how complicit they are in their own racism. Said made it impossible to overlook." Everyone nods, even Danny; Hind realizes with amazement their balding tutor appears to be actually taking notes. The tractor beam of attention moves on further around the table, as the discussion then turns to how to prep for the first exam.

Hind catches up with Sangita after class as everyone else trickles out of the building toward the pubs.

"How did you have time for all the reading?" she asks, pulling on her bangs in frustration as she shoots the girl a sideways glance, equal parts jealousy and admiration.

Sangita throws a companionable arm around her new friend. "I didn't," she admits.

Hind stops in their progression toward the door.

"You didn't?" Her red leather messenger bag sinks to the floor. Sangita returns her gaze without blinking.

"But you were so confident. And I knew what I wanted to say. I just didn't have the words." Hind's shoulders cave in. She blinks as her vision begins to swim in tears.

"Oh, come on, let's get a cup of coffee and I'll give you a crash course in Bullshitting 101."

Sangita drags the astonished Hind down the steps and into a nearby coffee shop. They sit on metallic stools, the only seats available to them, and watch passers-by as they wait for their orders to be called up.

"Skim," Sangita says. "Skim the headings, the intro, the conclusion, and you've got the essence."

Hind takes a huge sip of her cup of Earl Grey and contemplates the girl she has spent the past few weeks not noticing. Sangita is chugging a Coke from the bottle and has the text open to show her what she means. Hind pulls out her own already well-worn copy of the reader, embarrassed by the color-coded highlighting across the pages.

"You need to get macro," Sangita says, "not lost in the details." Hind gulps down more of her tea. "That's how you fake the readings?" Sangita nods.

Hind reaches for a pen.

She feels the girl's eyes lingering on her face, though she looks away quickly when Hind meets her gaze.

"Something wrong?" Sangita shakes her head.

Hind begins to underline the chapter headings of the next assignment.

"So here, in this section on Fanon, I would go off at a tangent about what?" She catches Sangita staring again, this time at Hind's neck and ears. "Anything related," Sangita says.

Hind puts down her pen carefully. In Qatar there is a substantial underground community of women with close female friends. Very close. She wonders if in her loneliness she has stumbled into a misunderstanding.

"Is there a problem?"

Sangita takes a deep gulp of Coke and shrugs her shoulders, eyes wide.

Hind gathers her things. The last thing she needs is a lesbian stalker. This must be the kind of look Noor tells her the boyas use at the university when picking their girlfriends. Butch Qatari girls or a girl-on-girl infatuation are not high on Hind's list of things to do. Though according to Noor, people tolerate this, as it is a sign of status to have a girl like you. What else can you do in a gender-segregated society, as Noor puts it. Well, she isn't there right now, so she for one can do something about it. Hind brushes away the thoughts of home.

"Thanks for your help," she says. "See you next week." Sangita grabs her wrist as Hind keeps putting things into her bag. At Hind's look, the girl drops her arm.

"I thought you had to wear a veil," she says in a rush. "But you're not."

Despite herself, Hind laughs at the furrow in the girl's brow. Her shoulders relax and she twirls the pen she was going to put into her bag.

"The veil is religious," she says. "For some people. For others, it's cultural."

Sangita leans forward, elbows on the table. "You're on the cultural side?"

Hind lets out a little sigh.

"There's no real point in talking about it. People's minds are already made up. Those who do, aren't going to stop... " She trails off, unsure of what else to say about this symbol that Westerners are obsessed by.

"And those who don't aren't going to start," Sangita finishes.

Hind nods.

"Couldn't have put it better myself."

Chapter 10

"The British system is so weird," Sangita says. "You don't even have to show your face. In the U.S. you get marked down if you don't go to class."

Hind looks up from her book. "That sounds like high school."

A rare shaft of sunlight illuminates the coffee table where the two girls are delving into a stack of used books they've just bought. Close to campus, Hind's sparse flat has become a replenishing hub for Sangita.

"Maybe, but think about it. Only about four of us, out of a dozen international students in the program, always attend section. We've met only two of the others in our own program. It's crazy."

Hind has to admit that the daily sessions aren't worth that much. Today, during their postcolonial African literature seminar, she doodled a map of the African continent. True, she's gotten to know almost none of the other international students. But she has no complaints. She has Sangita, this bubbling spirit of a girl with whom Hind has rapidly formed the first solid relationship she has ever known outside her family.

From the start, something told her that, unlikely though it was, they could be friends. Only a week after their first seminar meeting she did what she would only do for a friend from the Gulf or a relative. Instead of going out for coffee, she invited her over for tea.

A bit hesitant at first, Sangita made a breezy joke out of being both Indian and American, "which in the UK means I'm a two-time loser."

Hind wasn't sure how to respond. "I grew up with an Indian maid," she said after a pause, and couldn't help noticing her new friend's slight wince. She rushed on. "Anita. My grandfather found her during his trips to trade on the Kerala coast, and she's been with the family ever since."

"Well, our housekeeper is Mexican," Sangita replied, letting the pressure off. "My family is full of entrepreneurs, too. Dad's into hotels but I didn't catch that bug."

"Everyone in Doha wants to own a business," Hind said. "Cupcakes or *abayas* are the current rage. Oh, and magazines."

"Cupcakes?"

Hind laughed. "Qataris love to eat."

"You're getting this degree to design abayas?"

Hind stopped laughing. Sangita indicated she had clotted cream on the corner of her lip and she wiped it away.

"I want to be an ambassador." Something she had never said out loud to anyone else.

"Do Qatari women do that?"

Hind shrugged. "I would."

"Somebody has to be the first," Sangita said, as if this was the most normal thing in the entire world to want. She didn't list all the reasons this was a bad profession for a woman or why Hind was being too demanding of her culture. Instead Sangita chattered on about the eccentricities of her own family, how odd she thought her mother was for trying to instill a sense of domestic duty in her even though they had a housekeeper, how Saturdays involved being dragged to the Indian grocery store so that she could keep an eye on her mother's purchases.

"If I'm honest, Mom's attempts to domesticate me haven't really amounted to much. I can barely boil water. But I make some mean eggs."

Hind sighed. "Whatever it is, we always have people there to do it," she said, ignoring Sangita's surprise. "The cook cooks, the maid cleans, the driver drives."

Sangita's phone buzzed on the table between them but she didn't answer. This caused Hind to raise an inquiring eyebrow.

"Parents," Sangita said. "You know, checking I'm alive." She stretched her arms. "If you want to know the truth, I can't wait to get engaged. That will make them happy, and maybe then they'll leave me the hell alone."

Hind replied with a snort. "That's just the beginning." Sangita's eyes widened in surprise. "How would you know?"

Hind looked away, then back. "I'm engaged," she burst out.

Sangita froze. "What? Are you serious?"

"Totally."

"Your husband is going to travel around with you?" Hind took a sip of tea.

"Well! Forget all those career aspirations," Sangita boomed with fake delight. She put on the high-pitched voice and blinking expression of an old auntie. "Congratulations, dear, may you give birth before your anniversary."

They dissolved into helpless laughter, holding their sides.

"It's such a relief to tell someone!" Hind said, falling back on the red sofa that had been delivered just that day, bringing some much-needed color into the apartment. "You know white people; they'd think I was going to be chained to the wall or something."

"You mean you won't be?"

Hind paused for a minute, frowning. When Sangita didn't blink, the two burst into peals of laughter again.

༄

Now, looking back on that first awkward tea, Hind still marvels at how quickly she confided in Sangita. It's the last thing she would have expected. After all, they're so different in so many ways. She's given up keeping track of the contradictions. Sangita won't hesitate to take the Tube, which Hind would never do. Back home she drives her own car, even parks it herself. Yet here in London the girl has no idea how to do the grocery shopping or even make a cup of tea. She is full of twists and turns; one minute Hind thinks of her as a cousin or even a sister, then the next it's as if she is indeed the near-stranger she met only a few weeks ago. There is money in Sangita's family, no doubt, but the differences between their privileged upbringings are so stark that Hind sometimes wonders whether, if the two met in Qatar, they would give each other a second glance.

But their similarities are just as striking—a penchant for scouring neighborhood bookstores, for example.

"Can't they find something new to write about us?" Hind mutters, as she flips the pages on a book she picked up from a table marked "Essential Texts: Arab Women."

"Orientalism is not dead!" Sangita declares, picking out one particularly lurid tome with veiled women's faces on the cover, only eyes showing. She holds it up to Hind's face, squinting, as if to compare the two. As so often, they erupt in giggles that turn into loud guffaws. When they do this in a bookshop it touches off uneasy glances in their direction. White women hug their purchases tighter to their chests and wander quickly into another part of the shop. Hind has to grab her friend's arm and propel her out into the street before they are mistaken for hooligans.

The two never seem to tire of trading stories about parents who want them to find marital happiness, when what each of them really wants is academic or professional success. Before meeting Sangita, Hind thought the Gulf pressure to marry and have a family was second to none. Spouse-hunting at weddings was an Arab mother's specialty, or so Hind always believed. But Sangita has regaled her with stories of similar antics by Indian mothers in the United States. Matchmaking and constant introductions of eligible bachelors, all nauseatingly familiar.

"I want to see a book about similarities in Gulf and Indian marriage rites," Sangita says. "Why don't you write it?"

"Maybe I will."

Hind knows Sangita doesn't approve of her engagement to Abdulla. She tries not to liken it to the old-fashioned custom of arranged marriages that used to be widely accepted in India as well. "We had a little pressure, yes," she says, "but it was generalized. *Just get married* was the message. Nothing specific was actually arranged. It was our decision. You have to admit there's been a little progress."

Sangita won't have any of it. "It still sounds coerced to me. I can't tell you how many of my cousins have been in marriages like that—arranged marriages," she says, shaking her head. "Still, in this day. And to keep their parents happy."

"But ours is more like… a marriage of convenience," she explains.

"Convenience?" Sangita says. "Like the old Europeans? Land deals, pure and simple."

"You mean like in the fifteenth century," Hind says, scoffing.

"You know what I mean."

"He's family. The money, the land, the name. Yeah, I guess it is like the medieval Europeans."

"Is he at least hot?"

"You sound like my sister. Who is a teenager," Hind says, laughing. "You can judge for yourself. Here, I'll show you the engagement photos."

Hind reaches under the sofa and pulls out a photo album. Looking at it with Sangita, she tries to view their official portrait from a non-Qatari perspective: on a low, highbacked cream sofa with green paisley wallpaper in the background, a youngish man, handsome but stern-looking, sits stiffly beside her.

"You'll come to the wedding," she says, looking up at a surprised Sangita. "There will be six hundred other women there, so you'll fit right in."

Sangita smiles slowly and nods. "Well, why not? I'll come. Actually, it could be fascinating. I mean, I've never been to a wedding without everyone my parents ever knew being there. And the idea of an all-female reception, without any photography? Rather intriguing."

"Who knows who you might meet," Hind teases. "On the other hand, my sister always says 'Don't go to a wedding to find a wife, go to a funeral. That's when you know what they really look like.'"

"I don't think I'll share that gem with my mother," Sangita says. "One of the reasons I left home was because the whole family decided to take on the mission of finding me a husband. I wasn't safe with anyone. I don't want to give her any more ideas about where to find a potential groom for me."

For the first three months of their program Hind left the walls of the flat bare, the polar opposite of her wall, indeed every wall she's ever seen, back home in Qatar. It gave her a quiet feeling of liberation.

But for the past two weeks, as Hind has written a paper for the media and popular culture seminar, a rolled-up poster has sat on the island in the kitchen. Sangita, who has had enough of bare walls, has decided to frame it during reading week as a way to commemorate their survival of the first term. She talks Nigel the security guard into letting her enter the flat one afternoon while Hind is still in class, and hangs it above the sofa as a statement to offset the apartment's dismal lack of décor.

Hind, when she walks in, laughs until her sides hurt at the installation of teenage heartthrob Robert Pattinson, whom she calls "as pale as a bad shade of foundation." But Sangita's tactless push to get Hind to decorate the walls galvanizes the haute couturista in her, though the poster retains its prime placement in the apartment even after the painting of various rooms and the introduction of actual framed art, including Arabic calligraphy.

Hind realizes Sangita has become almost a roommate. She is as used to Sangita as she is to Noor, and when the obvious conclusion strikes her, she's amazed it took so long. "Look, Sangita, I should have realized this long ago, but you should have the spare bedroom."

"Oh, I can't."

"No, no, it's yours. Really."

"No, I mean I can't… Well, I just don't think I can afford it." Hind waves away any thought of sharing the rent.

"I'm not trying to make money," she says. "I'd be paying the rent anyway... But with you here I'd have a friend to share things with. Not just now and then, but all the time." Sangita's hesitant smile turns weepy as she throws her arms around Hind.

Yes, Hind thinks, *this is what I need.* Company, as the second term draws on and the chill of the British fall hardens into winter. Workload is bound to increase, and exams will call for intense late cramming. The lonely anxiety of all this would be eclipsed by having Sangita here, ready to listen to her deepest thoughts, worries and fears without judging them through the lens of what-will-so-and-so-think?

"So, that's done?"

Sangita looks up and nods vigorously, her face wet, full of gratitude. "Done."

Chapter 11

Incredibly, Noor's presence in Essex for the past six months has turned out to be no problem at all. Hind had expected her little sister to be all over her, but besides a "Hi, let's meet soon," there have been no cries for help.

Her mother, who helped Noor move in during the winter, actually came and went without Hind having to host her for tea or otherwise subject herself to interrogation, thank goodness. Her mother texted that she wanted to visit, or at the very least meet Hind at Heathrow on her way home, but Hind made sure she was unavoidably busy during the narrow window of time her mother had available.

Meanwhile, Noor has hardly been in touch and seems to be doing fine, which is definitely a relief, though behind the relief Hind has to admit she is a little irked, maybe even disappointed. Noor doesn't need her? Well, fine.

Still, as big sister, she really ought to do her duty and at least drop in for a visit. Things aren't always what they seem. What if the poor girl is floundering but too proud to call? Hind decides to skip another day of classes—she's already skipped so many she's lost count—and pop in on her sister. It means a tedious train trip to Essex, but if she's needed, she's needed.

"Skipping again?" Sangita says, noticing Hind is still in bed. Sangita, of course, is all ready for class and probably has been since dawn.

Certainly the two of them have been exceptionally good roommates, but as the third term has dragged on, the differences in their approaches to class attendance and studying have become more and move evident.

"Please don't go on at me," Hind groans from the bed. "I have to check on Noor today and you know we don't have to go to the lectures."

"Listen, if we were in America we'd both fail if we didn't show up," Sangita calls back from the front door. "But as my father would say, words of wisdom going down the drain." She pulls on her boots. "And I doubt Noor needs as much help as you say. You just like riding the train."

"To Colchester, seriously?"

But the door has shut. Hind rolls back over in bed and pulls down her eyeshade.

There hasn't been a text from Noor in days, which can only mean Sangita is right and her sister is finally settling into her undergraduate program. Poor mother. First one daughter abroad, now the other. From the silence in the days since her mother helped Noor move in, Hind knows she blames her for the liberalization of the family.

As the tantalizing degree comes ever closer, Hind is starting to think about the welcome reception brewing at home, the one that will shortly usher in her new life beside the stranger she is already half-married to.

A knock at the door wakes Hind up, and for a moment she doesn't know where she is. She must have dropped off, because the last thing she remembers is trying to decide which train she needs to take to visit Noor. If, that is, she is going to keep to her plan, which is becoming less and less attractive as she thinks about it. She must have dressed and then flopped on the bed again, studying train schedules.

More knocking. Sangita is out, so she can't yell for her to get the door.

"Is Sangita here?"

Still half-asleep, Hind stumbles to the door and cracks it open. Peering out, she sees a tall, very dark, extremely handsome man with hair thicker and blacker than her own. Could it be one of her cousins? He looks so familiar, and not at all threatening.

"Sangita," he repeats, smiling slightly. He raises his voice a bit, and enunciates carefully. "Is she here?"

"Sangita? No, she's in class." Hind feels herself blush as she studies him. No, he's not Arab. He looks more like…like Sangita, she decides. Indian. And, like Sangita, his accent is oddly American.

"You are?"

"Ravi," he announces, as if this explains everything.

They linger in the doorway. Hind is thankful she fell asleep with her Armani jumpsuit on and not the tattered jeans she normally lounges around in when she stays home all day.

"Nigel let you up?" she asks, stalling. Usually their security guard is much more attentive. She doesn't want to be rude, but if Sangita has a boyfriend this is certainly the first she's heard of it.

"Didn't seem to have a problem." Ravi gives her a smile that, though practiced, still has the desired effect. She somehow feels more at ease, if not positively intrigued by the appearance of his dimples. There is something about the grin that is familiar, though she cannot put her finger on it.

"Sangita isn't home yet," she says.

"You're in the middle of something," he says, as if just realizing the awkwardness of the situation. "I promise I'm not a serial killer."

"The thought hadn't occurred to me," she says with a laugh, although of course it had. Is she imagining the tension in the air? Not one of fear, not in the slightest. If anything, she is mildly excited. She is caught up in the evenness of his teeth, the confident way he holds himself.

"Well, come in and wait, then," she says, opening the door to a male stranger in a way she would never be able to do in her father's house. If her mother knew, Hind thought, she would have a meltdown to rival any Arabic soap opera.

He follows her into the apartment.

"So this is where it happens," Ravi says. Hind hovers in the kitchen.

"That's an odd thing to say," she remarks. "Where what happens?"

"Marathon studying," he says. "Which I assume is why she never calls anyone back."

Hind chuckles, partly at his sarcasm, but mostly because she knows "studying" is the excuse both of them use to dodge any familial duties. But if Ravi is her boyfriend—she stops herself short, surprised at the thought on several levels.

"Sangita is a busy girl," she says.

"So busy she hasn't even told me much about her roommate." Hind isn't sure how to take that observation. She puts on the kettle to distract herself from his direct gaze.

"I'm Hind," she says. "We're in the program together."

Ravi doesn't say anything, just follows her into the kitchen and leans on the island, which makes her more nervous. He is lean, unlike the men in her family, with the exception of Abdulla, but her mind shies away from focusing on Abdulla, and instead contrasts this stranger generally with most of the men in Qatar above the age of twenty-five. She isn't going to look at Ravi's arms again, at his snug t-shirt. She really isn't. But of course she does, as she hands him the cup of mint tea. He raises it in thanks and they both take a long, contemplative sip.

"You live in London?" she enquires.

He laughs and shakes his head, setting the cup down. "That's very nice tea," he says. "What is it? Mint?"

"Moroccan," she says.

"I'm here on a visit. Checking up on Sangita. On my way from the States to India."

"India?"

He regards her closely, breaking into a slow smile. "You don't know who I am, do you?"

Before she can follow up on this bizarre question, the door is flung open and Sangita barrels through, arms laden with books, a messenger bag slipping down one arm.

"Ravi!" she squeals, dropping everything to rush over to him. "You technophobe. Have you heard of email?"

"What's wrong with actually answering a ringing phone?"

He laughs, as if at a child. Hind, totally confused, takes another sip of her tea and turns sideways to give them privacy. She braces for Sangita to clasp him in a passionate embrace (as she would do, she has to admit, if this specimen of manhood were hers—and if she did that kind of thing). Instead, the girl takes him by both hands and holds him at arms length, as if to size him up.

"You're getting fat," Sangita says.

Hind coughs as her tea goes down the wrong pipe. She's always thought Arabs were the only ones to be so direct. Whatever the case, if this is fat, then she'd love to see him skinny. She flushes at the thought, though no one but her is aware of it.

"I was going to say the same thing about you," Ravi retorts. Now they embrace, but again it's not a body-crushing thing, no fingers in her hair, like a lovers' reunion in the movies.

"Mother sent you?" Sangita asks.

Mother? Needing something to do with her hands, Hind pours Sangita a cup, knowing it will likely go untouched. Ravi leans down to pick up the books she tossed aside in the entryway.

"Hind, you already met Ravi—"

"I'm going to the orphanage," he says, his eyes widened. "You want to come?"

"Your mother?" Hind bursts out, unable to contain herself any longer.

Ravi and Sangita turn their attention back to her, as if having forgotten she is in the room.

She bites her lip and continues.

"Your mother set you up with someone and you didn't tell me?" She hates the peevish tone that has crept into her voice. But the sight of them together, their warmth and delight in each other, reminds her too much of Abdulla's coldness waiting for her back in Doha.

"I'm sorry," Sangita says, realizing the problem. "This is Ravi, my brother." She squeezes his arm. "Ravi, this is Hind."

Ravi casts a teasing look at first one then the other. "As you said, we've met."

Still in semi-shock, Hind swallows her tea. She couldn't have been more stunned if her tongue had gone down with it. Ravi and Sangita laugh at the obviously flustered look on her face.

"I'm sorry," Sangita says again. "How could I have never mentioned him?"

"How indeed, Gita," Ravi says, drawing himself up in fake umbrage. "Not once? Not even once?"

"As for the orphanage," Sangita says with a wave of her hand, thrusting on with business, "I'm afraid I have to be here for lectures. In case you've forgotten, I'm a full-time student, brother. You need to count me out."

"Oh, that's bull." Ravi laughs dismissively.

"No, it's not. I've got to finish writing my thesis."

Hind takes in the two of them, their playful bickering. Ravi has looped his right arm around his sister's shoulders, and it's a lovely image, his burnt umber complementing her cinnamon, their dark hair and dark eyes a perfect match. The more she looks, the more the family resemblance strikes her, as does Ravi's attractiveness, which seems to grow on her every time she looks at him. One or two times she meets his open gaze, but draws her eyes away at the unsettling thought that the man is infinitely more interesting now that she knows he isn't her friend's boyfriend.

She tries to distract herself by contemplating Sangita, a pencil stuck in a bun at the nape of her neck, her long-sleeved plaid shirt untucked over leggings and greenish boots. A lot of work still to be done, Hind observes, where her friend's fashion sense is concerned. But who knows whether she has enough time left? "Married?" Hind asks, immediately wishing she could take the question back. But if Ravi is startled by her frankness, he doesn't let it show. "Nope."

"Different rules for boys and girls," Sangita sing-songs, raising her eyebrows at Hind. "You should be familiar with that idea."

There is an impishness rising in Hind, maybe brought on by the sight of Ravi's dimples. "I've heard of it," she says. "But I think it sucks."

"No society is exempt from it," Sangita says, persisting.

"Is that such a marvelous thing?" Hind snaps back, and the two friends hold each other's gaze for a moment.

"So, girls," Ravi slaps his thighs and sighs, glancing at his watch. A typical man, he seems oblivious to the slight tension between the women in the room. "I'm around for a few days. What're we going to do?"

"I think you mean 'ladies'," Sangita says, drawing out the word. "And in case you missed it, I meant what I said. I really am busy."

"Dinner," Ravi says, oblivious to the vibes. "Mr. Chow's?"

"I love Mr. Chow's," Hind pipes up.

"Can't," Sangita says. "Too much work, but maybe tomorrow?"

Ravi flicks a glance Hind's way. "You clearly have taste. Dinner it is."

He turns his back for a moment. *Your brother?* Hind mouths. Sangita shoots back an annoyed look.

"You're coming to dinner too, Gita," Ravi says. "Maybe I can't make you come to the orphanage, but the least you can do is listen. We have some issues there. The tsunami kids that are too old have to move out."

"The Japanese tsunami?" Hind says, with a quizzical look.

"Indian," Sangita replies.

"But that was ages ago," Hind says. "In 2004, wasn't it?"

She senses new interest in Ravi's surprised nod of assent, but keeps her eyes on Sangita. Something about looking directly at this man makes her uncomfortable. There is an intensity there, like an energy field radiating out from him.

"My grandfather was very upset by it," Hind explains. This is true. She remembers the rare sight of Jassim watching television non-stop for two days as the coverage unfolded. Once, she entered the living room unannounced and could have sworn he was wiping away tears. "He used to trade in India when he was younger."

"Perfect." He beams at both women. "So it's decided? We'll go, then?"

"I've never been to India," Hind says. She can't pinpoint which of the vibes coming off him—adventure, playfulness or, she has to admit (if only to herself), attraction—is causing her, or a part of her she's only read about in books, to come to life. But there is definitely a charisma about Ravi. When he turns to you, you are the center of the universe, if only for that brief moment.

"I think he means go to *dinner*," Sangita says, clearly needing to deflate the moment.

"First," Ravi says, "where's the bathroom?"

Sangita points in the direction of her bedroom before wheeling back to Hind, eyes narrowing.

"Don't take him seriously," she says, as soon as her brother is out of earshot. "He thinks everyone's a free spirit."

"Must be a great way to live," Hind says, "making your own decisions on the fly like that. Going wherever you want, whenever you want."

"Listen, woman, you have a great life too," Sangita says, almost hissing it. "As soon as you finish, you'll be a wife, and then—"

Hind dismisses the thought with a wave of her hand. "You sound like Noor."

"She has a point."

Hind turns on her. "Since when do you think matrimony is the answer to all of life's questions?"

"I didn't say that."

"You implied it."

Now Ravi is out of the bedroom, rubbing his hands. "Great, I smell like lavender fields, or something. Whatever happened to regular, plain-scented soap?"

Hind and Sangita hold their stand-off silently, facing each other across the kitchen island, Hind defiant, Sangita poised as if holding herself back from springing at Hind. Ravi joins them at the top of the island. Whatever tension he may or may not sense, he doesn't let on, but he's positioned himself between them like a referee.

"Ready?" he asks.

Hind breaks off her friend's glare. "Let me get my bag," she says.

Chapter 12

Seated at Mr. Chow's, heavy menu in hand, Hind can't remember the last time she had Chinese food. She has no idea what half the names of the dishes are. "Chicken and broccoli," Sangita is saying. "Anything with eggplant." Ravi murmurs in assent as if these are good choices.

"What would you like?" the waiter says to Hind. All eyes turn to her and she almost blurts out the first thing she sees, but thinks better of it.

"What they're having," she says.

"What?" Sangita says.

"We'll share, right?" Hind says, employing their favorite way to calorie-count.

"Pork in red sauce," Ravi says. "Sure we can."

Hind is so flustered she can't answer. Nor does she know how to take it back.

"Pork, Hind? Really? Don't you want to order something else?" Sangita is giving her a look that says she wants to take her temperature.

"Oh, *inti ba'ad*," Hind says, slipping into dialect. "Anything is fine," she corrects herself with a shrug. She hardly recognizes herself.

"She'll have chicken," Sangita says to the impatient waiter.

"About the orphanage," Hind says hastily, to preempt whatever Sangita is going to say as soon as the waiter has retreated. "How many times a year do you go there?"

Ravi passes a plate of dumplings to his sister, who takes one and stuffs it into her mouth.

"At least once, more if I can," Ravi says. "But we rotate. Whoever is nearest."

"Why not get involved in something more local?" Hind says. "I mean, in America. Like New Orleans?"

The dumplings plate comes to her and she takes one, ignoring the look in Sangita's eye. "Even the Emir gave money after Katrina."

"I saw that special on CNN," Ravi says, taking the plate from her. "He's a tall guy." They munch for a minute in silence. "But that's just it. Long after a crisis, the survivors still need sustained interest to stay afloat. Donor fatigue sets in, the news moves on, and everyone forgets."

"Ravi's taken the orphan thing to heart," Sangita says, some of the tension melting from her as she puts a hand on his arm. "He saw the kids when he was a teenager and he can't forget them."

"Sounds intense," Hind says, realizing she has no idea what it feels like to take a cause to heart.

"Hmm, but from the flatness of your tone I know you think it's anything but interesting." Hind takes a sip of water, taken aback by his bluntness, but she has to admit he's right.

Orphanages aren't at the top of her list of fascinating things to think about.

"He's just passionate," Sangita says. "He can't help it. These are young girls, mostly. They have no one."

Hind feels her devilish spirit rising.

"No parents?" she says. "Some of us might appreciate not being pushed around by intrusive power figures."

"Hardly a comparison," Ravi says. "There may be consequences if you defy your parents, but you won't be sold as a sex slave."

"Really? What do you think marriage is?" she fires back without thinking, an increasingly frequent effect this man is having on her.

"You mean forced marriage?" Ravi dismisses it with a wave. "It's illegal in most countries."

"No one is forcing you," Sangita says. "I mean, it's not like he's going to lock you up in a closet or something."

"I don't care. It isn't the same thing as a life of companionship," Hind shoots back.

"What are you talking about?" Ravi says, his face radiating confusion.

Hind signals Sangita to leave it. "I'm just saying arranged marriage is another form of sex slavery."

Ravi is already shaking his head. "You can't compare the two. There's no sliding scale of suffering that makes one better than the other."

Sangita casts a skeptical look at Hind. "I'd say wearing designers, not having to drive, that doesn't sound so bad. Do you know what a nightmare sex slavery really is?"

"No, and I don't want to." Hind is aware how bitchy she must sound, but she can't stop herself. "If you think arranged marriage is so marvelous, why don't you give it a go, then?" she says. "And let me know how things turn out."

"Stop making this fuss about yourselves," Ravi says. He taps a fist on the table. "Neither of you has any idea what these girls face. Graduate students? Seriously?"

"What am I supposed to do, feel guilty?" Hind asks.

"If you saw what I've seen you would know the answer," he says, his brown eyes blazing.

"Well," she hedges, "I've never been to Asia."

His eyes widen with excitement. "Come with me," he says, looking from one girl to the other. "Neither of you is doing anything as important as this."

"Ravi – "

"No postcards, or photos, or documentary will ever give you the sense of being there, looking into their eyes. Your degree can wait. All this," he gestures broadly at the European décor of the restaurant, "will still be here."

"I can't," Sangita says. "I know I owe the orphanage a trip, but I really can't just now. Almost done, but not done enough."

Ravi turns to Hind as if waiting for her to give her own, separate answer.

"Ravi, don't be an idiot. She's in the same program as me," Sangita says. "Remember? And on top of that, she's..." Sangita breaks off, glancing sideways at Hind.

"What? She's what?" Hind closes her eyes.

"Getting married."

"Engaged," Hind corrects her instantly.

"Yes, you're engaged, but..." Sangita falters, turning to Hind in confusion.

"But the date hasn't been set." Which, she consoles herself, is more or less true, though she knows the family will want it to take place as soon as possible when she gets back, as soon as Ramadan is over. Then, to distract them as much as herself from thinking any further about it, she adds, "I'd go to India."

The reaction on Ravi's face, a mixture of shock and boyish delight, gives her a rush of satisfaction. She doesn't look at Sangita, who she knows is aghast.

"I mean, why not? You can't just categorize me as a spoiled rich kid," she says.

"Whoa, time out." Sangita puts her hands up. "No one is categorizing anyone as anything," she says. "Orientalism is dead, remember?" She looks from one to the other. "Nerdy joke-induced truce?"

Hind laughs, a shaky sound of assent. The food arrives and she gobbles up as much of the fried rice as she can before pushing the dish with the forbidden meat as far away as possible. As they eat, the overt tension abates, though she avoids eye contact with Ravi.

"I don't see what the buzz is about," Sangita says. "There's nothing Chinese about this place. The waiters are Italian."

"Been here forty years," Ravi says. "Twice as long as you. The food's good, right, your plate is empty."

Of the three plates on the table, Hind's is the only one with anything on it. "Yes, it was," Sangita says. "How was yours, Hind?"

"I'm just going to head to the toilet," she replies. Ravi has to stand up to let her squeeze out. Their table set for three is only a few inches from the one next to it, where two men, stuffed into suits a size too small, are eating piled platefuls of fried meat with gusto.

"I'll come with you," Sangita says.

"Aren't you a bit old for that?"

Hind has never been so thankful for an interfering older sibling. She leaves the table and, pushing the swinging door into the bathroom, heads straight to the sink. She splashes water on her face, heedless of her mascara or makeup. *India, traveling, a man.* So many parts of this are waving red flags, and yet she's reacting to them as though color blind. Something about his condescending attitude reminds her of all the articles she's read about the world's richest country, the unearned paradise of which she has the nerve to be a citizen. That and the very real clock ticking away her freedom are propelling her to make the most of her last few weeks as a single woman, which, in proportion to the rest of her soon-to-be married life, seem like mere moments.

The door to the bathroom swings open and in comes Sangita, her hair free from its coil, swaying over her shoulders like that of the goddesses whose photos line her bedroom walls.

"Don't let Ravi get to you," she says. "He's all heart, and he never understands why everyone isn't."

Hind straightens from the sink and pats her face dry with some paper towels.

"Oh, no, it's fine," she says. "He's given me a lot to think about." Hind tries to straighten the quiver out of her voice, hoping her friend won't hear it.

"Like what?" Sangita enters a stall.

"India," Hind says. "I mean, this stuff in India. It sounds important." She balls up the paper towels and throws them in the hole in the counter.

"India?" Sangita flushes the toilet and comes out.

"For study days. Could be fun."

Sangita approaches the sink and holds her hand under the soap sensor.

"You know, I wasn't kidding," she says, scrubbing her hands under the running water. "I can't take any time to go with you. I need to do revisions. They've basically said I won't pass if I don't find a better case study."

"You don't need to go," Hind says.

Sangita looks up sharply, and their eyes meet in the mirror. "You can't," she says after a moment. "What if someone finds out?"

Hind looks at herself. She opens her compact and applies powder to the bridge of her nose.

"Mabya'rafoon," she says. "They won't know."

"Seriously, Hind. What about Abdulla, and the rest of your family?"

"They'll never know," Hind says. "Who's going to tell them?" She snaps the compact shut and regards her friend. "Ready?"

Sangita follows her out of the bathroom, reciting the reasons why this is the absolute wrong thing for Hind to be even contemplating. But all Hind can hear is her own heartbeat picking up speed the closer they get to their table, back to Ravi.

Chapter 13

The cream interior of the Emiri Diwan glows in the ever-present desert daylight as the Trade Ministry delegation sweeps through its corridors. Abdulla trails behind the rest of the men in their ministerial black robes. He is spent from greeting the Emir of Abu Dhabi and his team, an all-day affair. Avoiding the endless "you first," — "no, you first" that diplomatic manners dictate, even amongst their own party, he has chosen to loiter at the back.

Surely no one will notice if he slips away, back to his office. There is the Spanish delegation to receive at the end of the week, then the trip to Libya to check on any post-civil war assets that might be developing. Entering his office, he goes down the checklist of things he needs to get done before the end of the summer. He undoes his cuff links and the top button of his thobe.

Abdulla is brought up short by the sight of his Uncle Saoud lounging in the office entryway in a burgundy brocade armchair, scanning the pages of *Al Raya* newspaper.

"There you are," Saoud says, standing to his full height, just a few inches taller than Abdulla.

"*Al salaam alaikum, 'Ammi,*" Abdulla responds automatically, hiding his surprise behind the standard formulation. He bumps noses with his uncle in greeting, and Saoud follows him into the inner office, past Hamad, the male secretary, who is drinking tea and reading another of the Arabic dailies.

"Wa alaikum al salaam," his uncle replies as he takes the chair in front of Abdulla's desk. He casts around for something to do and pulls back one of the metallic balls of the Newton's cradle toy Abdulla keeps on his desk, a silly gift Luluwa gave him as part of her campaign to make him lighten up. The ball swings on its thin wire, crashing into the others with a sharp click that breaks the silence, followed by others as the toy plays out a perpetual motion scenario.

"What would you like to drink?" Abdulla asks after a while, picking up the phone to summon water, tea, or coffee from the kitchen boy.

"Ramadan has begun," Saoud reminds him, and declines the offer with a wave.

"Of course." Abdulla puts the receiver down and presses all his fingers onto the desktop so he won't interrupt the clicks of the balls as they swing back and forth at the end of the desk. He has revealed that he is not fasting and now waits for the recriminations.

His uncle clears his throat. "I was just here for a meeting about the new procedures for marrying foreigners."

Abdulla picks up a pen, wishing someone would barge into his office declaring an emergency.

"How are things at the council?"

"More applications than ever," his uncle replies. "Young men want to marry, but not their family members any more."

Abdulla shakes his head as if deploring this, but his heart isn't in it. The idea that anyone would voluntarily submit to marriage is beyond him.

Saoud stands as if to leave, then turns back.

"We're planning a summer trip at the end of the month," he says, almost an afterthought. "To London, for Eid. Come with us."

Abdulla avoids his uncle's gaze. *London in summer. With family.* He has been hoping for a quiet Asian getaway after Ramadan, maybe a beach in Thailand for the ten days of the Eid al Fitr holiday before returning to the reality of his impending marriage.

"I can't take off quite yet," he replies, reaching for the computer mouse to check his email.

"Ramadan will be over before we know it," Saoud says. Idly, he glances down at the Newton's cradle, now almost at rest. He pulls the ball back and sets the toy in motion again. "This year the family wants to travel instead of paying visits to everyone."

Abdulla nods, because of course his uncle is being sensible. The temperature outside is upward of thirty-five degrees Celsius and school is out, two reasons why every Qatari family who can is taking off for their annual summer respite.

"It would be good to see Hind before she comes back," Saoud mutters.

Abdulla leans forward, despite wanting to sidestep the entire subject. He nods as though he hasn't been avoiding this topic and his uncle for this very reason.

"You two should go out, do something fun, before the wedding." Saoud, dropping his gaze, gesticulating in Abdulla's general area.

"We don't do that really in our family," Abdulla says carefully. Neither man has mentioned Fatima.

"It's what some young people do now. Get to know each other."

Saoud clears his throat again. Apparently his uncle wants to have this talk even less than he does. "You know, visit her with her sister."

"I'll think about it," Abdulla says, not unkindly. He doesn't have it in his heart to refuse him outright. He does have to see the lawyers about signing with the medium-sized organic farm he's opted for instead of a bigger chain. They're in London, so maybe two birds with one stone. But then he would have to entertain Hind, take her out to eat, plan for their life together. Maybe he'll just take care of the documents by fax.

Satisfied, Saoud raps his knuckles on the desk and turns to go. "We'll be at your dad's apartment when we get to London," he says at the door. "Unless you boys are using it?"

"No, no, you're welcome to stay there," Abdulla says. "But there are only three bedrooms, so it will be tight if Khalid and Noor are going as well."

Abdulla comes around the desk to give his uncle the series of farewell kisses customary for close friends and relatives.

"All right, well, it is the Olympics," Saoud says, "so if you get stuck let me know. You can always share with Khalid."

Abdulla nods as if staying with his teenage cousin and dating his fiancée are two of the things he is most looking forward to in the coming weeks.

But it is undeniable; his uncle has a point. The wedding is coming up. Hard to imagine nearly a year flying by, but here they are in Ramadan again, and almost at the end of Hind's master's program.

London, he thinks bleakly, returning to his desk and pressing his head back against the top of the chair. Like most of the Qataris on staff, Abdulla has grown up going on family vacations to London, later sharing rooms with his brothers in the family apartment during his sleep-deprived student days at LSE and, more recently, on numerous diplomatic trips since taking up his government post. England holds very little mystery any more. It certainly is the last place he would choose for a voluntary holiday.

But if it means permanent freedom from the nearly year-old bargain his father has forced him into- now that the respite afforded by Hind's desire to study is almost over, they will soon have to set up as happy newlyweds- well, then, perhaps it is time to pay his cousin a discreet visit.

His phone buzzes, an SMS from Luluwa reminding him of their promised driving lesson today. After nearly a week of dodging, there is no more avoiding it or her. He wraps up at his desk, jotting notes for tomorrow. Most of the staff have gone anyway, because of the shortened hours during Ramadan. The roads are clear on his way home, since the city closes down in the afternoon during the holy month; and the sun is at its height, even more punishing when you can't eat or drink. He pulls into the compound expecting to see Luluwa hovering in the courtyard, but the heat has kept her inside as well.

Still, she must have been lurking somewhere near the window, because she comes bounding out of the side door as he puts the car into park. As she comes around to the driver's side, he puts the window down.

"Are we going now?"

He opens his door without answering, because her dancing eyes remind him too much of another pair that lit up in mischief throughout his childhood. They trade places and she slides into the driver's seat with only a minimal adjustment to the mirrors.

"Around the houses first," he says, not keen to take her out onto the roads, even though they are virtually empty. "Slowly."

She leans forward with excitement and noses the car into motion, the engine purring as they crawl around the shared grounds their grandfather built for his three sons. Inside their respective houses, the rest of the family sleep the afternoon away, waiting for sunset so they can break their fast.

"Reverse," he says, when they are misaligned with the front gate, "or we're never getting out of here."

She complies, her eyes going to the mirror as he has taught her before backing up. Her skinny arm comes around the back of his seat as she swivels half-around and looks back to make sure no one is behind them.

As they move slowly through the compound gate, the front of a white Mercedes edges in next to them, closing distance until the passenger side is even with Luluwa, the tinted window lowered. Narin, the family driver, is at the wheel.

"What in God's name are you doing?" says a voice from the back seat. It is Abdulla's mother. He pinches the bridge of his nose.

"Driving," Luluwa answers her aunt, whose lips flatten into a thin line.

"You're too young for a license," Maryam shouts. "And who knows if your uncles will agree?"

"Khalid drives," Luluwa replies. It is true that her cousin, almost the same age as her, is often seen driving around the neighborhood with one of his brothers.

"He can drive at sixteen," Maryam retorted. "You have to wait until eighteen."

"With someone in the car," Luluwa said. "He should be practicing with someone."

"In this heat—aren't you tired from fasting?"

"On my period, '*Ameti*,'" Luluwa smiles at her. "Not fasting this week."

The breach of conduct gives Abdulla and his mother pause. He looks at Luluwa's profile. He isn't the only rebel in the family. Luluwa fidgets, having used what he guesses is her strongest weapon, shock value. Abdulla regroups.

"Won't be a moment," he says, waving through the window. "What if she's stuck at home one day and has an emergency?"

"What if her driving causes an accident?" Maryam calls after them as Luluwa pulls through the gates and past her car. "Don't let the neighbors see you."

They both pretend they haven't heard and, at a safe distance, break into giggles.

Chapter 14

Tap, tap, tap…

Sangita groans, only half-awake, but the empty apartment offers no sympathy. Tap, tap, tap…

The invasive sound goes on, despite her best efforts to pull a pillow right into her ears. It's Hind's latest phase, Nature Conservationist, inspiring a bird feeder directly outside the only window in their London flat, the pane of glass mere inches from the cotton canopy draped over Sangita's bed. In the week of Hind's absence Sangita hasn't bothered to take it down, but now she's regretting the oversight, certain every hungry pigeon in central London knows exactly where to get a good meal. Sangita throws back the covers and stretches, because this morning a particularly persistent bird is making enough noise for a gaggle of Thanksgiving turkeys.

Photos of her life in America are propped along the ledge of her bureau and scattered across the lilac walls of the un-air conditioned room. She misses the climate-controlled summer on the East Coast of the U.S., cool even indoors. Well into her first summer here across the pond, she still isn't used to it; she would die of heatstroke if the bedroom door weren't flung open to the living room, where the apartment's only wall unit whirs away.

The Brits may have built an empire, but they have one of the worst possible climates for home base, she thinks for the hundredth time. Along with bad teeth and an aversion to deodorant, this is their worst failing as a people.

She sits up, knocking over a photo of her mother and her hoisting up their hands in a victorious grip, as though Sangita were a prize-winning pugilist and her mother the coach. It's graduation, of course, the black sleeve of Sangita's gown unfolding on her elbow. Those university days date back nearly six years now, but she treasures that photo as one of the rare moments when her mother broke out of the characteristic South Indian pose she usually uses for photos, reminding Sangita of the black and white snapshots from India where people stand in a line, rarely smiling, and assume the fig leaf position. Placed in a clear magnetic frame in the middle of the window, the 8x10 inch photo helps keep the sun from streaming in. She lays it aside and pushes the window open to confront the noisy bird offender, only to find the feeder swinging tranquilly with just one quiet visitor ignoring her in the warming air and encroaching daylight. But the tapping?

Tap, tap, tap…

Now she identifies it. It's not a *tap*, but a *rap*. And it's coming from the apartment door.

Someone is knocking.

"I'm coming," Sangita calls out.

Hind isn't in her room to answer the door, of course, even though in all likelihood it's for her—an early morning delivery of an Eid card from one of her parents' contacts, or else the embassy. Even though the end of Ramadan is still over two weeks away, maybe this sender wants to be prepared, like Sangita's auntie who always sends birthday cards from India a month in advance to make double-sure they won't be late. Not that either of the roommates cares at all for the formalities their families observe. An Eid or birthday card is more likely to be used as a placeholder in a book they are reading than displayed on the refrigerator.

"Wait one second," Sangita shouts, getting irritated as the pounding on the door increases in intensity. If the delivery guy would only stop pounding for one minute he would be able to hear her.

She pulls her arms through the slip-robe her brother Ravi brought back from his last trip to China, embroidered petals unfurled in black silk across her shoulders and down her arms and to the edge of where the fabric swirls around her ankles. It's a long garment. Hind often compares it to the black abaya Qatari women wear in public. Except for one thing.

"Of course, that bit would be covered up," Hind gestures to the plunging neckline.

So here is Sangita heaving herself out of bed first thing on a Friday morning, with no lectures or any other obligations, to answer the door for a deliveryman with Hind's latest order of Tariq Ramadan books or Cat Stevens, a.k.a. Yusuf Islam, for some project on Muslim modernity. Sangita ignores the clasp that won't close on the front, leaving some cleavage exposed, cut off by the edge of the sheer tank top she wears on top of spandex boy shorts. *Who cares*, she thinks. It will only take a second to sign for the package.

"Here," she says, pulling open the door, expecting to see Andrew, the regular DHL guy, and his wolfish smile. Andrew is one of a growing number of English boys with a thing for the Arab fashionista, not that any of them could have Hind. And don't think they haven't taken note of Nigel downstairs, the two hundred pounds of muscle who guards the front door in lieu of a call button.

Sangita opens the door wider and stops cold. Instead of the expected blue eyes and dimpled grin, brown irises so dark they rival Sangita's, stare back at her out of a face so stern he might be an angry god. The man, immaculately dressed and nearly six feet tall, looms in the apartment's entrance. "You answer the door in this way?"

Abdulla draws in his breath at the sight of the flesh this petite woman has spilling over the opening in her robe.

Sangita steps back as if it were her father, and not an impeccably-groomed young Arab man with furrowed eyebrows.

Her hand clutches at the robe's open neck, but the fabric has been cut to reveal her flesh, not conceal it.

"Who are you?" she asks, tucking her chin to her chest, her stance unconsciously widening as she's learned in those self-defense classes Hind insisted they take. She grips the knob, ready to swing the door shut in his face if he tries to force an entry. Even on this side of Hyde Park you hear stories.

"I should ask you that question," he says. "Where is Hind?" His spine stiffens to his full height, at least a foot above her. She curses the gods under her breath as his eyebrows rise

even higher, disappearing into his hairline. From the stories

she's heard of Hind's well-connected family, Sangita is pretty sure this man, whoever he is, could have her extradited and

jailed if he wanted. Even in London.

Relaxing her militant stance and death grip on the doorknob, Sangita moves aside in a universal sign of grudging welcome. Which he is either unaware of or ignoring, since he makes no move to enter.

As the awkward silence widens, Sangita shrinks further back from the door, caving her shoulders inward in hopes of hiding what little of her is still showing. Without looking directly at him, she covertly assesses the man who, she has realized, can only be Abdulla. Although his precise haircut is shorter than the curls in Hind's engagement photos, there is no mistaking the slant of that jaw or those smoky eyes. His handsome features are non-Western but otherwise indeterminate. Out of his traditional starched white *thobe* and *ghutra* flipped over a coiled black *'agal*, he could be South Asian, Latino or Arab, with a tan many men in Chelsea would pay good money for.

He peruses her only briefly. His eyes stay trained on her face, avoiding the pile of hair at the nape of her neck, or indeed any other part of her, though there is a lot to look at. She is conscious of every inch of her exposed flesh.

"Where is Hind?" he repeats.

Sangita's mind swirls in a range of emotion. Surprise, that instead of roving to the inviting neckline and making use of his height, he doesn't break eye contact with her. And fear, a growing sense of doom in the silence that stretches between them. She clears her throat.

Is she really going to tell him, now that he is here in the flesh, that his fiancée has run off to the tsunami-ravaged villages of South India with a man, unchaperoned? And not just any man, but Ravi, her brother. Why? Well, Hind went to find herself, of course. And Sangita is the one who is going to tell him this. *Oh, God*, she thinks, *I am dead.*

"She has...gone to visit her cousin Nejude in Essex," she offers, proud of herself for getting out their planned alibi without her voice or knees shaking. "But of course you know that, since she's your cousin too," she fumbles on, thrown by his blank look. He remains on the landing, standing motionless, as though he were a vampire waiting to be invited into a human domicile.

"I didn't know we had a cousin named Nejude," he says. Sangita could have stabbed her own eyes out. First principle in lying, Alice in their cohort always says, don't bother with too many details.

"Please come in," she says. "Would you like to have some tea while we wait?"

That line is sure to work on anyone, British, Asian or Arab, she thinks. It will have to do. Not waiting for an answer, she turns and makes a beeline for her bedroom, leaving Abdulla standing in the doorway, teetering as though his top half wants to enter but the bottom half of his body won't cooperate.

Chapter 15

In the safety of her bedroom, despite the increasing heat from the rising sun, Sangita shuts the door and takes a breath, her mind whirling. She scans the closet for something suitable. Cellphone in hand, she sheds the silk robe and pulls on a turtleneck tunic dress that falls to her knees, covering up her pajamas, all the while frantically holding down the number three on her speed dial. Hind's number goes straight to voicemail. She waits for the beep.

"He's here," she hisses, looking over her shoulder as though she were in some version of *Poltergeist*. "You'd better get back as soon as possible."

She slides up the top half of the BlackBerry and types in the message as a BBM and then an SMS, then copies and pastes it as a Facebook message and a direct Tweet. Her communication options exhausted, Sangita snaps the phone closed before tossing it onto her bed.

She takes a breath and spends a moment checking herself in the mirror. Her legs are still exposed, but the most important bits – arms, chest and neck – are now properly hidden under a layer of grey wool.

She spins back into the living room.

He has taken two steps in through the door and is staring in bemusement at the framed theater-size poster of Robert Pattinson that hangs over the red, wide-armed sofa.

"Does the sheikh take sugar?"

Sangita whips the kettle onto the stove and begins gathering the elements of a tea service. She and Hind are opposites in their drink tastes: Hind's preference is for tea or water while Sangita has an American immigrant's love of Coca-Cola. But she's seen Hind and her own mother do this a million times when ecstatic, gloomy or mellow, and hopes she can replicate the movements.

"No tea," Abdulla says. He's all the way in now, and his hands are flat on the marble countertop of the bar that serves as the apartment's dining table. With no task to occupy them, Sangita's hands drift to her hips, and her elbows bow out as if to give her more bulk and thereby more gravitas.

"You live here?" Abdulla says, still incredulous.

Sangita mentally notes all the ways she is going to maim first Ravi, her own blood, and then Hind for putting her in this predicament. She told them again and again during the hatching of their simple plan that discovery was likely. But they laughed off her cautions like those of a worried grandmother.

"I'm a good friend," she says. "I stop in often."

She has reminded Hind a number of times to tell her family that the two of them are living together. It isn't a secret to Hind's cousins and friends spread across England studying for various degrees. So why should it amaze or scandalize the older members of the family? She should have realized this would be one last secret her roommate would keep from her relatives in her bid for one last year of independence before they throw her into "the dungeon of marriage," as she calls it.

Now the man who is to be her keeper, Abdulla, is standing right in the apartment, flicking a non-existent piece of lint off what she is sure are Hermes cuff links, and demanding explanations from Sangita.

"I, ah, I'm her best friend," she tries again, knowing it's a pathetic way to explain her presence in the apartment at dawn, with her friend nowhere in sight.

Abdulla slams his hands on the countertop, letting out a sound of frustration. Sangita winces, having hit her funny bone there many times. Yet his face remains impassive.

"We're not lesbians!"

"The thought hadn't occurred to me. But since you mention it..." From his look, eyes narrowed as though he were a hawk sighting its prey, Sangita knows he is in dead earnest and not joking. Whether from hysteria at the thought of being deported, the sleep deprivation of exams, or being a truly awful liar, Sangita can't catch her breath. She bursts into laughter, and the giggles keep coming until she doubles over, clutching her stomach, unable to care that her dress is riding up the backs of her legs. Helpless, she slides down the length of the island until she is sitting on the floor.

He leans forward on his forearms, over the countertop, watching as if she were a stray animal.

"Sorry," she manages to gasp before she begins to hiccup. "I'm her roommate."

He leans away, drumming fingers on the counter so fast that, with her eyes closed, it conjures the sound of raindrops.

"When will Hind be back?" Abdulla says.

The threat of having to explain bad news, like the idea of going home in *Mary Poppins*, erases her mirth in a single moment. Instead of floating down from the ceiling to the ground, she pulls herself up by the lip of the island to her feet.

"The sheikh must believe I don't know," she says.

Abdulla sighs, and for the first time the guarded expression slips; she sees lines around his mouth and under his eyes.

"Tea," she says. "The sheikh needs some tea." She turns back to the stove.

"You're not Muslim," he says, a second non-question. "And you're not from the Gulf, so stop calling me 'sheikh.'"

Sangita considers this progress.

They regard each other as the kettle boils.

"Let's look at your process of elimination," she says, as if evaluating an exam question. "If I were Muslim, I would have come to the door with more clothing on and likely something on my head as well."

She rushes on, taking her cue from his pointed gaze and curt nod. "In particular, if I were Qatari, I wouldn't have answered the door without looking through the peephole, and, finding a strange man there, maybe not at all. But since I did, and since I was wearing so little, I'm not a Muslim, nor a Qatari."

He says nothing. It is her turn to drum her fingers on the countertop.

"I've lived with someone who is both for almost a year," Sangita says into the silence, suddenly realizing she has released valuable information. There. It's out. She winces slightly. She hadn't intended to give him that much detail. They have been roommates, not lovers, although Hind has told her stories of it being hard, in gender-segregated Qatar, to tell the difference. Sangita makes a note to file this one away and laugh about it later with Hind- if, that is, they ever make it out of this. "Did you know the world's largest minority population of Muslims lives in India?" she throws out as she turns to the whistling kettle. She hopes she can get this right, never drinking the stuff herself, despite being Indian.

The invisible steel string holding up Abdulla's perfect posture gives a little, and he shrugs, his shoulders slightly sagging.

"Fine. Tea."

Chapter 16

Abdulla lifts the flounced rim of the teacup to his lips, lips (Sangita knows) that many women in Hollywood would die for. Sangita holds her breath, crossing her fingers behind her back as she always does after telling her parents a lie. Well defined, the stunning lips pull back, after the briefest sip, into a grimace, and her fingers uncross.

"Have you ever made tea before?" he asks, covering a cough by patting his lips with a red kitchen towel.

She shakes her head. "And you're Indian."

"I grew up in America so I don't drink tea," she says by way of apology. "More sugar?"

Abdulla pushes the embossed teacup away and shakes his head.

"No amount of sugar is going to save that," he says.

At the look of dismay on his face, she rubs one hand over the knuckles of the other and tries not to feel wounded.

"Well, it's not like we knew you were coming."

He lets out what sounds like another mangled cough.

"I've watched Hind do it a thousand times," she says.

Almost immediately she regrets saying her roommate's name, seeing Abdulla's face, which isn't exactly ugly when relaxed, grow taut.

"How long do you expect her to be gone?" he asks.

Sangita clears away his teacup and saucer, putting the kettle in the sink and running water over everything.

"She didn't say," she answers carefully. "They were going to do some shopping."

"They usually like to shop here," he says, rubbing his chin.

With her back to him, she clenches her jaw for being so stupid. Of course, London and Paris are the two important summer destinations for Qatari women. Well, and men too, for that matter, from what Hind has said of her family's shopping sprees.

"I'm booking a room down the street until she comes back. On Park Lane. Tell her to call me when she gets here."

She hears a roar in her ears like after jumping into a pool and adjusting for the air pressure.

"What?" she says, turning around as he rises from the stool and heads toward the door. "You're staying?"

"Not that it's any of your business," he says pointedly, "but I have some important things to discuss with Hind and it must be done in person."

Sangita grips the countertop for strength.

"You'll have to wait until after the marriage," she blurts before thinking.

This brings him up short in the doorway. He turns slowly, his eyes narrowing, as though seeing Sangita for the first time. "I see Hind has not been as discreet as she should have been," he says, pausing as if not sure whether to say anything more. "Again, it's outside the scope of your need to know, but I did not come all this way to consummate in secrecy."

Sangita ducks her head, thankful for not being white; otherwise the slow burn of embarrassment flushing across her face would show as bright red. He is right. It's absolutely no business of hers if he is here to have sex with his future wife.

"I would appreciate your discretion," Abdulla continues, almost in a monotone, as though it pains him to ask Sangita for a favor. "Say nothing to her if she calls and is anywhere near her sister. No one knows I'm in London."

Sangita nods her agreement, although the door has already shut behind him. Great. Now she is involved in two conspiracies. Abdulla is here to talk to Hind about something so secret he doesn't want anyone else in either family to know.

Her mind whirs through what she knows of Qatari culture and Qataris, but the only ones she is acquainted with are women. Aside from incognito sex, or shopping, she can't come up with a sensible reason for his impromptu visit. And even sex doesn't fit, since the wedding is planned for the end of the summer, just a few weeks away. Anyone who has waited as long as they have during a one-year engagement could surely wait a little longer. Sangita shakes her head and puts away the signs of her failed tea. She only hopes she can keep track of what she is not supposed to say, as well as to whom she shouldn't say it. A tall order.

Chapter 17

While Abdulla is out of the apartment, Sangita showers, dresses again, then begins trying both Ravi's and Hind's phones. After a dozen times she tries the satellite phone they are supposed to leave on for emergencies. No answer. She leaves the same message for them on BBM, Twitter, Facebook and WhatsApp: *EMERGENCY. Call me ASAP.* But no response. There's no answer from the NGO village contact. The way it seems, the way it will appear, is that Hind has run off with Ravi and vanished into the villages of South India where people still do not have television or indoor plumbing.

"Did you find a hotel?" Sangita asks, back in the living room.

She isn't sure what kind of conversation one makes with a fiancé confronted by his beloved's disappearance.

"These bloody Olympics," Abdulla says, shaking his head and pouring tea into a purple coffee mug that says BITCH in large black letters around its circumference. "The whole city is full. People are even camping out across the West End and in front of the stadium for the opening ceremony."

Sangita sits in the red armchair, both feet firmly on the ground, watching Abdulla brew tea in the kitchen. In her linen tunic and leggings, her braided hair still wet, she's actually relaxing as he issues instructions in Arabic on his phone. From the bits that she can catch, Sangita realizes he really hasn't told anyone in Qatar that he's in London. He is running his office long-distance, as though he were only a few doors away or taking a personal day at home. He's talking so fast, and mostly in slang, that it's impossible for her to keep up, despite months of lessons at university. The vast difference between written and spoken Arabic is a constant challenge, one that Hind has been helping her with by teaching her the Gulf dialect.

"It's a magazine," she says, when Abdulla pauses to peer at the mug's provocative slogan. "*Bitch*. We subscribe and sometimes write for it. Not that we've ever had anything accepted," she adds hastily, in case the look of puzzlement on his face means dislike.

Whatever Hind decides to do, Sangita does not want to be responsible for ruining her friend's marriage and future. She tries to sit up straight and not fidget as she mentally reviews the many discussions she and Hind have had about Qatari marriages. Discussions held in the very room where Sangita is now studiously avoiding eye contact with the other woman's fiancé.

Taking in his tense shoulders, Sangita is beginning to wonder if Abdulla hasn't also benefited from the non-communication over the past year.

His machinegun Arabic instructions have been going on for quite a while; from the time she let him back into the apartment, the onyx phone case has sat on the counter while he has moved freely around the kitchen with the Bluetooth perched on his ear.

"*Tabeen shai?*" He is now talking to Sangita, asking her whether she'd like some tea, but he hasn't switched out of Arabic.

"*La oreed shai'an.*" She hastily declines the offer, jumping up and heading into the kitchen. Sangita's mother would be horrified if she knew her daughter had failed in her duties of hospitality. Then again, her mother would be slightly puzzled that any Asian man — she lumps "Asian" in with "Middle Eastern" — would offer a woman something to drink.

"You speak Arabic?"

She pauses in front of the aluminum fridge, and mutters uselessly "*na'am*", "yes" in Arabic. Formal Arabic.

He laughs again, but this time without restraint, so that her ears grow hot. Hind and her Arab visitors have similar reactions to Sangita's use of *fus-ha*, the classical and most formal type of Arabic.

"That makes it difficult for me to throw you out," he says, a tiny smile playing at the corner of his lips.

She laughs in return, shakily. He hasn't divulged the purpose of his visit, but it must bear some relationship to the rising anxiety Hind has been feeling as the date for her return to Qatar has drawn closer. For the most part he seems friendly, not like an irate bridegroom. But of course he doesn't know where Hind really is.

"*Shukran,*" she thanks him and opens the heavy fridge door, taking out a bottled Coke, the glass frosted. Pulling down the bottle opener, a tiny red English phone booth, she pops off the top and guzzles down the first thing she's had all morning.

"You could say *mashkoor,*" he says. "Dialect is a lot easier to learn."

"Okay, but which dialect?" she sighs. "Arabic's not one language; it's more like fifteen."

They contemplate each other, this time openly, as they sip their drinks.

He has rolled up the sleeves of his pristine white shirt, revealing ropy forearms sprinkled with wiry hair. The sound of a passing police siren startles them both. He smiles again, a not unfriendly smile, and gulps down half the contents of the mug. Her stomach growls loudly enough for both of them to hear. Neither of them has eaten anything since their first encounter, which for Sangita means she's had no food since lunch the day before.

"Let me make some sandwiches," she says, wishing Hind were there to do the shopping for them. Fresh Market is one of Hind's favorite places in London, though she's confessed that in Qatar she never does the shopping or cooking.

Food in general is not Sangita's strong suit, despite her mother's best efforts. Opening the fridge again, she misses Hind even more keenly. This is irrational, because if Hind were here Sangita wouldn't be making small talk or sandwiches. They would be packing and saying their goodbyes.

Abdulla too contemplates the contents of the fridge: two bottles of Perrier (Hind's; Sangita has never liked mineral water), one box of baking soda in the door, two sticks of butter, and twenty bottled Cokes in the tub marked VEGETABLES.

"Let's see what you can do with this," he says, coughing to cover what sounds like a laugh.

She lets the door swing shut and bends down to open the freezer, located counter- intuitively underneath the fridge, European-style. She's careful to use her knees, the way Hind has often reminded her, to bend down, not over.

She plucks out a box of frozen tandoori that is hiding in a corner, and shakes it, attempting to loosen up the freezer burn clinging to the package. It falls with a dull thud on the countertop.

They regard it instead of each other.

"December 2011." Sangita reads the expiration date with a straight face.

"We're going out," he says.

She tosses the tandoori back into the icy depths, shuts the freezer, and straightens to face him. Her uncertainty must show on her face. They are of the opposite sex and not related; he is engaged, and it is Ramadan. She can't think of a more unlikely set of circumstances for a lunch date.

"I have no place to stay, you have no food, and it's still my first day," he says, answering her questions as if they were written on her forehead. "I can't shake this migraine from the plane," he adds. "Food might help."

"Food is called for," Sangita agrees.

Whatever else he is, he's not an unreasonable guy, she thinks, as if taking notes for Hind. "Afterward I'll figure out what to do."

"You're staying?" she asks a second time.

He pauses for a minute as if considering an invitation.

"I mean, I just thought you'd have a driver, and a place, you know, in Bayswater or something…"

He rolls his shoulders into a shrug. "I could call someone," he admits, "but then I'd likely get questions about why I'm here and requests to go places I'd rather avoid."

The downturned corners of his mouth make him seem almost

sad, and for a moment Sangita actually feels sympathy for him. "You'd rather be anonymous," she says.

"If it's okay."

"You're asking my permission?" There is no hiding the surprise and glee in her voice.

"I assume you pay rent here, so it is technically your apartment too."

Now it's her turn to nod and cross her arms as if she were weighing the possibilities. "And if I say no?"

Abdulla pulls out his BlackBerry.

"I'll call the embassy. They can surely find me something. But when someone asks me why I'm in London and where Hind is—"

"This neighborhood has a bit of everything," she says, grabbing her bag from the table to the right of the door. "What do you feel like?"

"Indian," he says reflectively, to the spot just above her head. "That's easy," she replies, heading out the door with him and pulling it shut behind her, hoping to leave behind the burgeoning feeling that she is starting to enjoy bantering with this stranger.

Chapter 18

After a few Tube stops and a brisk walk into the Soho area, they are sitting at Ragam, her favorite South Indian restaurant, with its hot pink interior and green trim. Sangita and Abdulla pore over their large wood-casing menus. If they were to hold them up it would be impossible to see each other across the table. She lays hers flat, pretending to scrutinize it as he is doing, though she knows most of it by memory. She's just grateful for a few moments to focus on something other than making polite conversation.

Abdulla seems relieved Hind isn't likely to show up imminently. He is considerably more relaxed since their morning encounter and is becoming almost interesting.

"You two ready?"

The waitress appears, the streak of pink in her hair a match for the restaurant's interior. "Do you have *biryani*?" Abdulla asks.

The girl's answering stare can't be read as either affirmative or negative.

"*Dahl makhni*, butter *naan*, chicken vindaloo," Sangita says, falling back on her favorite meal with Hind. This is the heavy carb version they've relied on when working through the night on qualifying exams, usually sending Nigel out to pick it up.

"On the menu it says lamb."

"Tell the cook Gita asked."

The girl turns away unimpressed, but the move gets Abdulla's attention. He closes the shutters on his menu and looks inquiringly at Sangita, his head tilted to one side as though he's assessing a painting.

"We come here a lot," she says.

Sangita has to remind herself to stop sounding like she and Hind are a couple. In fact their friendship has mostly allowed them to avoid family pressures to become grown-up women and hurry along their path to being wives and mothers.

"Drinks?"

A woman with a long braid, wearing a yellow sari, appears and Sangita kicks herself inwardly. She looks at her watch – three o'clock. Normally Maya Auntie doesn't work the lunch shift but leaves it to her nephew to manage. She thought they would be safe, but the already strange lunch has just become public news. Not to the Qatari community, maybe, but Sangita's life has just gotten enormously complicated.

"Orange juice," Abdulla says, waving off the wine list when the woman returns with one.

"The same please, Maya Auntie," Sangita echoes, trying to avoid eye contact with the restaurant owner, a friend of her parents. Perhaps coming to Ragam wasn't the best idea after all, but she took a chance, same as Hind. And, same as Hind, she has been caught out.

"Of course, dear. Nice to see you again. Please say 'hi' to your parents." Maya Auntie speaks as if it were just Sangita dining alone, but her eyes linger on Abdulla, taking in the gleaming flat dial of his watch and the starch in his white shirt.

Sangita wishes painful death on her brother and missing roommate for the second time that day. Maya Auntie has been playing a major role in helping her parents find "the one" for their daughter, even though she is far away from their nest in the U.S. All it needs is for her mother to find out she's had dinner with a good-looking man in London, and in two days she'll be sending out wedding invitations. Can Maya Auntie tell that Abdulla is Arab? Has she heard Sangita say his name?

"You okay?" she asks Abdulla, hoping that Maya Auntie will keep her distance if they make conversation; otherwise the matron will be unlikely to hide her curiosity.

"Flight catching up with me," he says, rubbing his long fingers across his face. She can see the signs of travel fatigue and something more, years of pressure maybe, in the fine wrinkles around his eyes. His pinkies rub down the length of his nose on either side.

"She'll come back," Sangita says, hoping it's true, and resisting the urge to touch his hand, which is now lying inches from hers. Reminders of her Hindu upbringing and life with Hind help restrain her boundary-crossing American tendencies. Rule number one is simple. Never touch non-relative males. Of course, there's also "do not dance, eat or have sex with them," but these Sangita has managed to bend every now and then. Although not, she reminds herself, sitting up a little straighter in her chair, with other people's fiancés.

"And then what will I do with her?" Abdulla says, pinching the bridge of his nose.

"You'll talk it out," Sangita offers diplomatically, and raises her chilled glass to him in a toast. "More than that I can't say, because I don't know what you want to talk to her about," she adds carefully.

"It was a rhetorical question," he says drily. "No need to bring out your inner Oprah."

Sangita laughs. She both does and doesn't want to get further involved. In the midst of her frantic calls to Ravi and Hind she hasn't had much time to worry about what exactly it is that Abdulla wants from her roommate that can have brought him all the way to London. For now, just sitting across from him is a welcome distraction from the threat of Maya Auntie hovering in the periphery.

He clinks glasses with her, his lips turned downward in a sardonic grin, as the waitress arrives with their *masala papad*.

"This isn't the fifteenth century," Sangita says, emboldened by a few bites of the first food she's eaten all day. "You two can come together and figure things out."

Abdulla contemplates her over the rim of his glass, places it back on the table, locks his fingers together, and seems to consider her statement. Sangita shoves more tomato and papad into her mouth so as to avoid saying anything else ridiculous. She swears she can hear a clock ticking on the wall.

The throat-clearing of the waitress announces more food has arrived. The girl with the pink streak serves spoonfuls of each dish as though putting out feed for farm animals.

"I'll do it," Sangita says, as a meager plop of rice lands on her plate. The girl shrugs, as if to say *It's not rocket science.*

"I always get *biryani* because I never know what else to order," Abdulla says. They attack their food as though in agreement to suspend any serious discussion. Sangita shovels rice into her mouth and rips a piece of *naan* in half. *Sangita, do not get in the middle of this,* she reminds herself sternly, as her mother often used to do when disciplining her brother.

"I don't even know your name, to be talking about such personal things," Abdulla says.

She rubs her forefinger around the rim of her now almost empty glass, causing a tiny hum from the vibration.

"My name is Sangita," she says.

"Does that have a meaning?"

"Musical."

"Abdulla is—"

"The slave of God," she completes for him.

"I feel more like a slave to my family," he mutters.

"I thought men had all the power in Qatari society," she says. As if to save him from revealing any further secrets to this perfect stranger, Maya Auntie shoos away the reluctant waitress and refills his glass herself. He immediately drains it again. This is all the excuse she needs to hover around them and refill it.

Her presence stills their repartee. Maya Auntie avoids Sangita's side of the table until Abdulla inclines his head to indicate more for her as well. Sangita knows her mother's phone will be ringing as soon as daybreak hits the American East Coast. Her life as an independent woman is doomed.

"You seem to know a lot about me," Abdulla says. The waitress comes around again to refill their plates, but he waves her off and picks up the serving spoons himself.

"Hind talks about you all the time, and how strange it will be to go back. To be married…"

Something about the sound of Hind's name stills any playfulness in the conversation. Abdulla spoons out the dahl and rice, first to her then to himself. Sangita could kick herself for sharing anything about Hind's private ruminations. He goes perfectly still, leaning his knife and fork together against the side of the plate.

"It's not just her life that is changing," he says, and takes a large gulp of juice.

"It isn't that she doesn't want to marry you," Sangita says, almost at a whisper. "She just needs time to get used to the idea."

He seems to consider her point as he chews a large portion of chicken vindaloo.

"It's not easy on the guy either," he says finally. "And we have run out of time."

It is her turn to raise an eyebrow, but she has a feeling it looks nowhere near as elegant as when he does it, partly because she has never figured out how to raise just one.

"You don't know what you'll get. What if she's lazy, refuses to work, spends all your money to keep up with her aunties and cousins and sisters? Or changes her mind after you've spent a million riyals on the wedding and goes back to her family's house, and you have to go through it all again?" He counts off the various possibilities on his fingers.

Or she could die, Sangita thinks, when she sees him staring at his ring finger.

Abdulla's pause is almost imperceptible. "Or end up giving you only girls," he goes on, "so you have to marry again. And then you're stuck with two wives. I can't think of anything worse." He feigns a shudder.

Another wife? Sangita puts her knife and fork down carefully, reminding herself that an assault on any person would likely result in a jail sentence, let alone stabbing a foreign semi-dignitary.

Abdulla notices her flash of anger. "It's a joke," he says, tapping her on the back of her hand. "Lighten up. Most people our age don't practice that custom. Unless they are from really conservative families."

She lets out a cautious breath, assessing him from under her eyelashes.

"Don't tell me you're like the Westerners, always obsessed with the idea of multiple wives," he says. He continues eating, grinning. "Not so open minded, are you?"

She sits up, ready to defend herself, then at his laugh, her posture deflates a little, because he can so easily get a rise out of her. "I watch *Big Love*," she says. "I know Muslims aren't the only ones who practice polygamy."

At his blank look she laughs.

"It's a show on HBO about some extreme Mormon types who have multiple wives, but secretly, because it's illegal in America."

He seems dubious, and the eyebrow rises again. "Excellent source for accurate cultural information," he murmurs. "HBO."

"Why are you here?" she asks.

There is a small silence as he casts about for something to say.

"The divorce rate is really high," he says. "Too high. I just want to make sure we are still on the same page."

Sangita chews a bite of potato and rice, considering the stories she's heard about women leaving their husbands the morning after the wedding reception, going back to their father's house.

"This is when it might be good to be poor," she says, finishing her piece of *naan* as he pauses, waiting for further explanation. "When the family has money to take the girl back in, she may have less incentive to work things out."

He sweeps the last drop of curry from his plate with the last piece of *naan* and seems to consider.

"There is such a thing as too much money," he agrees, to her surprise and pleasure. "As a country, we are suffering from this."

She drains her juice, thinking the next time she sees Hind she will tell her she could do worse than this man. Of course having lunch with someone is not the same as living with them every day for the rest of your life…

"Dessert?"

Maya Auntie is hovering again, the glint in her eye giving Sangita an uneasy feeling. What if she has already woken up her mother? The sighting of her daughter at lunch with an unexplained male might be an occasion worthy of such an early morning phone call. What an irony—lunch is still going on, and the ladies may already have discussed everything from the proximity of arms on the table to how much the two have eaten of each dish.

I should have introduced him as a classmate, Sangita thought belatedly, smiling weakly. Her teenage skills at deception have faded since she moved out of her parents' house.

"No, thank you," they say in unison.

"The bill, please," Abdulla says to the waitress when she comes to clear the mostly empty dishes from their table. Maya Auntie frowns and waves at Sangita as if to say *Don't be a nuisance.*

"We're going to pay, Auntie," Sangita begins, but instead of arguing, Abdulla simply leans back, pulls out a roll of fifty- pound notes from his pocket and leaves a few on the table. The waitress brings a small tray of fennel and sugar in place of the bill. He tosses a few pieces of crystallized sugar into his mouth, pushes his chair back and rises to leave. He's all the way to the door before seeming to remember something, and turns, waiting for Sangita, who rushes away from Maya Auntie's inquisitive gaze with a perfunctory murmur that the food was delicious, and precedes him into the street.

Chapter 19

As they enter the building, Abdulla nods at Nigel, who is reading on his Kindle—most likely how to convert a nuclear reactor into an ecologically friendly device, or something equally obscure. Sangita is amazed at how knowledgeable the door guard is about world events. Noting the understated exchange between the two men, she makes a mental note to Google his photo and see what former military branch he might have served in. His bulging thighs and ramrod-straight posture give away what she suspects he would never share with her if asked.

She slides the key into the lock and then takes out a second one for the top part of the door, the one Hind usually leaves undone. Abdulla silently takes it from her, as it is half a foot above her head, and then they are back in the apartment.

He seems as lost as she is as to what to do next.

"I've called Hind a hundred times," she says, slinging her bag down on the end table.

"And she isn't answering," he says, stating the obvious.

Sangita takes care not to mention that the phone in question is a satellite phone, which would clue him to the fact that she's thousands of miles away.

"No point in my trying then," he murmurs, scrolling through emails on the ever-present BlackBerry.

She has to consciously resist sprawling in the chair, the usual position she assumes when she and Hind are discussing everything from the future of the two-state solution to getting their first periods to why Hind going to India is the worst decision she could ever make. Instead, Sangita perches on the red sofa, straight-backed, erect, careful not to cross her legs or show the bottom of her feet to Abdulla, who slumps down heavily across from her in Hind's leather armchair.

"I must make some office phone calls," Abdulla says, popping up again almost as soon as he has settled. "Excuse me."

Sangita points towards Hind's room where he can make them in relative privacy. As soon as he's out of range, Sangita reaches frantically for her own phone to try the satellite again. This time someone answers.

"Sarfraz!" Sangita shouts in relief, and then lowers her voice, trying to speak intelligible Tamil to the in-country program coordinator.

"Sarfraz, it's me, Sangita."

Sarfraz's static-filled reply sounds more robotic than human. "Tell Ravi to call me," she says, knowing it's futile to hope anyone could make sense of what she is saying over the static of the line.

Still, it's a start. She's made contact. She can try again, when the connection might be better. She's gotten their attention; now maybe they'll leave the phone on. It was only meant for this, after all. No one in the villages calls each other; most people use SMS because it's so much cheaper than voice calls or a landline. She types out another furious email and short direct messages on both Twitter and Facebook, noting that neither Ravi nor Hind has updated their status on either. They must know now that it was an overseas call.

Sangita prays that Sarfraz will think to call her first and not her parents, who are major benefactors of the school reconstruction project. It's been almost a decade since the tsunami devastated the area so near their native village. Most people have forgotten about the destruction, but not her parents, nor her brother. This is his annual trip to check on the orphanage and school his parents started immediately afterward.

She's startled by the voice of Abdulla, just behind her. "She has been living with idols," he breathes.

Sangita follows his gaze to the small altar she has made in her bedroom, a single poster of Lakshmi, the goddess of wealth, sitting cross-legged on her lotus flower, and above it a small shelf with a bronze Ganesh and a basalt Shiva.

"These are Hindu gods," she says, as he approaches them warily.

Abdulla links his hands behind his head and stretches, taking the room in at a glance, the raw silk bedspread with a sari border, the mini-rainbow of color spurting from the clothing in the closet, the piles of books on every available surface marking a path to the door. "There is no god but God and Mohammed is his prophet," he says automatically, hollowly, as if half-wondering why he is bothering, since no one is there to tell on him if he doesn't. The words have probably been fed to him from his earliest days, Sangita thinks, a Qur'an behind his head in the bassinet from birth. From the ashen look on his face, Sangita half-expects him to take out a string of garlic and a stake.

"Change that to 'Jesus' and you'd make a fine Christian," she says.

He laughs, this time without trying to disguise it, even though his eyes return to her altar.

"How do you come up with these one-liners?" he asks. "You have an answer for everything."

"The world's largest Muslim minority lives in India," she says for the second time. Even though her family isn't overly pious, they would be proud if they knew she was defending their religion.

"A pluralist," he says, but it sounds more like a question.

Sangita shrugs both at the title and at his scrutiny. "That the divine is everywhere is a tenet of Hinduism. You can pray in there if you like," she says, pointing again toward Hind's room. "There should be some rugs that visitors use."

"That's very thoughtful of you," he says, but makes no move in that direction.

Abdulla looks tired, and Sangita realizes he is battling not only the knowledge of whatever he wants to discuss with his carefully-chosen wife, but also an early morning flight and slight jet lag.

"I'm going to take a nap," she says, faking a stifled yawn. Sangita doesn't know if it is just her imagination or the tension of entertaining him, but somehow she is starting to like him, his taciturn ways, his precise manners. She trails into her room and moves to shut the door, only then remembering he has nowhere to stay.

"She has a queen bed in there," Sangita says, poking her head out the door, and once again waving a hand toward Hind's doorway.

The summer evening sun still burns bright through her tiny window, and yet, at eight o'clock, the day is spent. And she has a man, a relative stranger, in the apartment. Sangita suddenly feels weary, still full of food from lunch, wanting to climb back into bed and pull the covers over her head. Maybe when she wakes up Hind will be here, brewing mint tea and going on about how poor people could hold on to their dignity if they had more clothing.

"Wherever you are," she sighs, a tiny tear slipping out of the corner of her eye before it closes in sleep, "you're gonna get it when you get back."

⧜

Abdulla eyes Hind's door with a mixture of horror and fascination, starting a little when Sangita shuts hers firmly. He hasn't ever been in a woman's bedroom, if you don't count the single rooms at university he and his friends snuck into on weekends. Fatima was not a fussy person and kept their apartment in measured tones of Armani rather than feminine gone berserk. Since moving back to his parents' house, he hasn't really spent that much time around women. Luluwa is well past the age where he or his brothers can roam around her freely unless she seeks them out. He has no idea what sort of person Hind really is. Would she have frilly pillows on the bed, or more posters like the one in the living room?

As if entering a sacred temple, he turns the knob and enters.

Chapter 20

Again, for the second time that day, the sound of rhythmic pounding in the apartment wakes Sangita from a deep sleep. But it's only been minutes, she thinks, rubbing her face. She ignores the pool of moisture on her pillow, a sure sign of her exhaustion, and unrolls from the bedspread. Stretching, her arms reaching for the ceiling, she's aware of something urgent, something forcing her out of bed, prompting her to move quickly. She wakes slowly, taking in the objects she's spent the past few months placing in their respective spots: the precise line of perfume bottles and makeup brushes, the earrings hanging from a mesh wire jewelry holder, the full-length mirror slanted at an angle. No time for ambiance.

She pulls on an oversize t-shirt and leggings and steps outside her room, where the sight of her roommate's fiancé-turned-surprise-visitor brings the events of the day rushing back. He is pacing in the living room. Abdulla moves with the litheness of a caged predator, his long strides taking him across the teak flooring.

The pounding this time is from a tennis ball he is bouncing along the floor as he walks. He must have dug it up out of the couch cushions, a relic of one of the many times the roommates have vowed to make exercise a part of their weekly routine. "It's London," Hind would say pragmatically. "We walk all the time—those are our workouts. In Qatar we only drive." Sangita wasn't convinced by this rationale, nor by the ensuing stories of how in Doha it is possible to drive up to a McDonald's, beep your car horn, and have someone take your order from the parking lot. The Qataris apparently have an even faster idea of fast food than most people.

Abdulla has not been occupied in the same way as Sangita. "Sleep at all?" Sangita asks, though the lines on his face tell her otherwise.

He pauses in his stride and shoots her a look that says he hasn't forgotten any of the day's events, including her first early-morning appearance at the door in more than she has on now. Too late, Sangita remembers the tunic sweater dress crumpled on the floor next to her bed.

"Everyone spends the afternoon asleep, waiting during Ramadan," he says, taking a seat in the brown leather armchair. "I never could."

Sangita trails over to the sofa as he dangles his arms across his knees, bouncing the ball against the opposite wall.

"Isn't that like cheating?" she asks.

He catches the ball and rolls it between his palms.

"You sound like my grandfather," he says, laughing. "Are you religious?"

"God is with us," she says, "in many forms."

He tilts his head back and looks at her sharply.

"How did you say you come up with these one-liners?"

"Big family," she shrugs. "You always have to be ready to defend."

Abdulla seems to contemplate this. For some time he has been watching her, with peripheral vision, as she moves around the apartment. Perhaps she knows. He doesn't think so. He almost doesn't care. The truth is, Abdulla is re-evaluating this slip of a girl he didn't even know existed before this eventful day. He has come to find Hind, and hopefully a loophole through which he can call the whole thing off. Instead, he finds himself engaged in a completely unanticipated encounter, and is intrigued by Sangita, who stirs in him an interest he can't remember feeling for at least the past year or so.

"How many brothers and sisters?" he asks.

"Just the one," she says softly.

Sangita feels some of the defiance leaking out of her straight spine. She eases against the cushions, wondering if the mention of Ravi will somehow destroy their growing rapport. Can he somehow sense the connection between her brother and his absent fiancée?

"Not so many," Abdulla says, his mouth loose, apparently never suspecting anything.

"Lots of aunties and cousins," she goes on, "but only the one brother."

Sangita draws a deep breath to ward off the sudden stab of longing she feels for her older brother at that moment. His certainty has always paved the way for her. Without it, she would never have made the journey here. She would never have found her kindred spirit, Hind. Now she needs Ravi more than ever.

"I have an adopted sister," Abdulla says, almost as if he is admitting weakness. He is no longer hiding the weight of his eyes in the corners of thick lashes. His gaze rests fully on her now.

"I thought Arabs didn't believe in adoption," Sangita says. "Her father is one of my uncles. He sort of abandoned her after my wife…" Abdulla falters and breaks off. He clears his

throat. Sangita sees this is hard for him. It occurs to her that he probably hasn't spoken of Fatima outside his family in all this time. Hind hasn't said much about her, either.

Abdulla steadies himself and continues. "Her mother, you see, went to her brother's because, well, frankly, her father…"

He trails off momentarily, searching for the right word. "He…remarried and didn't want anything to do with her."

Sangita nods, realizing from the gruffness of his voice and his sudden awkwardness that he is not used to telling this story.

"Luluwa is the only girl in our house of five," he says, the tennis ball now wedged between his thigh and the chair.

She smiles at the thought of a young Arab girl, maybe not unlike

Hind at that age, dangling a household of men from her pinky finger.

"She never liked the idea of my marrying Hind," he says suddenly, as though their confessional mood has jostled something within him.

All at once Sangita realizes this is going beyond being simply a polite social call with a handsome man who has happened by her apartment. The subtle outrageousness of it hits her in an instant. She is sitting with Hind's fiancé. Said fiancé hasn't the slightest clue he is talking intimately with someone who is complicit in helping his affianced break one of the biggest taboos of Gulf Muslim society: traveling alone with a non- relative male to another country. And, in slightly altered form, it is the same rule Sangita herself is breaking with Abdulla at this very moment.

"The sun's down," she says, jumping up, and then turning to look at him as he remains immobile. "Aren't you going to pray?"

Abdulla moves away, as if she struck him. "I haven't fasted properly in a long time," he admits. "The last time was nearly four Ramadans ago, when Fatima was still alive."

Fatima. Had her death robbed him of his faith? Does he think God abandoned him?

"Praying and fasting aren't the same," she says.

"I'm not religious," he said. His voice had a slight tremor. He didn't meet her gaze.

Abdulla drops his head, those ever watchful eyes closing as if in defeat.

"Neither am I," she said. "But I don't feel guilty about it." He turns to her, frowning.

"God will be there whenever you are ready," she says.

"In Islam we can never lose faith," he says. "We can't object to God's will." The droop of his shoulders says he already has.

"God can take it," she says. "Otherwise what's the point of being God?" He doesn't answer.

"I'm going to make some food."

Abdulla pulls himself out of the chair and begins rolling up his sleeves.

"I'll wash up."

Sangita busies herself in the kitchen, opening and closing drawers, though they both know there is little there in terms of nourishment.

"Want some eggs?" she says, but before he can accept or decline the offer a rush of vulnerability overtakes her, and she shoots across to the kitchen to be closer to the exit. She is, after all, an unprotected female, and no matter how well-mannered he might be, he is a male. But Abdulla doesn't fit the profile of the lecherous Arab. At least not yet. The fact that she has again come out half-dressed, as polite Muslim society would see it, doesn't seem to faze him as much as it did this morning. Then, as quickly as it came on, the feeling turns to what it really is—panic at being separated from both her brother and her best friend, and alone with this man who seems so fragile, his grief fresh on his face.

"Eggs?" he is saying, holding a half-full egg carton as he comes back into the living room.

"Sure," she says, taking the egg carton away from him and going for a spatula from the drawer, a skillet from a cupboard and butter from the fridge—anything to avoid the rising feeling of doom.

"I hope your eggs are better than your tea service," he says. His lips bend into what she is learning is his version of a smile. She replies by sticking out her tongue. He laughs, and this time his laugh is looser and less strangled than before.

She curses the placement of the stove's burners, set into the top of the island itself so that it's impossible for her turn her back on him like her mother does when avoiding the rest of the family. In the modern kitchen there is no room for secrets.

She turns the knob halfway and waits for a slab of butter to melt.

"If it weren't for eggs," she says, "I would never have made it through the first term. Protein in a one-pan meal."

She cracks four into a glass mixing bowl, grabbing the whisk from the utensil holder on the countertop. She is about to begin beating when he comes around to her side.

"Let me," he says. "I can at least do crepes."

"You know how to cook?"

He smiles, this time a smile stretching across his face. "I'm an excellent assistant," he says, reaching out a hand. "Pass me the bowl and whisk."

This is hard for her to imagine—Abdulla being helpful to anyone beside himself.

"No maid?" Sangita probes.

"Not at LSE," he replies.

She lets him take over, wondering why Hind has never mentioned that her fiancé is one of the few non-Western men who can actually be of use anywhere near the kitchen. One broad palm cups the bowl as the other beats the eggs at a pace so dizzying that the peaks form within a few seconds without him sloshing any yolk on his shirt or on the counter.

"While you were sleeping, I got Nigel's advice on a grocery," he says. She looks on with raised eyebrows as he begins measuring flour and sugar for the batter.

Sangita is surprised but delighted by his foresight, because she's ravenously hungry. She starts on a large red onion that has turned up in the fridge's veggie box. She chops, almost absentmindedly, as Abdulla uncaps a small bottle of milk and pours half a cup in with the whipped yolk. She adds the onions to the warm butter, turning them as they became iridescent, and makes way for Abdulla, who is pouring crepe batter onto a second warming skillet. Pouring carefully, he waits a moment, and then peels them up just before they turn brown.

"Scrambled eggs," they both say in agreement.

It is strange, the sound of water behind her as he fills the kettle, then the hum a moment later as it turns on, the precise way he chooses a knife from the block to slice a baguette. Strange because these are the companionable things one does with a roommate— or a spouse, she reflects, thinking guiltily of Hind. How much longer can she delay the news of her friend's disappearance? They have reached the end of one day. Maybe one more? Sooner or later she will have to explain.

They settle into preparing a modest breakfast for dinner as if the elements were commonplace. Hind should be here, Sangita thinks suddenly, when Abdulla begins opening cupboards and looking for serving dishes.

"Careful," Abdulla is saying, and she realizes she hasn't stirred the eggs in a while. They are starting to stick, a congealed mass. She scrapes the skillet until the clumps break up, bits of onion distributed all around.

Meanwhile he has a stack of golden, neatly folded crepes. The kettle sounds. She turns off the heat.

"Toaster?" he asks. She shakes her head. He sighs. "What do you women eat?"

She tries not to laugh as she scrapes the scrambled eggs onto slices of bread that he has arranged on two blue and white dinner plates. Each of them spears two crepes, which Sangita has doused with butter and pats of chocolate from an opened bag of miniatures.

"She'll come back," he says, as if continuing their conversation from earlier in the day, "and then we'll see."

She nods in agreement, not wanting to give voice to her doubts or to the increasingly tangled emotions she feels. Irony that he is trying to comfort her, when he only knows half the truth. Fear that something serious may have happened to Hind and Ravi and there is no way of knowing. Anger that the two people she loves most in the world have put her in this incredibly awkward position. And confusion at the polite and easy manner of this man who, till now, has served only to embody male repressiveness in her friend's stories of home.

"Let's eat then," he says with a smile. "You're right. Never a bad idea."

She slides into a seat next to him and smiles back.

Chapter 21

Sangita finds it even more amazing, after they have finished eating, that Abdulla helps clean up, clearing the dishes, drying while she washes, and even putting them away. But as soon as the tasks end, the easy camaraderie ends with them. In the growing silence, the two of them are back to being complete strangers instead of the amicable acquaintances they were becoming.

When the phone on the wall rings, they both flinch.

"Hello?" Sangita says, half-wondering where to start, when all at once she hears: "Gita! Who is this man you were eating with in Maya Auntie's restaurant?"

"Hiya, Ma."

It's just like her mother to launch into a conversation as though it were already going. And just like her to have the most up-to-date information. Sangita looks at the clock on the microwave. Only ten hours can have passed since the meal under discussion occurred. Sangita is surprised her mother has waited this long.

"Don't you 'hiya' me," Mama says, not to be distracted.

"How are you?" she persists, wishing she could switch into Tamil but knowing it would alert her mother that someone else was in the room. They only speak Tamil when foreigners are around, in the movie theater line or when deciding how much to pay for something at the flea market.

"Maya says he was very handsome," she says, unperturbed. "A friend, Ma, just a friend."

Sangita senses Abdulla wandering away from the countertop towards the living room and unhunches her shoulders. He takes up the BlackBerry again and scrolls through his contact list, or emails, she can't tell which. She cranes over at the top of Abdulla's bent head, hoping for a better angle.

Maya Auntie has sharp eyes, Sangita gives her that. At least her facts are right. What she doesn't know—and Sangita hasn't volunteered— is Abdulla's name... That's all anyone in her Hindu community would need to hear before screeching from the room. The slave of God, *abd* of Allah, could never be a potential marriage partner for a high-caste Hindu girl.

But he's not my fiancé, she reminds herself. I don't have to feel guilty about anything.

A noisy sigh. Sangita pictures her mother worrying the thick rope chain from which hangs her five-gram *thali*, the Hindu woman's equivalent of a three-carat diamond.

"You have enough friends, girl," her mother is saying. "Find a man who will make a commitment to you. Speaking of which, I found two more potentials this weekend at Monica's wedding."

Sangita rolls her eyes, glad her mother can't see her. She looks over her shoulder to see Abdulla is studiously looking out the window. *He's as bad at eavesdropping as he is making small talk.*

"I have to go, Ma," she says, wishing her mother didn't have such easy use of technology and resources when it comes to keeping tabs on her only daughter.

"Have you talked to your brother?"

Sangita flinches. If only Ma knew that Ravi was showing up in their natal village with a Qatari woman, there would be no stopping her from flying over on the first available plane, damn the expense, to drag the poor boy home by the ear.

"I'll tell him to call you," Sangita says, her standard line whenever the parentals expect her to be the go-between to their only son. Sometimes she wishes her parents had more children so that they could share the attention. She lays the phone back in its cradle and places both hands on the countertop.

"Mother?" Abdulla asks, and lifts both eyebrows, waiting for an answer. She shrugs as though to say *you've lived abroad, you figure it out*, surprised by his interest.

"Just tell them what you're eating. That usually throws them off the scent," he says, not unsympathetically.

Sangita drums her fingernails on the countertop. *But not always who you're eating with*, she adds to herself.

"Usually she gets off the scent pretty easily," she says, thinking aloud, "but lately she's just got it into her head that I'm on a time clock. And it's not fair: Ravi is three years older than me."

He comes around behind her, rummages in the fridge for two Cokes, pops them open using the bottle opener on the fridge door, and offers her one. They clink bottles in the unspoken commiseration of children with meddling parents.

"I thought only Arab parents were this interfering," he says, leaning a hip against the marble island.

She shrugs again, taking a long gulp, as though the Coke were something more fortifying than carbonated water and sugar.

"From what Hind says, I gather they're about the same. Non-Western parents want a say in everything."

I've got to stop doing that, Sangita thinks, as she sees his posture stiffen. A casual mention of Hind's name, and look at the pall it casts over the conversation. "Do you do arranged marriages also?"

"The love comes later." Sangita mimics her mother's stance, one hand on her hip. "You learn to love each other."

"Sometimes it's true," Abdulla murmurs, without the usual irony. From the look on his face, he has surprised even himself with this admission.

"Did you love your first wife? Hind wasn't sure."

He hangs his head for a moment, and then shakes it from side to side.

"Wasn't long enough to tell."

In the silence, she reaches out and presses his trembling hand flat on the marble countertop with her own. For a split second she thinks she sees a shine of tears as he clears his throat.

"You're the girl. It stands to reason they would pressure you," Abdulla says, as though stating a universal fact.

Sangita feels the hair on her neck bristle and the moment passes. She snatches her hand back.

"Well, that would be fine if I grew up in a village in India. Or in Africa. In…you know, Sudan. For example," she shrugs. "But I didn't."

He raises the eyebrow again, glancing at her, then goes back to finishing his drink.

"So they need to back off," she adds, making it, she hopes, less personal.

Abdulla sets his empty bottle on the counter. Sangita sighs and drums the counter with her fingers. Abdulla hasn't spoken.

"They just want to make sure I'm happy," she goes on, "but they don't realize how hard it is to meet someone. What should I do, go down to Tesco and pick out the right one?"

"I've got no sympathy for you, dear," he says at last, his voice laced with sarcasm. "Look at the whole reason why I'm here."

They regard each other in silence for a heartbeat, then two.

This is not your friend coming to visit, Sangita reminds herself. *This is the man your roommate will marry, whether either of them likes it or not.* She can think of nothing to say to that chilling thought. Turning attention back to herself would just seem selfish compared with what he and Hind are dealing with. Her dilemma is abstract, theirs immediate.

All of which is a rude reminder that the fiancée in question is nowhere to be found and the fiancé in front of her hasn't the slightest clue that this is the case. Surely all the camaraderie they have built up will vanish in a second if Hind doesn't show up fast. Sangita gulps down the rest of her drink, murmurs something about having an assignment to finish, and retreats to her room. There's very little to say.

☙

Abdulla watches her retreat and can't help but admire what he sees. But here he's done it again, run her off with his prickliness. She likes his fiancée, cares about her. She's probably decided by now that he's insupportable and, if she hasn't already, will send off a hundred text messages telling Hind to call off the entire wedding. Which of course would suit him fine, but what would it say about him? That she's evaluated him and found him impossible, a complete downer.

Suddenly, for some inexplicable reason, he doesn't like the idea that this girl, this irrelevant Indian girl, finds him flawed.

Chapter 22

Abdulla is having difficulty keeping his balance in the claw-foot tub in his fiancée's bathroom. Standing up isn't so bad, but having to hold the showerhead with one hand and the soap in the other makes his balance on the slick surface precarious. He curses the English for their crowded lifestyle and, just as he feels his heel starting to slide for the third time, he turns off the water.

His eyes narrow as he catches a glimpse of his wet hair in the mirror above the sink, which is so small even a bird couldn't take a bath in it. Hind is tall, like him, so the mirror is a good height, easily framing his face. He can see the dark circles under his eyes starting to show. Three days, and the girl who was his childhood playmate is still nowhere to be found.

He steps out of the bathtub slowly, first one leg, muscled from years of riding his father's horses, and then the other, until he is back on the even black and white tiles of the bathroom floor.

Hind, unlike Abdulla's mother or his aunts, has taste. She has never gone for the gold glitz you find in most Qatari homes, but instead sticks with one or two colors, generally solids as far as he can see, augmented with complementary fabrics. The bath towels are black, the hand towels white, picking up the color scheme from the floor. There is no place here for the accoutrements of womanhood that fill Sangita's bathroom. Any potions, lotions or perfumes Hind keeps in the massive dresser across from her bed. In the bathroom proper, it is all business.

He towels off and runs a hand across his chin. After three days it's populated with wiry black stubble. His mother wouldn't appreciate a bearded face; this was one of her favorite features of her young sons in contrast to the curled beards of his father and uncles. He mentally adds a shaving kit to the list of things Nigel needs to pick up. But no rush. Abdulla has not been in a hurry for years. Even after returning to Qatar from his final year at LSE, just before his marriage to Fatima, he never really came to heel in the ways that are proper for a man soon to be married and the head of his own household.

He steps closer to the mirror. Down the right side, on a yellow post-it note, Hind has written a to-do list in neon pink highlighter: GET NOTECARDS BEFORE FINAL. DRINK WATER. DROP LAUNDRY. CALL HOME. The last one brings him up short. If she has been calling home regularly, how do they explain her silence? Where do they think she is right now?

His sigh sounds like an old lady's, but he can't help it.

He dresses, pulling over his head the white t-shirt Sangita has given him.

That Hind has befriended an Indian girl isn't the biggest of surprises. Like their grandfather, she has never been a slave to convention—a girl who speaks English fluently and graduated from an international university with high hopes. He should have known his mother had her eye on Hind as a backup, if only because of the occasional email she would pass to him with a news photo of his cousin next to Her Highness at some red carpet event. Not every Qatari family wants its daughter's image printed for the eyes of the country to roam across. A girl who allows herself to be photographed has to be made of stern stuff. She must know her family will stand by her, and the girl in the photos clearly did. It was in her face, even in the grainy news images. The once-chubby cheeks of the young girl who used to eat sand in the family compound had receded into angular, assured cheekbones. A judicious touch of eyeliner, not the all-too-common heavy band of black on top and green on the bottom, played up a sparkle in her eyes that the black and white of the newspaper couldn't dull.

He should have known it was really Hind his mother was suggesting.

"Hind will need a firm hand," his mother said. "She has ideas, as all young girls do, and needs a good man as her husband."

Abdulla said nothing, merely inclined his head, thankful that no reaction was expected of him. He thought of Luluwa, still five years away from this kind of haggling, and repressed a shudder as he and his father rose to kiss the cheeks of his future male in-laws to seal his engagement. *Will it be better in half a decade?*

Pushing the thought aside, he resolved to pretend to be the best husband-to-be he could to a girl he hadn't seen in five years and had no intention of actually marrying. That she wanted to study for her master's was a good sign. Perhaps she wouldn't depend on him to be home every night, as his friends' wives did, always bothering them with some story or other about the maid's laziness or a bargain in the mall.

Abdulla pulls on his trousers and buckles the belt. Both are well worn. He will need something else for however long this stakeout is going to last. He decides to call ahead to Thomas Pink to order shirts, but just as he tries to leave the bathroom he finds the knob is frozen. After trying it several times he considers pounding on the door, but thinks better of it. The girl might come, so sleepy that he will feel guilty for waking her. Maybe half-dressed.

Maybe the shower was too hot.

What if she has bolted the door from the outside? Why would she do that? She hasn't had a problem with him sleeping a door away from her, as any of the women in his family would. She just trails into her room and shuts the door.

One more try, and this time the handle gives slightly. He cracks the door open to the sound of female voices, but there is still resistance from the other side, something pushing back.

It's the girl. She has her back to him, her hands behind her, and is holding the doorknob tight. Abdulla, a foot taller, can see over her shoulder into the living room where, only a few feet away, someone is speaking.

"Hanoodie knew I was coming," another girl is saying, big lips flopping over into a pout. Something familiar in her face tells Abdulla he should recognize her. "Why would she go volunteer in Essex when we're supposed to be shopping?"

A Qatari friend of Hind's, perhaps, come to visit, or...

"Sorry, Noor, you know how she gets," Sangita is saying. "She hears of someone in need and just drops everything and goes."

"Are those guys' shoes?"

Noor. Abdulla contemplates the bright pink lipstick and tight jeans. He hasn't seen any of the girls since before they were all teenagers.

"Is there a guy here?" Noor begins scanning the apartment.

"My brother was," the girl offers. "He forgot those. I need to get around to mailing them back."

"Good taste," she says, eyeing the leather loafers.

"I'll tell Hind you came by."

"So my own sister would rather do good than spend time with me," Noor pouts, her pink lower lip sticking out. It is indeed Noor, the skin-and-bones youngest girl cousin in the family, now a budding young woman.

Abdulla sucks in his breath and holds it, even though neither of them seems able to hear him. He's not the only one in the family looking for Hind.

"Look, if she turns up, tell her it's almost time," Noor is saying, examining immaculate inch-long fingernails. "She may have a visitor."

Abdulla shrinks back into the recesses of the bathroom. "Is that right?"

"Well, *Ubooy* is trying to convince her fiancé to come, since they haven't seen each other in so long."

Sangita coughs.

"You know, the reception will be soon after Hind gets back, and no one wants it to be awkward."

"I'll be sure to tell her," Sangita strangles out.

Noor's eyes narrow as if taking her in for the first time.

"I figure you know this already from Hind. And you're not Qatari, so this is okay."

"Your secrets are safe with me." Sangita leans forward in a conspiratorial whisper and tries to fake a laugh. It rings hollow.

"Can I use the toilet?" Noor asks suddenly. Abdulla hears her moving towards them.

"No!" Noor pauses, very likely puzzled by the girl's startled tone. Sangita coughs again and shoves back on the door. "I mean, the toilet is broken in this bathroom. Use mine, please."

Abdulla waits until he hears the other bathroom door close, then snakes his arm out and yanks the girl in with him.

"What is Noor doing here?" he hisses, pinning her arms on either side of her.

"She's here to buy Hind some saucy underwear for your honeymoon," she shoots back.

Dumbfounded, he releases her arms and she sags against the bathroom door like a ragdoll.

"She doesn't know where Hind is either." Sangita shakes her head.

Abdulla leans on the sink behind him, afraid to give it his whole weight. "If Hind isn't with her..."

"Sangita?" Noor calls. "Is there someone else there?"

Sangita claps a hand over his mouth. The contact of her slight frame against him is like an electric shock as they freeze in place. She presses a finger against his lips, unnecessarily, since speaking out loud is the farthest thing from his mind. For a moment, all he is aware of is the feel of her, slim and soft, poised against him. He is like a schoolboy, he thinks, at the first sight of a swimsuit magazine.

She moves toward the door and opens it a crack.

"No, I was just getting into the shower," she says through the crevice. Noor doesn't seem convinced.

"Are those cuff links on the counter? And what's with all the phones?"

Abdulla could have smacked himself for the uncharacteristic sloppiness. Everything about him seems different since he arrived, so much so that he is starting to not recognize himself.

"I'll tell her you came by, Noor. You know how she is. I'm sure she'll be back in a few days."

"All right." Noor is eyeing the teacups drying in the dish drainer. "Do you want me to call someone about that toilet?"

Sangita peeks around the door and shakes her head vigorously, her coiled hair falling away from the top of her head.

"No, I'm okay. Thanks!"

Abdulla joins her at the crack in the door, and together they watch the slow sway of Noor's retreat out the apartment door, not moving until the click-clack of five-inch Gucci heels in the outer stairwell has died away.

The instant they hear the front door shut, they come out of the bathroom gunning for each other.

"What was she doing here without her sister?"

"I don't know. What were you trying to do, get us caught?" They are now toe to toe, which would be less ridiculous a face-off if Sangita had her heels on. As it is, face-level is somewhere near his collarbone. Nevertheless, in the fury of his frustration, Abdulla has to let loose and give it to her. She tilts her chin up in defiance, but what Abdulla actually notices is not the defiance so much as the curve of her throat. As his fury recedes, he realizes he is having a hard time deciding whether he wants to strangle or caress her at this vulnerable spot. For the second time that morning he hears himself sigh like a grandmother, and grits his teeth to maintain his resolve.

"Never raise your chin like that to an enemy," he says, mock-clipping her with his fist. "You're exposing your jugular."

She takes a step back, considering him.

"Noor had a key and she let herself in. I thought you said you didn't want anyone to know you were here."

His head snaps up at this, but she is already in the kitchen, dangling a silver key from a crystal strap.

"You have it," he realizes, relaxing a bit.

"So she can't walk in again like she just did, with no warning, and find you alone here."

"With you."

She shrugs. "With me."

"Clever," he says, breaking into a slow grin. Sangita frowns and turns away.

"Hey, I just gave you a compliment," he says, following her into the kitchen.

"Try it with my name."

He pulls down the coffee bean canister and pours some beans into the grinder, glancing at her once or twice. Apparently Noor gave her enough warning to pull on a hooded sweatshirt and yellow cotton pants. Across her chest it says: BITCH. He looks away, realizing he's finding reasons to look even when the flesh is covered up. *This is getting out of hand*, he thinks bleakly.

"Same fundraiser as the mug," Sangita says, mistaking the lingering gaze. She slides onto a stool and picks at the grapes Abdulla brought back along with the bagels and newspaper, which she begins leafing through, ignoring him.

He starts the coffee, glancing occasionally at her. He has to admit that if it weren't for this girl's cleverness a few minutes ago he would be in a lot of hot water now, and not just with Hind. Questions would be flying from both sides of the family about this clandestine trip of his that he still has no explanation for.

"Thank you," he says, "Sangita."

She straightens up a little and gives him a look, then goes back to the paper with another shrug.

"I don't want Hind to get in trouble," she says.

"Neither do I," he says, and immediately wonders what he means.

She looks up at him for a long moment, as if considering how to take what he's just said. He decides he means exactly what he said, and he can see that she believes him. Her nonchalance dissolves and is replaced by panic. And the weariness of keeping a secret that isn't even hers. He can see in her eyes that she wants to unburden herself.

"Tell me," he says, leaning across the countertop, sipping coffee from the matching BITCH mug. "Please just tell me."

It all comes tumbling out. A brother, Ravi. Who came for a visit.

Hind's fascination with his NGO work with children in India. Abdulla feels a tightening in his gut as she goes on about Hind always wanting to help others but never knowing how, and Sangita's delight at finally having a sister to rein in Ravi's boyish obtuseness.

"They are lovers," he blurts out, stopping her short. It isn't a question.

Sangita flushes, apparently knowing this was coming. "My brother is an honorable man," she says. "He wouldn't do that."

Now Abdulla really loses it, bursting out with a maniacal laugh.

"He is a man," Abdulla says, stating what he thinks is the obvious, "and an American."

Sangita straightens herself and comes as close as she can to staring down someone still half a head taller than she is.

"He is a man with principles," she says. Abdulla shakes his head.

"Hind is engaged—"

"That didn't stop him from running off with her!"

Sangita sags against the countertop. "They went as friends," she mumbles. His eyes fly up in what is quickly becoming a standard reaction. "This very contradiction has plagued me for so many nights since Hind and Ravi left ten days ago..." she trails off at his stunned look.

He takes another gulp of coffee, breathes, and waves a hand, indicating that she should continue.

"Finals, graduation paperwork, and finding a job... I've had no time to think about this. I had to put my doubts away. So the two people I love the most in the world are together. What can be bad about that?"

His coffee is gone. He feels his arm trembling as he resists the urge to smash his mug against the far wall. He wonders, has he ever felt so strongly for anyone that he would risk everything?

"But you're one living, breathing, powerful reason this is wrong, no matter how innocent they are." She rests her forearms on the countertop as if she would like to put her head down and weep.

Abdulla feels a softening toward this girl that he doesn't know what to do with. Of course it is wrong, but so is the rest of it. The whole bloody mess is wrong and he knows it. And here is this girl clearly prepared to suffer for other people's behavior. She doesn't deserve this. But even so. . .

"I wasn't really sure about her," he says. "But Hind is naïve to think she can possibly have this adventure without anyone finding out."

"Your family is going to kill them," Sangita says, the sound of tears in her voice.

"No, they're not. We don't do that sort of thing in Qatar."

She looks up at him, then down again. Perhaps she believes him. But there is still fear. To his amazement, Abdulla realizes he feels the need to justify himself.

"Don't be absurd," he says bitterly.

"They'll lock her up—"

"Stop it, please." Abdulla glances at his BlackBerry, partly so he won't have to look at her. "What happened to being a friend to Muslims?" he adds dryly. "I thought you knew all about us, that we aren't the barbarians Westerners always claim we are and so on."

She looks back at him, still wary. "Sorry. The sheikh is right."

"Nobody is going to kill anyone," he says finally, looking hard at her. "And by the way, didn't I tell you to stop with the 'sheikh' business?"

For the first time since they met, her mouth snaps open and shut without a speedy rejoinder.

"You're not Qatari. So call me Abdulla."

Speechless! He can't help breaking into a laugh, in spite of everything.

But how can he laugh? Why is it he's feeling almost jolly? Could it be that the dire news she has confided in him is only dire in her eyes? He must be careful not to seem pleased, but still, he can't help but brighten at the notion that Hind might have given him the exit clause he has been hoping for. But he can't let on.

"Anyway, we don't even know where they are," he says. "But I'm sure our agencies can find them easily if she's using her passport." He watches her response, a tightening in her face. "Unless, of course, they are traveling on fake documents?"

"Look, they aren't running away together," Sangita says. "They're installing computers in a school for street children."

Abdulla didn't expect that. But instinctively he knows it's true, and suddenly all the air goes out of his tough-guy act.

"All right," he says with a sigh. "I know what I have to do." He straightens his unwrinkled cuffs.

"You're going to report them to MI6," Sangita breathes, keeping herself from fainting by gripping the edge of the counter.

"They have more important things to look after," he retorts, striding to the door. "Don't watch so many soap operas. We don't involve other governments in our family affairs."

"However you bring it off, you could drag her back to Doha and she could be punished. Haven't there been cases where the girl is kept a prisoner in her own home?"

Shaking off her absurd paranoia, Abdulla tries to clear his head and think. Hind, by her indiscretion, has given him the perfect excuse to break off the engagement. No one could ever fault him for divorcing her. That's what it would be, even though they haven't lived together yet, not technically. In the courts, and under Sharia law, she has been his wife from the moment they signed the contract at their milcha.

He turns to look at Sangita. She's clinging to the countertop, trembling.

"Don't lock your knees that way, you'll faint," he says, feeling guilty for the sheer joy tumbling through him at the prospect of being free, contrasted with the fear he's caused in Sangita. Reaching out awkwardly, like a thirteen-year-old boy, he pats her on the shoulder.

This startles her for a moment, but then she perks up a bit. Looking down at her knees, she tries to do as he says.

"Okay, I have to get a hold of myself," she breathes, gulping in a long breath. "It's just that –"

"No, no," he says. "Not necessary."

"Let me say this." She waits for him to nod. "I'm torn, you see, between protecting my friend and letting go of this secret that isn't even mine. Do you understand?"

"Of course I do," he mutters in the face of her candor. "Give me some facts. When did she leave?"

"Ten, maybe eleven days ago," she says.

"Car? Train? Boat?"

"Plane," she says, using the tips of her fingers to massage her neck. "They flew into Bombay."

"Mumbai," he corrects her.

Sangita eyes him from her slumped position.

"My family has done business there for over thirty years," he mumbles, entering some notes into his BlackBerry. "My grandfather was there first, as a pearl merchant."

"Really?"

"Stop trying to change the subject," he snaps. "Airline?"

"I don't know. Qatar Airways?"

They go still.

Surely Hind wouldn't have been so stupid as to use the national carrier for her dream misadventure. She would attract attention, perhaps even be recognized. He would have no choice then but to repudiate her. And no one else would be likely to marry her, at least not as a first wife. Hind knows all this full well. For a girl from a family of high social standing, it would amount to public humiliation. *She leaves me no choice*, he thinks, grinding his teeth, his fingers worrying the rounded scar beneath his watch. *And then? Then it will all just start over again*, he admits. *They will not rest until they have found me someone.* He pinches the bridge of his nose at the thought of going back to his father and uncles for a third time.

"I managed to get through to the village earlier this morning," Sangita is saying, "but they couldn't hear me." She's trying to distract him. He follows her gaze to his hands, which he realizes have been twitching at his sides.

He reaches for his phone and wakes up the officer at the airport immigration desk.

"They had reservations on Qatar Airways but never showed up," he says, following her back into the living room. "What does that mean?"

"I don't know," she whispers.

"What am I supposed to do? I can't go to the embassy," he says, squaring off with her, "for obvious reasons." He looks her dead in the eye before setting off again to the other side of the room.

Sangita stays perfectly still, not even flexing her shoulders, as he swings back toward her, his broad frame filling her sightline to the apartment door.

"No one must know that Hind is missing," he tells her, though she hasn't asked a question. "For her sake as much as mine."

He must be the one to break the news to the family, to his uncle, so he can tailor the circumstances just right. That way no one will blame him for dumping her, and he'll have bought at least another six months in the cycle before having to meet yet another girl.

Abdulla firmly puts thoughts of Luluwa's warnings and his grandfather's shaky gait out of his mind. "Sooner or later they'll know I'm here and expect us to show up at the house, or there'll be questions," he mutters as though to himself, again pacing the length of the living room.

"It could be a few more days," Sangita says.

He pulls one hand through his hair, which, despite its lack of length, still pops up in tufts, as though this weren't the first tug of the morning. Clearly, of the two of them, the girl has gotten more sleep.

He considers Sangita for a moment. She is uncharacteristically silent, hands shoved into the back pockets of her jeans, shoulders hunched up near her ears. She too is weighing the consequences of discovery and, if her silence and the guilt in her eyes are any indication, already blaming herself. Abdulla feels his head begin to pound.

Wherever she is, Hind is doing what she wants. Isn't this the right he has promised himself he will fight for when Luluwa's time comes? Maybe the roommate is right and nothing is going on with the brother. Maybe Hind feels as trapped by their pre- determined fate as he does, but she has had the courage to do something about it.

"Let's go out," he says, startling them both. The words hang in the air between them.

Sangita raises an eyebrow as if to say: "Where could the two of us go?"

Where could two strangers who aren't supposed to know each other and don't have a clue about the whereabouts of their missing link go and not be noticed? Where could Abdulla hide in a city crawling not only with Qataris, but with relatives from all over the GCC?

He raises a forefinger and picks up his phone from the countertop. As he speaks to the cultural attaché at the embassy, she idly rinses out the coffee mug and water glass.

"Done," he says, disconnecting the line.

She hands him a new cup in a gesture he is beginning to find familiar.

"They do medical appointments and social engagements too?" she asks, not entirely surprised.

"Where might we go and not be noticed?" Abdulla waits, relishing the suspense. "We're going to the Women's Floor Dancing."

"The Olympics?" Sangita's hand stills halfway through drying the glass.

"Not great seats," he warns, nipping in the bud any idea of ringside box seats or nearby celebrities. Fatima may have been reasonable in all other areas, but having the best tickets to shows was one of her delights in life.

"We want to blend," he reminds her, and himself as well. "To disappear in a sea of anonymous spectators."

He can tell she likes the idea. But he is doing this for reasons she can't possibly appreciate. He wants to have the advantage when finally bringing out the news about Hind. Even the smallest rumor of any indiscretion of his own would make it difficult for her to be judged severely. *Not that this will be anything of the sort*, he corrects himself. *We're waiting for Hind to return. Nothing more. Three days alone in the apartment is enough.*

"We're going to the Olympics!" Sangita shrieks, jumping up and down, throwing her arms around him and squeezing, evidently not bothered by the fact they'll be watching a ridiculously minor sport from terrible seats, much less that she is having physical contact with a non-relative male.

Is it his imagination, or has his pulse just doubled at the brush of her body against him and the nearness of her perfume—orange, laced with a hint of jasmine? Instinctively he shrinks from contact, but she is already across the room and jumping up and down in circles around the apartment. Despite himself, he smiles.

Evidently they both could benefit from getting out of here for a while.

Chapter 23

In the taxi Sangita says, "I always wanted to be a gymnast. Turns out I'm not so flexible."

Abdulla smiles at her, and this time he can feel the smile reaching all the way to his eyes, relaxing his face. The years of his reticence with others begins cracking under her exuberance.

The stadium is nearly empty save for the two of them and the parents, coaches and friends of the competitors, but the girl is loving every minute of the colorful twirling ribbons and the lithe bodies that tumble, dance, and race their way across the mat. She watches the dancers with pure delight, while from under hooded eyelids he watches her, her profile, the even white teeth, the dimple in the curve of her cheek, the flash of red lips when she smiles.

He stretches his legs as Sangita bites into yet another hot dog. She obviously enjoys eating. And he can't think when he's felt more comfortable around someone. The silences between them aren't awkward at all, but companionable. Then Sangita's spirit rises up, as when she vehemently disagrees with the judges' scoring, once or twice drawing looks from the ushers, and he can only smile with admiration.

After hours of sitting, and sampling at least one of nearly everything on offer at the concession stand, Sangita looks like a kid emerging from an all-day double feature festival. Unexpectedly, Abdulla is having so much fun he can hardly complain when she wants to stay all afternoon, even sitting through the floor change for the men's competition the next day. All of it fascinates Sangita. Or maybe they are both just relieved to be outside the confines of the apartment.

They are finally standing up to leave, stretching the kinks out of their legs, when Abdulla reaches suddenly for her hand and jerks her back down.

"What in the world...?"

"Keep low," he tells her. "We have to go quickly, but stay down."

His larger hand grips her bony one and begins dragging her forward. Bent double, they weave through the mostly empty row towards the nearest exit. As he picks up speed, almost in a semi-jog, she finds herself doing double time to keep up with him.

"Why are we doing this?" she almost wails in exasperation.

"Co-workers," he says. "Don't look. Keep moving."

They are ducking past janitors sweeping trash and concession stands closing for the day when a large man coming out of the bathroom brings them up short. Abdulla drops Sangita's hand as though it was on fire, flinging it away from him, and at the same time takes a giant step away from her.

Sangita looks for somewhere to disappear. The elation of the day has evaporated and she is reminded just who she's spent this special afternoon with—a Qatari civil servant destined to be her friend's husband. "Abdulla?"

"Hamad!" he exclaims, with more excitement than he has ever shown his secretary before.

"You're on this trip? I thought you declined to join the official delegation."

Abdulla spreads his hands out searching for a plausible explanation.

"Backstage tour," Sangita cuts in, using a professional tone. "Up-close view of the Olympics for hopeful future host cities." She gives them such a conspiratorial wink that Hamad almost reacts with a classic double-take.

Unable to help himself, Abdulla breaks into a grin, and coughs to cover a laugh.

"We better keep moving along, sir, if we're going to keep up with the others," Sangita says to Abdulla, as though they have just met. She indicates forward with her head and Abdulla nods, thankful yet again for her quick wits.

"Yes, yes, excuse my haste. See you soon, *insha'Allah*." Abdulla waves and is off before Hamad can ask when or where. They take off again, now so close to the exit he can almost smell the fresh air, and hit the crash bar of the double doors together, bursting out into the dusk.

Sangita has her arm out, hailing a black cab, before he can check behind them again to see if they are being followed. They tumble in as she says "South Kensington."

He takes a seat across from her on a pull-down chair; she sits on the bench. Abdulla looks out of the window, rubbing his chin. No sign of anyone he knows.

She leans her head back, and begins to giggle.

"Sir?" he says, breaking into a laugh.

She joins him in a full-scale laughing fit, their sides heaving. The cabbie slides the partition shut as Sangita begins cackling.

"We're lucky that was Hamad," he says, wiping his eyes. "He'll probably forget he even saw us when he gets back to the hotel."

Sangita pays the driver and accepts the change, and they tumble out on the curb in front of the apartment building.

"Who else was there?"

"I thought I recognized my uncle in the front row," Abdulla replies.

She stops in the stairwell a step above him. This makes them almost the same height and he can't avoid looking into her eyes. "Thank you," she says, placing a hand on his chest. "For not getting Hind into trouble."

She seems to be about to say something else, but only gives him a pat before they resume tromping up the stairs to the flat. Sangita passes Abdulla the key, leaning on his forearm to keep herself up.

He enters the apartment behind her as she throws her bag down on the counter and kicks her shoes into a pile by the door. He doesn't mention that he would have as many questions to answer as his missing fiancée if the family saw him and Sangita together alone in public.

"You do that too?" he says absent-mindedly, watching her flop into an armchair as though there wasn't a bone in her body. "Do what?"

"Stretch out… like that."

She looks at him with an odd smile and pulls a small blanket from the back of the sofa, covering herself from mid-chest to knees. Turning his full attention to his own shoes, he scrupulously avoids the line of sight that could fully take in her supine female form from head to toe. Abdulla realizes he hasn't seen such a sight since he was a husband. Luluwa wouldn't count, and in any case she has too much energy to lie down ever; and his mother is always watching TV upstairs in her room. How could this American girl know that women in abayas never lie down in public? It means nothing to her. Is that why he is not shocked?

Then it strikes him that in truth, he hasn't been this at ease with a female in his life ever, other than with Fatima. His dead wife. *Fatima, Fatima, Fatima.* Maybe repeating her name will bring him to his senses. He stands up, his back still to the sofa, pressing his hands against the wall as though warming up to run a 5K. He tries to shake the mounting tension from his body and settles into the chair opposite Sangita, feet on the floor, legs casually extended in front of him, hands to the side, as though he can't hear the blood coursing in his ears. After their little outing he has no plan. A few hours' distraction was all he wanted, but as the day wore on, and the longer they stayed, the less sure he was what to do next.

"We have a lot in common, Indians and Arabs," the girl is saying. "You know, the Mogul dynasty of Muslims ruled India for hundreds of years. Where do you think you got samosas and henna from?"

He gives her a deadpan stare.

"Do you break out in these mini-lectures often?"

"I get that from my dad," she says with a laugh.

Suddenly he is struck by an image of his own father, Mohammed, at his second *milcha*, grinning like a child with candy in the midst of Ramadan. *I should have called home the minute she told me the truth about Hind's whereabouts*, he thinks. But then what? Explain he has come to London to do what? Consummate it, as Sangita boldly pondered? His father would see right through that, knowing full well he had no desire for this marriage in the first place. No, if his family knew he had come here alone, without her family's permission, without a chaperone, they would instantly know the truth, that he had come to end it.

And whatever Hind's mistakes, nothing would be able to save him from going on the marriage market again.

"Eggs?" he says, to fill the growing silence.

So there are his choices: marry Hind, or break it off to do it all again another day. His future, the one his family always sees as so rosy, unrolls like a tableau before him. Rumors, recriminations, and whispers at the mall, at the office, at restaurants, that *he* is the guy whose fiancée ran off on him. He is the man. There will of course be other families happy enough to make an alliance with his, but the torment of another beauty parade of victims is more than he can bear to consider.

Sangita giggles.

"We're in London. Let's order something."

She points towards the kitchen where an array of take-out choices is taped to the side of the refrigerator.

"What do you fancy? Chinese?" he asks, his fingers darting over the menu collage that covers the entire left side of the fridge above where it meets the counter.

Sangita shrugs and pulls off her headband. A shiny wave of black hair spills across the sofa arm, sweeping to the floor. Abdulla can't help but notice how much she resembles an odalisque in a painting. The shape of her face, the color of her hair, even her skin could be mistaken for Moroccan. And the pose. It is the pose of the harem woman.

He clears his throat and tries to concentrate on her face, excluding the rest, but the V of her t-shirt defies him as it dips lower when she stretches. It has been a long time since he saw, much less touched, a woman's body. Not since Fatima's pregnancy, when she was too worried about the baby.

Just as he is watching Sangita's lips say "Chinese sounds good to me", the phone rings and he makes a stabbing reach for it.

"Hello?" he says, turning toward the wall, his back to Sangita. "Who is this?"

He bristles at the male voice on the other end of the line.

"I could ask you the same question," says the man. "I want to speak to Sangita."

Abdulla hands the phone over, since she is already hovering at his arm.

"Hello? Ravi!"

Abdulla eyes the menus on the fridge and flips out his phone, dialing absently. Sangita can feel his eyes trained on her face.

"Where are you? What? Slow down." She turns her head toward the receiver as though this could amplify the sound of her voice. "I tried calling you, they said you were out."

While she listens, Abdulla calls the Chinese take-out place and asks for one of everything on the menu. Whatever they don't eat they can give to Nigel or freeze for later.

Sangita closes her eyes when she hears the panic in her brother's voice. Unflappable Ravi, who was always the first to arrive at disaster scenes, who broke his leg during the state final football match and went off the field smiling, who looked in the face of poverty once a year on visits to their family's ashram. Ravi sounds like he hasn't slept in days.

"Sangita, it's been a roller coaster," he is saying, as Sangita feels her heart slightly breaking.

"I don't know how you can have lived with her for so long. She's so sheltered it's shocking."

She leans her head against the fridge slightly and rubs her throat. "I told her to go home," he says.

She feels a brief moment of elation. Maybe Hind is on her way home that very minute.

"That's what turned it all around." He laughs. She can imagine him shaking his head, as her father did when Sangita refused to go to any of the half-dozen universities in New York. "She loves a challenge."

Warmth has entered his voice, as if talking about the quirks of a friend—or a new infatuation.

Sangita closes her eyes again. Her only brother is falling in love with her friend. Who is already engaged. And whose fiancé is standing right behind her. In the apartment he has paid for.

"Ravi, I can't really talk about this now," she says for the first time in their lives, halting his rhapsody in midstream.

"Who was that earlier?" he asks.

Sangita bites her lip. Abdulla is doing the predatory walk again across the living room. She pinches the bone of her nose between her eyes.

"I need to talk to Hind," she says.

"She's not here, Sangita," he says, as though she were daft. "Do you think I'd be ranting about her in front of her face?"

"Come home," she says flatly. "You both need to be here and settle this."

"It's the guy," he says, whistling through his teeth. "He's there."

Sangita nods, even though Ravi can't see her and Abdulla hasn't asked her a question.

"We're a day's drive from the city," he says, "in slums. And I don't know if there are flights."

"We'll get you a flight," she says. Abdulla already has his phone back up to his ear. "Just get to Mumbai Airport as soon as you can."

Ravi is about to say something earth-shattering, she is sure, like "Hind is having my baby," or "we got married two days ago" when the line cuts off, as it still so often does in India. She places the receiver back in its cradle and massages the back of her neck.

The doorbell sounds. Abdulla deals with the delivery boy who has brought six bags of food that neither of them feels like eating. He drops them on the countertop.

"Heavy rains predicted for the weekend," he says, fingers drumming on the countertop.

"It's the monsoon season," Sangita says, lifting plastic containers out of the brown paper bags. "They'll get out as soon as they can."

Abdulla doesn't reply, merely punches the countertop, thumb tucked under his fingers, knuckles meeting the marble.

"Egg drop soup?" She lifts up the quart-size container, which is nearly as big as she is. He shakes his head no, but his lips manage a slight twitch at her attempt at humor.

"We have to eat," she says.

They play with their soup. Neither of them makes a move toward the solid food.

"Who knows what they'll say when they get here?" Sangita says.

"What are they going to do," Abdulla snorted. "Show up, arms intertwined, confessing their love for each other?"

"What should she do," Sangita retorts. "How is this marriage going to play out if you live in Qatar?" She tapped a finger on her lip as if playing a game of Clue. "Your mother would take to her immediately, of course, able to spot a fellow-appreciator of brands, a fellow-Gucci-lover. Your father, not really interacting with the world of women, except to see his eldest son married, would be satisfied by her mere presence."

"Things will never reach that point," Abdulla said sharply. "Disinheritance is most likely on the horizon for one if not both of us."

There, that was the anger Sangita expected. His playful tone was swallowed up in the near growl.

"And then there will be no way to fund Hind's designer addiction," she said softly. He did not reply.

Chapter 24

Satiated with a little taste of everything, Sangita takes up her customary seat in the living room. Only this time, stretching out across the coffee table opposite her are two muscular saplings in place of Hind's lean legs. Abdulla flips through channels after grumbling about the position of the TV, which is half the length of the room away, semi-obscured in a wardrobe across the room from where they sit, and nearly impossible to see from the more comfortable sofa.

"The living room is for conversation," Sangita says.

They haven't spoken about the phone call, or the flurry of follow-ups when Abdulla made a complicated series of flight arrangements and backups for Ravi and Hind in case the monsoons cause more delay. Sangita is glad of the silence. She is still trying to process the breathiness of her brother's voice and gauge the wonder she could almost see in his eyes.

They would be such an odd couple, her best friend and her brother. So different—he shunning their family wealth to make his own contribution in India; she using her wealth to establish the life she wants for herself, away from the prying eyes of her culture.

Going to see Ravi in action was one thing. Living day in, day out, amongst the poorest people in the world, as he was planning on doing full-time, would be another.

She sighs at Abdulla's channel-surfing and stretches. He doesn't seem able to stop on any one station for more than ten seconds.

She catches him glancing over his shoulder at her. He sniffs the air. "What is that?"

"Jo Malone, Lime and Basil," she says. He sniffs again.

"Like it?"

"It's fresh," he says. "Not like oud."

She leans closer to ask if he's wearing oud, the oiled perfume of the Gulf, but he turns swiftly away.

"What are we going to do tonight?" he asks. "Since there is no satellite to save us." Sangita can't help but notice it is the first mention of "we" since the truth came out.

Perhaps he doesn't think of her as the enemy after all. Though nothing shows on his face, she senses a restless energy building within him from the way his scratches the back of his neck.

His turn to stand and stretch. For a moment the breadth of his arms places the top of her head only a fingertip away.

"We're in this together," he says, "whatever they come here to say."

Sangita resists the chill that creeps up her arms with this reminder of how serious the whole situation really is, despite the bad tea, eggs or Chinese food. She is sitting next to a government employee of a state that still has beheadings on its law books. This is true, no matter how much he dismisses their existence. A quick scan on Google proves as much. Her brother is running around India with the fiancée of a cousin of a cousin of the brother of the ruler of a country that still allows beheadings. Or something like that.

But Sangita can't reconcile the misogynist tendencies of a state that would do such a thing with the living, breathing man who stands before her. He seems... reasonable. After all, has he gone screaming to the authorities or turned her in as some kind of accomplice? Maybe she's going to have to reframe her opinion of the sheikh.

Her eyes fall on the calendar that also serves as a placemat on the glass-topped coffee table.

Alice's shebang is written in black block letters.

"There's a party tonight," she says. "A silly party with people from the department. It'll be full of grad students." She doubts the appeal or wisdom of this option.

"As long as it's not Harrods or Hyde Park," he says, pulling himself up. "If there's no chance we'll run into any Qataris, we're safe."

They disappear into their respective rooms. Quickly Sangita dabs on perfume before shedding the jeans and V-neck from the Olympic event and stepping into a red linen dress, spaghetti straps hidden under a see-through white elbow-length sweater. A change of earrings and she is ready.

In the living room, Abdulla's skin and hair look vibrant against his white button-down shirt. He's wearing jeans so artfully faded she would have thought he had spent hours picking them out if she hadn't seen Nigel hand him the Thomas Pink bag herself.

He waits for her to exit the apartment then follows her down the stairs. They melt into the crush of people out on a Friday evening in the summer, most of the girls in skirts short enough to make Sangita blush.

"Walking is the only exercise we get," she says, trying to fill the silence but also relishing the fact that there is someone else to talk to. Normally she and Hind share the minutest details of their reactions to daily events. But Hind has been gone for what feels like ages.

"No one walks in Qatar," he responds. "There isn't a sidewalk in most places."

"So it's true," she says.

He shrugs as though it were obvious.

"Too hot to walk, I guess."

Abdulla considers it. A plausible theory, but doesn't go far enough.

"That's only three months of the year," he says. "The rest are actually fairly pleasant. Most families have enough money that they won't let their women walk on the street. They get driven."

"Even for exercise?"

He nods at her, rubbing his neck.

Driving, women, Qatar, talking. The act of connecting with him should be difficult; he's been taciturn in the apartment, but here, in the middle of this London street, it feels easy somehow, normal even. She looks away for an instant, trying to rid her vision of the angular profile.

"Careful!" She pushes against his chest to pull him back from the curb as a red double-decker bus roars by, filled with tourists craning their necks out of the open top. The bus driver honks once and most of the people on the sidewalk don't flinch but carry on as though nothing happened.

"I hate this about the British," Sangita says, seething. "They never involve themselves in anything."

"Yes," Abdulla says. "But you admire it, too. Don't you?" Sangita waits for her heartbeat to slow. "I suppose—"

"Stupid Paki! Look where you're going!"

Her head swivels around as she tries to figure out which direction the snarled statement came from. On her left is a blonde teenage girl chatting on her iPhone, on their right a boy in a hoodie, despite the warm weather, with the signature cord of an MP3 player trailing into his pocket. She turns around to see who is behind them, but Abdulla takes her elbow and guides her across the rumble strips. The pedestrian light is green and they are enmeshed in the swell of humanity.

"Doesn't matter," he says, as they come to the other side of the street. "I'm Arab, not Asian."

She halts in mid-stride and looks over at him to see if he is serious. Seeing her disbelief, a wolfish smile spreads across his face.

"You can't get upset about everything some ignorant bastard says."

"I know, I know."

"This is our story with the West. We know it."

Sangita rubs her hands over her face.

"They can't get away with that," she says finally. He shrugs.

"They do."

"They colonize the world and don't even bother to notice that we're different?"

He chuckles and resumes walking, which only fuels her irritation. She has to step double to catch up.

"Brown is brown. Sometimes brown is even black," he says. Words are eluding her. The lack of a rejoinder is something new for her, and only seems to happen with Abdulla, because often he is right. How many people surprised her by telling her how much they loved Indian food in the first few weeks she moved to London? None. Unlike in America, here in England people know all about India. They think of it as part of their heritage. A heritage they can pick and choose from on a whim.

She starts walking again, ahead of him, into Soho Square. He increases his stride and now they walk side by side across the green lawn of the small park, keeping to the brick path and avoiding the squatters on the bench who are settling in for the night.

"That's Paul McCartney's office," she says, by way of a distraction, pointing at the glass front of a building.

He nods noncommittally.

They amble up a side street to a tall, narrow building and she pushes the buzzer.

"Condos," she says, "converted from offices."

The only person in the department with more money than Hind is Alice, the daughter of an entrepreneurial British family, who was the first to buy in the renovated building. As they are buzzed in, Sangita has a fleeting thought that Alice will likely wonder why she has been hiding someone as good-looking as Abdulla. As they approach the open door of the apartment she realizes, too late, that they should have organized a cover story.

"We're cousins," she hisses as the door opens. "You're visiting."

He cocks the now familiar eyebrow but doesn't otherwise disagree.

They slip into a party that's shifting into high gear now, as drums beat out a rhythm for a long-haired girl and skinny boy dancing in the middle of the room. About thirty other people are hanging around, some smoking cigars, others drinking, a few men trying to negotiate both activities simultaneously.

"Sangita!" A thin blonde shrieks from across the room and runs to embrace her. "We're done. We're done."

Sangita lets herself be embraced, closing her eyes for a second. If only everything could go back to a few days ago and start over. They'd be here at Alice's party celebrating graduation and dreaming up the next step. The UN or embassy life for Alice, fieldwork in Mauritania for Sangita, starting a designer boutique for—

"Where's Hind?" Alice asks. A sheen of sweat glistens on her otherwise flawless face. Her inquisitive eyes drink in Abdulla and then swing back to Sangita.

"Not feeling so well," Sangita improvises. "We can't stay long."

Inwardly Sangita groans, realizing they haven't thought of a fake name for Abdulla. If Hind has invited them all to the wedding this is going to be hard to explain.

"Abdulla," he offers.

"My cousin. He's visiting," Sangita rushes to add. "Alice, do you have anything to drink?"

Alice leads them toward a towering cabinet on the far wall, her eyes never leaving Abdulla, taking in his smile, his broad shoulders, the tucked-in shirt and the tan canvas shoes. Across the room Jennifer, the department's longest-enrolled and most self-absorbed student, is holding forth. Catching her eye, Sangita waves her over. *Join us,* she mouths, glancing toward Abdulla. This, she knows, will bring her over, and the more Jennifer talks, the less airtime they will have to deal with Alice and the inevitable questions mounting in her eyes.

Sure enough, within a minute Jennifer materializes at their side, her bright pink lipstick at odds with the purple shirt and coordinating pants.

"Can you believe I lost my latest draft?" Danny, the department's oldest student, is saying as Sangita pours orange juice for herself and Abdulla.

"You didn't have it on a flash drive, did you?" Sangita asks, trying to stay in the conversation while she figures out how Abdulla has gotten into an intense tete-a-tete with Alice over in the corner. Irritation is rising and she busies herself by collecting discard plates around the table.

155

"How's it going?" Jennifer, another classmate strolls towards them.

"Explaining the latest in portable storage devices to Danny," Sangita mutters.

Jennifer stifles a giggle at the blank look on Danny's face. "Lost all my files," he mutters.

"Didn't even save it as an email attachment?"

Sangita swats Jennifer lightly on the arm. For once she is happy to let Danny's monologue of academic woes wash over her. More people crowd the dance floor now, students and some of the staff from the department as well. She sneaks another glance out of the corner of her eye at Abdulla, who gives her a small wave back as Alice leans up to shout something in his ear over the music.

"Doing a little bit of homework at the end of term?" She whips back around, giving Jennifer a startled look. "Oh, come on, that's not really your cousin."

Sangita chokes on her juice and Jennifer pounds her on the back.

"At least, I never looked at any of my cousins that way."

Sangita tries to deny the implicit accusation, but in the place of intelligible sentences only garbled sound comes out.

"Arab?"

Sangita sighs. There is no way to keep Jennifer in the dark except by making a speedy exit. Which Abdulla is not ready to do, judging by the way he is leaning towards Alice.

"Qatari," Sangita admits.

Jennifer whistles softly. "Great research potential. The mind of the modern Arab man."

"Yeah," Sangita admits. They drain their drinks. This has been her unspoken thought whenever she has mulled the possibility of a doctoral program in cultural studies. She hasn't told Hind, but there are so few studies published on Qatar that Sangita can't help thinking she's found the perfect place to contribute to the field.

"Go for it," Jennifer says, giving Sangita a fist bump as they stand there, the rest of the party swirling around them.

A blonde guy in the center of the dance floor does the moonwalk and then pretends to swing a robotic arm.

"The landlord's son," Jennifer shouts into Sangita's ear as the music goes up a notch. She points out a man with red hair talking to Abdulla in the corner.

Alice collects people like most people do stamps or dolls; this results in the oddest combinations at her gatherings. Sangita normally feels them to be tiresome, hating the compulsion to make repetitive insipid conversation. She misses Hind even more keenly, thinking how they would be dissecting outfits and mannerisms, determining who wanted in whose pants or who had likely already slept with whom and was now avoiding them.

"Ai! Shakira!"

Sangita tries to shake her head to say no, she'd rather not, but this is not a concept Jennifer understands. No point in resisting, she thinks, letting Jennifer drag her toward the dance floor.

"Let's do our routine from the belly dance exercise class," Alice squeals, leading them into the middle of the dance circle as the slightly whiny melody of the song takes over.

"Hips Don't Lie," she says, and smacks Sangita on her right leg as though there was a start button there. Unable to break out of the circle, Sangita surrenders to the beat of an old but familiar song.

Party yapping is one thing, but any excuse to dance is another. They rotate through the various moves of their cardio-belly dancing class, Sangita fully aware that when the time comes to shake, she will have much more to go around than Alice. Hoots from the onlookers confirm this, breaking into her dance haze. She pulls away from the circle as Wyclef wraps up the last notes of the song, to head for the bathroom.

"Better than a Bollywood movie," Abdulla says, appearing at her side, eyes no longer piercing but hooded and withdrawn. His teeth flash white in the semi-darkness.

Sweaty, Sangita flips hair out of her eyes and squints up, laughing.

Alice commandeers her and Jennifer into giving an impromptu belly dancing class for the whole party. Men and women are dissolving into giggles as the girls show them various techniques for isolating parts of their bodies: shoulders, hips and butts. Abdulla stays on the fringes, but she feels his eyes following her as she moves around the room adjusting one person's posture and another's rhythm.

"You could charge money," he says, "for your lessons. Women would die to show this off at Qatari weddings."

"I thought your weddings were segregated."

"Are you always so literal?" He flicks her on the arm. "Okay, so I don't know, but I assume from what Luluwa says."

The force of his admiring gaze is too much. Sangita holds up a finger, indicating she'll be right back, and slips into the bathroom without a word, jumping in front of Alice who is talking on her mobile. Inside the smallest room in the apartment, Sangita runs water over her hands and presses them to her flushed cheeks.

Is it her imagination, or did her heart pause then speed up at the sound of Abdulla's voice? It has been a long time since she's had a crush on someone, granted, so she searches back in her memory for the telltale signs. Another thing she wishes she could whisper to Hind if she was here right now: *Remind me again, when do you know he's interested?*

"Get a hold of yourself," she says out loud, staring her reflection down. "She wouldn't want you lusting after her fiancé."

Once the words are out, she sits down on the toilet lid. Maybe it is proximity or maybe she's been working too hard finishing her thesis. Maybe her mother is right, that several days in a row spent alone with a man can never be a good thing, but Sangita realizes she is in trouble.

When she comes out of the bathroom, however, Abdulla is nowhere in sight. She hasn't seen any cigarettes to date, but maybe he is outside for a break. The party has clearly hit that moment in the evening. The music is now even louder and nearly everyone is out on the dance floor. Even Danny is letting Jennifer move his hands to the beat of a Lady Gaga song. Sangita returns to the snack table, hoping to find some soda, settling for bottled water instead. She munches on a carrot stick, the only thing left on the platter that was earlier full of chicken wings, and watches the dancing. She nearly chokes when Alice leads Abdulla out onto the dance floor, his hands on her narrow waist, head bent to hear whatever she is prattling out of her mouth despite the volume of the music.

"Looks like your *cousin* made a friend," Jennifer says, elbowing Sangita in the ribs. "Better act fast or Alice may get the jump on you."

Sangita takes a large swallow of water and doesn't answer. "My uncles are always pushing women on me," Abdulla says in between dance numbers, coming over to where she stands frozen at the snack table. "But I think blondes may be my weakness." Before she can reply, he is gone again, back at Alice's side, in the middle of the dance floor.

Next to her, Jennifer laughs.

"Chapter one– opposites attract," she chortles into her drink. "Are you taking notes yet?"

Chapter 25

The first faint light of dawn is just beginning to pry its way through the murky gray London cloud cover as Sangita pushes open the apartment door. She zigzags her way across the living room, shedding her light sweater onto an armchair. She kicks off a shoe in either direction, teetering slightly from fatigue or anger, she can't honestly say which. Returning to the apartment alone isn't her only problem. What bothers her more is that she isn't sure if she is offended for Hind's sake or her own.

So it was okay when he was flirting with you, she tries to reason, collapsing face forward onto the sofa, *but not with someone else?*

She turns on the TV, hoping to replace the image of Alice and Abdulla on the dance floor, only to find *Dirty Dancing* on the movie channel. *Perfect,* she thinks, turning it off and throwing the remote across the room.

"Where did you go?" Abdulla's voice.

Sangita tries to sit up but only succeeds in cracking her head on the arm of the sofa. She is somewhere between retorting and crying, rubbing the back of her head, but Abdulla bats away her hands.

"Does this hurt?" he asks. His thumb and forefinger move up and down her scalp.

"No, no," she says. "I'm fine."

Sangita tries to rise up onto her elbows and off the couch. "I didn't know you'd left," he says.

"Doesn't really look like it mattered."

"Alice is an interesting person. Did you know she was born in Saudi Arabia?"

Sangita snorts, pressing her weight against him, trying to get up, but he isn't expecting it and they tumble onto the floor. He sits cross-legged on the floor as if ready for a long chat.

"You're angry with me?"

"You're not mine to be angry with," Sangita says.

The words hang between them, stretching into silence. She rubs her elbow, scooting back towards the couch.

"I'm going to bed," she says, getting up. He gets up with her.

"I'm not really good at fighting, you know. Not much practice."

She whirls around.

"You can drop the inexperienced routine," she hisses. "We know differently now." Abdulla spreads his hands out, palms up. "Hold on, what are we really discussing here?" Sangita glances up in mock disbelief.

"What you do with Alice or anyone else is your business," she says. "But I will have to tell Hind."

She continues to her room but he beats her to it, arms spread out in the doorway, chuckling.

"We were chatting and yes, I lost track of time. I thought you were dancing too somewhere."

Sangita tries to go around him but can't move his big frame. Having no choice, she listens.

"But then they told me you'd left, so as soon as I realized—" She shrugs.

"None of my business," she repeats, and tries to duck under his arms into her room. But they snake around her, halting her exit.

His red-rimmed eyes remind her that it's late, far later than good judgment warrants. *Nothing good happens after midnight.* Sangita can hear her mother's remonstration through her teenage years. For a second, everything is suspended in Abdulla's black irises. She feels his lips meet hers with force enough to clang their teeth together. Neither of them pauses. The contact is like the force of a punch in her sternum. She gulps air, only to draw him closer to her. She has never felt this electricity, this spark that has run up her arms to her head. From roving hands of teenage boyfriends to fumbling graduate students, none of them has caused the nuclear reaction going off inside her.

Sangita's heart is beating so powerfully she has to close her eyes to contain it. Seconds go by before she realizes Abdulla has moved away and is leaning against the edge of the couch.

"Did I do something wrong?" Sangita asks, running her fingers through her hair and twisting it back into a bun.

He shakes his head, resting it on his forearms, which are draped around his knees.

"Abdulla?"

There is a low, keening sound coming from him.

She hovers, not sure what the protocol is after you kiss your best friend's fiancé and he retreats into a near-fetal crouch.

Sangita lays her hand on his shoulder and feels it trembling with the force of his sobs. He raises his head, revealing a tear-stained face.

"She was pregnant," he says. "I killed them both."

Sangita sits back on her heels. Abdulla drags his fists under his eyes like a young boy. She takes a deep breath, releasing her hands from around her mouth. His breathing catches once or twice, and then slows.

She reaches out slowly and places a hand on one knee, then the other. Here on the floor they are able to see eye to eye.

"You didn't know," she says.

He bangs his head on their joined hands.

"Driving accidents are the number one cause of death in Doha," he says. "I should have picked her up myself. I should have died with them."

The floodgate is open. Sangita does the only thing she can

under the circumstances. She sinks down next to him and draws his head onto her shoulder. Shudders shake the length of his body. Trembling, she entwines one arm with his. Holding his hand, she feels a raised scar just above his watch.

After awhile, his breathing slows again, and she realizes he is asleep. She shifts her weight backward, onto the floor, so that his head and shoulders lie on her stomach. She hums a faint tune, one her mother loves to sing to the babies in the extended family. Sangita stares at the ceiling, her fingers riffling through Abdulla's hair, wondering how to chase away the sting of a lifelong regret.

Before long, she too slips into sleep, cradling Abdulla next to her heart, their breaths merging together. The circle of her arms around him relaxes. They spend the remaining hour or so of the night half on and half off each other, on the floor.

"What the hell?"

Sangita hears the familiar voice coming from somewhere, maybe the next room, maybe another time or place. But more distracting is the numbness in her legs and stiffness of her back as she jars awake.

"Sangita!"

Sangita tries to sit but bumps her head on the coffee table. Trying again, she scrambles upright before the open-mouthed stares of her brother and Hind, frozen in amazement in the open apartment door.

Abdulla recovers first, straightening his rumpled shirt and smoothing a hand over his eyes and then his mouth. "We have questions of our own," he says, standing tall in front of Sangita as she pulls her dress straps back onto her shoulders. "Where have you been?" he says, aiming a stern glance at Hind.

Sangita wrings her hands through her hair, twisting it into a knot. She keeps her eyes on Abdulla, avoiding Hind's gaze, which burns across his shoulder at her like a flamethrower. "You've been fucking each other," Hind says flatly.

With a swift stride Abdulla grasps Hind by the shoulders and shakes her once emphatically. "You have lost your mind." Even with her three-inch heels he can look her dead in the eye. "I come

163

home to find my half-naked roommate rolling around on the floor with my fiancé and I'm the one that's crazy?"

"You have a fiancé?" His face twists in mock amazement. "If anyone knew you went to India without a chaperone—" Running short of words, he shakes her again.

Hind slaps his hands, rubbing her arms as he withdraws them. "If I'd known she'd stab me in the back the moment I was out of sight, believe me," she mutters, moving away into the kitchen, "I wouldn't have gone anywhere."

"Oh? You would have remembered you're an engaged woman?" Abdulla shouts.

Looking back at him, the throbbing vein in his forehead, the clenched fists, Hind recoils, her eyes widening. Sangita lays her hand on Abdulla's elbow. At the touch he whirls away.

Ravi, who has stood silently in the doorway, clears his throat, reminding everyone there are two men present.

"But you don't even want him," Sangita whispers at Hind, coming around the island toward her.

Stillness settles over the four of them.

Sangita reaches for her friend, but Hind breaks her grasp and heads for her bedroom, past the two men, who are now eyeing each other warily.

"Hind, there was nothing. Nothing happened." she tries to follow her, but Hind turns on her with fierce eyes.

"Our definitions of nothing are very different," she snaps.

"We were talking, it was later and later. And then—"

"And then your arms found themselves around him? Your legs?" "Stop." Sangita makes a strangled sound and reaches toward her once more, but Hind sweeps into her bedroom, slamming the door so hard it shakes in the frame.

Sangita turns, appealing silently to her brother. Ravi manages a smile and hugs her briefly, planting a kiss on the top of her head, while at the same time eyeing Abdulla, who is now pacing again behind her.

"Ravi, I swear, we just…" Her voice sounds pathetic, even to herself.

What can she say? *We were bored, we went to a party, and he told me his darkest secret?* She avoids looking at Abdulla. Behind her guilt and shame is the knowledge that she has never been kissed by anyone with such ferocity. Or been so surprised by liking it.

"She was coming back," Ravi says to both of them, to the room at large. "She couldn't do a life abroad. She'd decided to live in Qatar."

Ravi squeezes her shoulder and disappears into Hind's room. Sangita sighs, running a hand over her face. She can hear Hind's angry sobs and over them her brother's warm tenor, trying to soothe her. This is a first. For once she is the cause of her friend's pain, not the solution. Sangita moves to follow Hind despite her protests, but Abdulla tugs her hand.

She turns in surprise.

"Come back with me," he says into her ear. "To Qatar."

She shakes her head as though to clear it of a stray radio frequency. "What?"

He rotates her gently so that she faces him, her chin tilted up. Already a slight bruise is forming near her collarbone from their brief encounter.

"We don't even know each other," she says.

"The love comes after," he says. "Remember?" Looking into his eyes, Sangita knows he is serious. The visceral feel of his fingers on her shoulder is its own argument.

Chapter 26

Tell them the truth, says a voice inside her head that sounds suspiciously like Sangita's. *Tell them that it's off.* Hind shakes her head and carries on applying eyeliner.

"Hanoodie, let's go."

She can just see her sister at the foot of the staircase, head thrown back, shoulders taut, raising her voice at her to hurry up. Noor will not give up, and she is letting the whole house know it. Hind momentarily considers flipping on the house intercom and whispering, "I don't like to be rushed."

The comfort she normally feels in the familiar routines of home seems distant, along with the other things she loves about living with her family. Her beloved Lisa has become irritating, for one. Lisa, her lifelong nanny (most of her cousins call theirs "maids") has taken to hovering around since her return as if worried she might disappear again. The solicitousness that Hind exploited in her childhood to sneak contraband snacks into bed is now cloying. Hind has begun to avoid Lisa and Noor, the two people who know her best and are most likely to quiz her openly about the brilliant horizons ahead in her new role as a wife.

They'll surely detect her palpable lack of enthusiasm for the wedding reception planned for this coming Saturday.

"If you don't go down there, she will leave you."

Her father's voice startles Hind out of her thoughts. He looms in the doorway, resplendent in a *thobe* with a red and white checkered *ghutra*. She rises from the stool in front of her vanity table, what he calls her "beauty arsenal," where she and Noor used to play dress-up for family engagements and wedding parties. To her surprise, he takes her by her shoulders and kisses her on top of her head, the very thing she is supposed to do to him to show respect.

"It's good to have you home, Hanoodie," Saoud says, "even if we will lose you again."

Her eyes fill with tears at the sincerity in his voice. Moments with her father are rare. They all fight for them like little kids vying for nuts and candy at *Garinga'o*, the traditional children's night celebrated in the middle of Ramadan.

"I'll be nearby," she says as they walk down the hallway towards the top of the staircase.

She focuses on his presence, not wanting to think about how she is likely to be living in her room for the rest of her life. Will her father support her as a divorced woman, or will she have to go through the same debacle again with another suitor after a few years? And when the wedding is called off, will he blame her for ruining Noor's chances, not to mention the family name?

"Hind!"

"Coming," she calls out with more force than she intended. Her father chuckles and squeezes her hand.

"Noor is upset too," he says. "The house will miss you. You just got back."

She holds on to those blunt fingers, feeling the rough skin that betrays his elegant appearance, the calluses revealing his upbringing as the son of a spice and pearl merchant. Now, only a generation later, he is a modern businessman, a civil servant.

Tell him the truth, the voice says again, and this time Hind doesn't override it. "Baba—"

"There you are."

Noor rushes up the steps of the curved marble staircase. On the landing she pauses to catch her breath and adjust her metallic-tipped heels, nearly hopping with excitement at the sight of Hind in her room.

"Mama needs Ramzan, so we have to go *now*," she says. The bell-shaped sleeve of her *abaya* is a black shadow against the white marble foyer as she points to the back door.

Saoud flicks Noor gently on the arm as he passes. "She's nervous," he says. "Go easy on the bride."

Hind lets out the sigh that has been building up all morning. If only her life were as simple as they imagine it for her. She will truss herself up like some ancient trophy and on Saturday be delivered to her husband, push out a few babies, hopefully boys, and then for the rest of her years meet her sisters and friends for elaborate meals at five-star restaurants, reliving the glory days of graduate school while on family holidays to London over Eid or during the summer. Racing from one sale to another, getting ready for one party or the next, her life will pass in a delightful succession of events marred only by an increasing number of wrinkles and growing children.

"You girls go," her father is saying, "or your mother will take the car for sure."

Hind descends the stairs to a small antechamber outside the garage where the shoes of various household members are strewn in the doorway. On a clothing rack hang several abayas on padded hangers. She fingers a plain black one, her mother's, devoid of any embroidery and long enough to cover her feet in the style of women thirty years ago. It is a stark contrast to the brilliant blue embroidery snaking up and down Noor's arms and the metallic blue stilettos peeking through the folds at every step.

Hind draws the cloak of black around her shoulders, smelling her mother's rose perfume. She has missed having oud rubbed into her temples if she feels a headache coming on. The light weight of the fabric on top of her clothes is familiar, yet so different from her carefree student days abroad. Noor makes a face without commenting. Normally the choice of such a drab *abaya* would be the cause of a mini-makeover, with Noor as stylist. But today getting out the door takes priority over fashion.

Her mother's *abaya* swirls over Hind's shoes, making her seem to glide over the marble floor as she follows Noor, who is somehow sprinting to the door even in her near-stilts. Hind trails behind, out to the car waiting in the circular drive. She stops for a minute to catch a glimpse of her father, at the side of the house near the separate entrance to the men's majlis, but his back is turned to her as he chats on his phone.

She pulls her *shayla* closer to her neck, gathers her abaya in the other hand, and steps into the black Cadillac Escalade reserved for the older women of the family. She glances out the window and doesn't see the Land Cruiser in the carport; the kids, Khalid and the cousins from Uncle Mohammed's house, must be out with their nanny.

"Your nails are awful," Noor says. "And you could do with a trim. Let's go to the salon after this?"

Hind makes a noise of despair at the tide of pettiness she has re-entered, which her sister takes as assent.

Noor starts making calls. She then gives Ramzan, the Indian driver, instructions on the upcoming shopping expedition, all the while continuing her beauty routine. He is wearing his trademark khaki baseball cap and bobs his head at each of her instructions, his eyes barely visible below the cap's rim.

Noor pulls a perfume bottle out of her purse and douses her arms, then the front of her *abaya*, before offering it to Hind. Hind takes the bottle and gives herself an obligatory squirt before passing it back.

"First take us to Landmark, and then Mama from Al Dana Club," Noor says as she checks her makeup in a tiny crystal-rimmed compact.

They wind out of the back gate and speed down the street. Ramzan deftly weaves through the roundabout and onto the North Road, taking them away from the West Bay area and towards the suburbs of the city. Sand whips across the windshield as the car picks up speed to keep pace with the increasing Thursday afternoon traffic. Behind the dark tinted windows, air-conditioner blasting, even in their *abayas* they are cool, defying the scorching temperatures outside.

"If only Villaggio was open," Noor sighs. "All the brands were there."

"I wouldn't go there even if it was," Hind says. "Who wants to shop with the ghosts of dead children?"

The news of the tragedy still stings Hind, even though she was away when it happened. People who could shop there unfazed are a mystery to her. Her sister is a mystery, like the rest of this once-familiar life she has left behind.

"It was terrible," Noor agrees. "But life goes on."

"Not for the dead," Hind says pointedly.

Thursday afternoon, and headed to the mall with her sister. By closing her eyes to the construction cranes on the latest real estate projects dotting both sides of the road, Hind can imagine it is almost any week in the years before her engagement. This same trip to the mall. Since the weekends are the best days to see and be seen at the mall by everyone, male and female, they would take turns doing hair, bunching up their buns for more volume under their *shaylas*. But those days seem like a dream now.

"Mama home, then back to pick us up," Noor continues.

At Ramzan's nod that he understands, Noor settles herself against the car's butter leather interior.

"One of us," she says, unwinding ear buds for her iPhone, "has to make sure you don't embarrass yourself during your henna night or your honeymoon. Since you didn't bother shopping in London where all the latest stuff is."

Hind bites her lip rather than tell her sister not to bother. There isn't going to be a wedding or a honeymoon or babies.

Instead she turns her head and watches the neighborhood she grew up in go by. What she sees now is mostly ripped-up roads and construction cones. That the plans for major overpasses and flyovers have made their way out to this part of the city, far from the center and heading towards the North Road and the oil fields, is an indication of the scale of Doha's expansion. She has seen the ads on Sky TV and in *The Guardian* about Qatar Airways and Chelsea Barracks and the hundreds of other Qatari projects abroad. But coming home, she barely recognizes her country.

"Hasna says not to bother with Nayomi or Jennyfer, all cheaply made," Noor says. "So I thought we'd start with the new Victoria's

Secret. The stuff may be cheap but it'll give you a big bang. You know, for effect." Another fit of giggles.

"They only sell perfume here," Hind replies. "Even I know that."

"There's dozens of other places," Noor says, waving a hand. "We've got the rest of the day to walk around."

Hind wishes she had an iPod to drown out her sister. Maybe she can get one today. The gap generation, that's how Sangita always described them. Hind and Sangita, the odd couple with their preference for reading books on the Tube rather than listening to music. She feels a hollow where she wishes she could summon sympathy for her guilt-stricken friend. The rational part of Hind knows she can't fault Sangita when she herself was in the middle of nowhere with Ravi; but the side who has been dragged back home to become a domesticated creature, a part of the household furnishings, is livid.

"If you still need stuff we can go on the Agent Provocateur website. I can't believe you didn't go before leaving London!" Noor hits her sister playfully on the exposed leg of her jeans, showing through part of her *abaya*. "Where were you the day I came to go shopping?"

"There's no need for all this foolishness!" Hind explodes and punches Noor back in the arm to avoid answering the question.

"Ow!" Noor rubs her arm and eyes her sister reproachfully. Ramzan and Lisa's eyes flick to the rearview mirror. Fights between the girls are legendary, but now they are too old to be admonished by anyone but their father.

"Chill out," Noor says. "Everyone says it's normal to be nervous."

Hind scoots closer to the window so she can press her forehead against it like she did as a child, when she would fall asleep looking at the sands on the edge of the city. Speaking the truth has drained all the energy from her.

"It's not nerves," she whispers to the window as much as to Noor. "We aren't doing it. I'm going to be divorced."

Noor's tinkling laugh causes Hind to turn to her sister again, just as the SUV pulls up in front of the mall's newly-opened designer section. Noor lays a hand on her sister's leg where only a moment before she delivered the offending swat.

"Abdulla is coming to see you," Noor says. "It's all been arranged with Luluwa so you can have some privacy. Away from the house. That's why we're really here. Maybe he can do a better job of calming you than I can. Now that you two are so close and all."

"What?" Hind asks, stunned.

A hint of pouty lips as Noor slides off the seat and out the door, adjusting her *shayla* and bag in the reflection of the car window. Hind snatches up her own bag and crawls across the back seat after her sister.

"What did you say?" she shouts at her, hanging from the car door.

But Noor is already striding toward the sliding glass doors. Cars behind Ramzan are starting to honk, waiting to unload their own female cargoes. Hind has no choice but to grip her *shayla* with one hand and her bag with the other and dismount.

"I go to parking," Ramzan says.

Hind nods absentmindedly and shuts the door. Lisa's flat Asian face is devoid of emotion as she climbs down out of the front seat and stands waiting to follow Hind into the entrance. For a desperate moment Hind wishes she were younger and able to grasp her nanny's hand and hold onto it as they toddle into the mall with all its wonders. Instead, Hind puts one foot in front of the other, sucking air through her nose as Sangita taught her during their home yoga sessions. She has to fight the urge to run as fast as she can in the opposite direction, in her three-inch brass-studded Gucci pumps.

Chapter 27

Luluwa enters the bedroom on tiptoe so as not to wake her grandfather, at the same time hoping he will already be awake to finish telling her about his mystery woman.

She slides into the armchair, the worn bamboo antique having been replaced by a sturdy new piece of furniture that her more sizable uncles have been taking turns in as her grandfather grows weaker. Now that Jassim is failing she knows she must compete with her uncles for his waking hours, so every moment is special.

Just as she feared, he isn't awake. His papery cheek is slack on the pillow as the sunlight fades from the room. She slides her iPhone from her pocket and takes a photo in the growing semi-dark: her grandfather. The flash causes his eyelashes to flutter. She holds her breath.

"Lulu?"

"Na'am, Yaddi," she says.

Jassim opens watery brown eyes and smiles at his youngest granddaughter.

"You came back to hear the end of the story," he says.

She smiles, though his voice is so thin she must strain forward to catch his words.

"The moral," he says, coughing, "is never part in anger."

"Is that what you did, *Yaddi*?"

"And it wasn't even her I was mad at," he says, inching his torso up onto the pillows, waving away her help. "It was the family."

Luluwa listens as her grandfather closes his eyes, telling her the story of his lost love Aziza, the name meaning "dear one," who was in fact his dearest, the daughter of his business partner, a wealthy businessman in Mumbai. A Muslim, yet somehow still not deemed good enough for Jassim.

"She wanted to stay at home to have the baby. I wanted them here, but I was living with your great-grandfather and there was nowhere for her to stay. I had no money; her father knew that, and he wouldn't allow her to leave."

His breath is growing ragged. Luluwa squeezes his hand where it lies on the duvet. She feels guilty that she doesn't stop him, but she wants him to continue.

"I thought I could come home, convince everyone to accept her, then go back, and..." His voice trails off into a whisper.

"Live happily ever after," Luluwa finishes for him, into the growing stillness.

Jassim tosses his head on the pillow as if the memories are too much.

"There were many storms that season, so many storms. By the time I went back she was already buried. Childbirth had not been kind."

Luluwa wipes a tear from her cheek, not bothering to check the others as they come quickly.

Her grandfather squeezes her hand and she runs her fingers across his knuckles.

"Lulu, *ta'alee*." Uncle Mohammed calls her gently from the doorway. Luluwa gives the weathered fingers one more squeeze and goes to stand by her uncle. He wraps an arm around her, as Anita goes in to check on the old man and the various machines in his room.

"Uncle, when did *Yadd* Jassim get married?" Luluwa asks. Mohammed squeezes her shoulder as they walk towards the top of the staircase. "You're too young to be thinking of these things," he says.

Luluwa lifts her tear-stained face. "Someone has to know all of this before he passes away," she sniffs. "All of his secrets."

Mohammed chucks her under the chin.

"His marriage to your grandmother is hardly a secret," he says. "Go down and eat with your brothers."

Treasuring the true secret Jassim has given her, for once Luluwa does as she is told.

Chapter 28

"You sure it's okay if I stay in your apartment?" Sangita asks. Sand-colored buildings whizz past as the taxi driver weaves through the traffic. They are on a long tree-lined avenue, the water to the left shimmering in the dusk. She can almost see sand roll across the street in the steady breeze. A dust storm, if she remembers Hind's stories correctly. At the thought of her friend, Sangita feels another sting of guilt. It feels so strange finally to be in her friend's country without her knowledge.

"No one comes here," Abdulla says, as the taxi crosses over a bridge onto an island shaped like the outer ring of an oyster shell. "No one has been here since…"

Since Fatima died.

She stretches, the effect of six hours of travel catching up with her in stiff joints, tangled hair and fuzzy teeth.

She knows they are coming to The Pearl, an offshore island built on reclaimed land, to Tower One and the apartment he shared with his wife. But once inside, rather than feeling suffocated by Fatima's presence, Sangita senses only the sadness of an unlived-in apartment sitting empty for nearly three years. She watches Abdulla walk around the suite with his familiar prowl. She watches him peer down at the street seventeen floors below. He shared this view with Fatima, the wife Sangita will never know and Hind can't help but resent.

Sangita rubs her arms. The apartment has the latest in finishes, from the crown molding to the floor-to-ceiling windows. The overall effect is not unpleasant, and she is glad of neutral ground away from the prying eyes of his family, including those of her former friend.

He stops in front of her and turns, standing so close she can feel the heat of his body. Unbidden, she thinks of Hind. What part of the city is she living in? What is she doing right now? Has she felt this kind of desire, and did the same temporary restraint keep her apart from him too?

But clearly Abdulla doesn't want to talk about Hind; it is as if he has never known her, as if she has died. Sangita turns away from his gaze, wondering if she has done the right thing in following Abdulla home. Perhaps it is a mistake, but how else will she know if she can live here, a stranger in this strange land, for love of a man she barely knows?

Even though she has disciplined her face not to betray any emotion, Abdulla seems to know she is unsettled. He comes to her, placing his hands on her shoulders.

"I'm going to take a shower," Sangita says, noticing a gleam in his eye. "You could probably use one too."

"I'll call you in a few hours," he says, backing away as though she were on fire.

They exchange tentative smiles.

Has she revealed her doubts? She hopes not. In Abdulla's eyes she sees only steely determination. *But that is a man's privilege*, she thinks as the door closes behind him. Men can always do whatever they want, and damn the consequences. Case in point: her presence in Qatar at this very moment.

The one thought she can hardly bear is that her friend Hind would be the ideal person to get her through all this. But Hind is lost to her forever.

After Abdulla leaves, she washes away the grime of the plane and falls into a light sleep, buoyed by the jet lag of her first few hours in Doha.

She awakes near dawn to a Skype call ringing on her computer. "Ravi," she says, pulling the computer off the end table towards her, flipping hair out of her face.

"How's it going?" Her brother's familiar face and voice make the plush Arabian surroundings even stranger.

"Fine," she says. "It's almost seven in the morning. The sun's been up since about five-thirty. Isn't that wild?"

There is silence from the other end as she pans the computer camera around the room. Daylight streams in from a bank of twelve-foot windows that she has intentionally left unshaded.

"Can you believe this?" she says. "This building wasn't even here six years ago. I'm on the seventeenth floor." The remnants of sleep fall away and she grows more animated in her tour. Back in the bedroom her eyes fall on the black robe draped on the armchair.

"And look, this is the *abaya* they wear. See how this one has gold threading up the sleeves? The women design their own. Their grandmothers were only allowed to wear black."

"What are you doing, Gita? Why would you start wearing that?"

Sangita pauses, since Ravi is looking at her, not the bell- shaped sleeve she has spread on the bed for him to view. His image breaks up for a moment over a bump in the connection, but she hears the sternness in his voice. She shrugs, even though she knows what her brother is hinting at. Her parents' questions ventured into a similar vein yesterday during her session with them.

"I think they're beautiful," she says. "Instead of hindering women they let them move freely. With their faces covered no one can even see where they are looking." She senses he isn't interested, but drapes a matching *shayla* over her face.

"This isn't some anthropological project," he is saying, hands clasped between legs where he sits on the denim-covered sofa in the den in their parents' apartment in New York. "Gender, Islam, first-hand and whatever." He waves a hand around his head as though indicating her thought cloud. "This is the rest of your life."

She blinks at him through the gauzy fabric. "Take that thing off your face!"

She pulls it down. Sangita knows he can't understand what she's doing, because if she is honest, even she can't really formulate how she has come to be in this apartment in Doha.

"What's that?" Ravi is pointing to a stack of legal pads on the end table behind her head.

She sits up, wishing she had put them in the closet before falling asleep last night.

"Oh, I'm just doing a little work," she says, putting them on the floor out of his line of sight.

"Work?"

"You know, taking notes." She flops back onto her stomach in feigned relaxation. "I want to remember every moment of this."

She doesn't mention that the notes contain a rough outline of what she hopes will be the first of many articles, maybe enough for a book even, on her experiences in Qatar.

"Have they made you convert yet?" Sangita fixes him with a stare.

"You know as well as I do, I don't have to. A Muslim man can marry a non-believer. A Muslim woman cannot. Sexism the world over."

Her brother laughs, but it is a harsh and broken sound. "No," he says.

"No?"

"They can marry Jews or Christians without any problem." Sangita clamps her hand over her mouth in regret for being so insensitive. He won't talk to her about what happened— or didn't happen— on his trip with Hind to India, or about Hind's decision to come home. A taboo subject is a first for them, and neither is handling it well.

"Seriously, it's not like that, Ravi," she says, "I'm just here to check it out. But did you know citizenship only passes through the father here? What a way to make sure the women behave."

"People of the book are believers," he says, enunciating as if to a child. "You're a Hindu. You're a non-believer. And you have to convert."

She chews her lip uncertainly. "Would that be so bad?"

"You're supposed to be the rational one," he says.

Now would be the time for a dropped call, she thinks, but of course the technology is fine just when you hope it won't be. He is right. In the escapade that was Ravi And Hind Go To India, Sangita had kept her head.

"Hind had her adventure," she says, hating the whine that has entered her voice. "This is mine."

Ravi sighs loudly and comes closer to the camera on his end."The kinds of notes you're taking," he says, trying not to skirt around the question. "Could you go to jail for what you're doing?"

"Jail? I'm here legally," she huffs. "Do you want to talk or just lecture me?"

He puts his hands up in surrender and agrees to back off. They talk for a few more minutes about the possibility of him coming to Qatar if things do go further.

"Can you honestly see yourself living there?"

Instead of answering she leans against the headboard and smiles at her brother, whose creased forehead belies how much he loves her.

"If not, I'll just come home," she says, blowing him a kiss, wishing she didn't have to involve him in this. But since he has taken a shine to Hind, he is the second-best thing to a gal pal for her, since he knows something of Qatari society.

"There's no future for you there if you don't marry him," he is saying as she signs off. "And technically, if you sign that contract and you break it off you'll be a divorced woman. At twenty-four."

His words echo in her head as she goes back to sleep. He isn't in favor of the marriage. She can't necessarily count on parental approval, and she isn't sure she can go through it with it alone, even if the American embassy does give consent for her to marry a Muslim man and make her marriage to a Qatari legally binding in the U.S.

Chapter 29

A blast of air-conditioning envelops Hind as the glass doors hiss shut behind her. After a moment's blindness her eyes adjust to the fluorescent mall lighting, in such stark contrast to the darkness of the tinted SUV windows. She wishes she had big-frame sunglasses like the two women who slide by wearing flame-red lipstick, the metal tips of their heels winking out with each strutting step of their *abayas*. A pimply-faced teenager is walking behind them, so intent on his mission he crosses Hind's path without noticing, his jade prayer beads dangling from one pocket, an iPhone in one hand.

"*Khamsa khamsa khamsa,*" he mutters, causing the girls to pick up their glacial pace. He keeps a few steps behind them, rattling off the digits of his phone number.

"He's so bold," Hind says. Having finished reciting his phone number, the boy's lips are still moving. He has begun again.

"Why don't they say something?" Hind asks, stopping in her tracks. "That's harassment."

Noor grabs her elbow and pulls her along.

"If you talk, they think you're encouraging them," she whispers. "He'll get tired eventually and find someone else to bother."

Despite herself, Hind swivels around. The teenager is still following the women, who are probably twice his age.

"He could be after them for hours," she says, but Noor's shrug indicates this is just normal practice.

"You know this is how it is," she says. "What's gotten into you? It's as if you've returned from Antarctica instead of England."

Hind feels sick to her stomach. This is home, and yet increasingly it seems a place she no longer knows. The churning in her stomach intensifies at the thought of seeing Abdulla again. This man, her cousin, her friend, and the person she is supposed to marry, has betrayed her with another woman; though if anyone knew where she herself had gone while Abdulla was cozying up to Sangita, they'd likely say the same thing about her.

"You guys didn't arrange to meet somewhere at home, while everyone is busy?"

"Like that ever happens," Hind murmurs back. She has avoided Abdulla's calls under the pretense of jet lag, but doesn't know how much longer she can keep this up.

They pass in front of a coffee shop. The white leather seats facing the mall arcade are already taken by groups of men, ostensibly there to chat, surreptitiously eyeing all the women that pass by, regardless of race. Hind, Noor and Lisa continue walking, caught in the game of pretending they don't know they are being watched. Hind longs for the streets of London, where anyone can watch just as casually as they might glance at their cell phone, and no one gives it a thought.

A man who doesn't ogle. She knows one, but he isn't Qatari. Hind tries to put Ravi's face out of her mind, realizing that what she feels isn't longing but guilt. The bald truth is that none of this has anything to do with Ravi. Or with Abdulla, for that matter. Ravi has become another person on her growing list of people she is avoiding.

No, in some way she hasn't fully grasped yet, it's about her. Marrying Abdulla is simply the easier thing to do. She turned off her UK mobile the minute she got on the Qatar-bound plane at Heathrow, and she hasn't turned it on since. All the emails,

Facebook messages and IMs Ravi and Sangita have been sending her have gone unanswered.

The pull of her life here, the rules, the order, seep back into her mind as easily as the fine grains of sand settle on her abaya. This is her place. This is the role they have set out for her. She walks after Noor, passing two women who glide by, their feet hidden by the hems of their *abayas*. Hind straightens. She has forgotten that posture, the tilt of the head that keeps you from making eye contact with anyone.

"*Yalla*, Hind."

Noor is at her side again, Lisa on the other arm, as they shepherd her towards the main avenue.

"He says to meet him near Carrefour. We'll come back here," Noor says.

How have they communicated? How does Abdulla even know she is back? When did he get back? The questions swirl in her throat as she and Lisa follow her sister's bobbing head. It wouldn't make sense to meet in a restaurant, where they'd be more likely to run into someone who knew them. Though it is perfectly proper for them to be speaking. They are legally married, after all.

"You spoke to him?" Hind asks.

This engagement is different from what she thought being an engaged woman might mean.

Hind shies away from thinking about the night she caught Fatima sneaking down the driveway, her shoes in her hand, and the sight of Abdulla's car outside the gate. Her cousin is dead and her transgressions with her.

Noor varies her gait, first walking briskly and then, realizing she has gotten ahead of Hind, slowing to let her catch up. As they pass the shiny black mannequins dressed in the latest fashions, Hind longs to duck into H&M with the other girls, out with their sisters and cousins. Instead, they keep marching, Noor so eager that Hind wishes it were her sister getting married, really getting married, and not this farce that her life has turned into. She is certain this is the fastest either of them has ever walked through a mall, past expat mothers pushing strollers, past the store guards who stare at passers-by, averting their eyes as this small juggernaut of women troops by.

They pool in the electronics section just inside the Carrefour entrance. Noor looks around, erect as a meerkat, her eyes scanning the arcade.

How have they set this up? Noor and Luluwa? Luluwa is as close to Abdulla as any of his brothers, some say closer. He probably used her to set the whole thing up. Hind tries to remember seeing the two girls together in the past few days. She racks her brain too for any sign that her parents know about her escapade, but they are blissfully ignorant, she is convinced. Her father hasn't asked to see her passport; her mother hasn't bothered with the official Supreme Education Council notice that she has completed her degree. After a few months, Hind can just pretend her passport is lost, destroy it with matches from the *bukhoor* burner and apply for a new one.

But now the one person in Qatar who knows exactly why she left England, and where else she went, is somewhere nearby. The real question is why? Most lovers do this because they are heartsick for each other. For Abdulla, she knows this to be anything but the case. She takes a deep breath. Maybe he hopes she won't show, just as she hasn't returned his texts.

"There he is!" Noor whispers.

Hind feels her pulse beat even faster, and this time not just from nervousness. He strides past, seemingly not even noticing them, heading towards the back of the store. He is with a woman, her face completely covered by the gauzy fabric of her *shayla,* which trails in clouds alongside him.

Noor, Hind and Lisa follow at a distance of thirty paces, all three pausing to feign interest in a blender as Abdulla greets another shopper, a sleek, official-looking Qatari in traditional dress. They pause for the nose-touching of close male relatives. A cousin? They exchange overlapping greetings as Noor stares unabashedly.

Hind pulls her *shayla* completely over her face, encasing herself in black the way conservative women do, which she normally hates, knowing that it confers the cheap privilege of seeing without being seen. But this is one time, one place, she doesn't want to be recognized. She gives Noor a sharp elbow to ensure she'll cover up too.

As the other man moves on, Abdulla resumes a measured pace. The group find themselves in the garden section of the French superstore. Abdulla wanders over to inspect the garden hoses. The entire aisle is empty except for a few Indian men who look like they could be related to Ramzan.

For the first time all day Noor hangs back, suddenly engrossed in hand-held shovels and pots of various sizes. Hind has come to a full stop. Lisa seems unable to make up her mind which girl to protect, looking back and forth between them. Hind wants to reach out and touch her hand, reassure her. But she can't reassure anyone, not even herself, about what is going to happen next.

Abdulla veers suddenly toward her. "Why haven't you told anyone it's off?" he growls in Arabic.

There it is, without the slightest preamble. Is this the economist-turned-diplomat they are writing about in the paper, sure to be minister one day?

Hind doesn't answer. She knows now why women love to cover their faces. All this time she thought they were oppressed, these poor walking versions of Islam, huddled against the world. But instead, inside the gauze she feels insulated and protected, and no matter how hard he tries he will never see more than the shadow of her face, will always have to guess where her eyes are.

His right eyebrow rises at her silence and the facial tic, the one that shows up whenever they tease him on Fridays, is starting.

"Tell people whatever you want. But tell them we aren't going through with it."

She is glad he is speaking in dialect because Lisa's Arabic is not good enough to keep up with the Gulf slang.

"Or else what?" Hind hears herself croak, watching the scene as though she were hovering on the ceiling of the store.

It's hard to grasp. In front of her is a person she didn't realize she wanted until she heard he loved someone else. Does she want him? Did she ever? Whatever the case, he is now a stranger, reduced to snapping at her in the aisle of a grocery store.

"Excuse me?" he asks, slipping into English.

"Or else you'll do what?" she says again.

The worst has already happened. She has ruined their chance for happiness. Emboldened by the thin layer of fabric separating them, and because no one can see the direction of her gaze, she stares back at him. Her eyes take in the line of his jaw and the stubble that says he is growing a beard.

"Listen to me," he says, as if to a stranger, drawing as close to her as he dares without touching her, years of training restraining him from shaking her as his voice says he wants to. "You are in the wrong here. I can do whatever I want. So I'm giving you one day to tell your version, whatever that is." He breaks off in a laugh so horrible Hind knows she never wants to hear it ever again "Or I will."

She recoils as if he has struck her.

"We both know this is your fault," he adds.

The tears start. Abdulla, the one her father chose for her. The hours of wrangling for her *mahar* as she and Noor lurked outside the *majlis*, listening in. Her mother's glistening tears as she kissed her before the *khutouba,* and the men signing. All for nothing.

"A woman's life is as hard as her husband's," her mother said. *"Insha'Allah,* yours will be easy."

Abdulla, her fiancé, once her playmate, now her enemy. Thankful for the hundredth time for her *shayla,* she doesn't bother to blink as tears course down her face. Many more years of this invisible public life await her. She can't help the sob that escapes her.

"It's not just my fault," she manages on a hiccup when she catches her breath. Unlike Abdulla, she makes no attempt to keep it quiet.

The aisle goes very still as both Lisa and Noor look up from their giggling and whispering. Noor throws her shayla back over the top of her head and her green-lined eyes flicker from Abdulla's stony face to that of her sister, who is uncharacteristically still.

Hind hiccups again, trying to get a hold of herself to retort something else equally heart wrenching, but her mind is blank. Lisa is coming to her, her tiny frame moving with surprising speed, given her plump hips.

Then a dark shadow, a mirror image of Hind, comes floating towards them, slowly, as though the woman is unused to wearing an *abaya*. She has a simple rhinestone cuff on each wrist and a *shayla* pulled over her face with the same edging, hanging just above where her collarbone would be if you could see it.

Hind feels the edges of her vision slipping away as she realizes Abdulla is already over her and out with another woman. Suddenly she feels wobbly, light-headed; she hasn't eaten anything since lunch, and then barely a scrap, since everyone has been about their business and not really paying attention to family meals during the week. She sways, and then steadies herself on Lisa's arm as her faithful friend stares daggers into the boy she once partly raised, at least on his visits to their house. Now he is a man hurting her favorite child.

"Abdulla, *khalas*. Really."

A woman's voice. Something in it Hind thinks she recognizes.

A cousin? Would he dare betray her with yet another cousin? Hind knows this happens all the time, but the thought that he could be so unfeeling is one more pinprick in her heart. Even sharing him with Fatima's memory is something she was never keen on, may her cousin's soul rest in peace.

Sangita warned her that the loss of face, should Abdulla discover her whimsical journey, would far exceed any fleeting pleasure she might gain from it.

The Indian girl lecturing the Qatari girl about Gulf culture. And she didn't listen.

The woman reaches for Abdulla with a slim, tan hand and grips his elbow. The simple gesture is enough to spring Noor into action. Stomping up the aisle, she takes up a position at Hind's flank. "Who the hell is that?" Noor hisses, watching Abdulla wrap his own fingers around those on the sleeve of his *thobe.*

"This isn't you," the voice says again, and everyone realizes she is talking to him, and getting through. His shoulders relax somewhat; his fingers leave hers for a moment to readjust his *ghutra*, pulling the front further down on this forehead.

"You heard me," he says to Hind, but this time in a normal speaking voice. "Take care of this soon or I will."

His gaze sweeps over all of them, Hind, Lisa, Noor, and then he turns away, intending to take his companion with him. But she shakes her head slightly and they murmur together.

Hind's tears, slowed in shock, now begin afresh and she feels them drip off her chin. "I'm staying for a moment," Hind overhears.

The words freeze her. The woman is speaking classical Arabic. There is only one person Hind knows who pronounces all the vowels so clearly, as if she were reading the news on the radio.

Abdulla seems suddenly uncomfortable, glancing several times back at their group. But he squeezes the woman's hand once and indicates with his chin he will wait at the end of the aisle. At the sight of the delicate wrist, even before she pulls back her *shayla*, Hind knows who this is. That she has to share him with the dead Fatima isn't enough. Now, alive and well, it's her best friend too.

"You! You bitch!" Noor shouts at the top of her lungs, so that the workers in yellow Carrefour overalls stop wheeling in stacks of watering cans to gape at these crazy women in abayas squaring off like Mexican bandits.

"Listen, I want to make this right," Sangita says.

Noor steps up, Hind realizes, part in horror and part glee, to slap Sangita in the face. But Lisa steps between them.

"You go now," Lisa says in her simple English, shooing Sangita as if she were one of the many stray cats that hang around their kitchen door.

"No. This is our chance for happiness," Sangita pleads, her eyes not leaving Hind's. "Please, Hanoodie—"

"Don't you dare call her that, you slut."

Breathing like a racehorse, Noor towers behind Lisa, hands fisted at her sides. Hind feels a moment's surge of love and pride, watching her sister, the young lioness, until it occurs to her that it is she, the older sis, who should be protecting Noor.

"Tell them soon, for your sake," Sangita is saying, "like he said. We're going to have news of our own soon."

"Whore," Hind manages, her voice gaining strength and sharpness. "I'm supposed to make it easier for you?"

Abdulla circles back and settles his hand on Sangita's shoulder, turning her away and bending down to whisper in her ear. "Tell them anything. Say he would have beaten you," Sangita calls back, her voice breaking, "but just tell them."

Hind starts shaking uncontrollably. Held steady by Lisa and Noor, she lets herself be led away.

Tell them anything? The phrase, the thought, keeps time with her stomach and heart, repeating, churning. Her mind starts turning over ideas.

"Call Ramzan," Noor tells Lisa. "Tell him to come to Gate 1."

Chapter 30

"The bastard!" Noor is still seething as the mall recedes behind them. "I knew something was weird that day I went to see you. He was there. I know it. He was there and they were—"

Drained of all feeling, Hind is still grateful for her sister's passion. Usually, the full force of her personality is focused on Beyoncé's latest fashions or the new Amr Diab single. Now it is a thunderstorm of pure rage raining down on Abdulla, her former favorite cousin, who might as well be dead to her now.

"Get Baba! Call Khalid," she spits into her phone as their SUV speeds out of Landmark's parking lot.

Sensing urgency, Ramzan drives even more manically than the rest of the Qatar traffic, even hopping a curb when the right lane is blocked. The Escalade bumps across the median in front of their house, veers through the iron gate, and zooms past the towering compound wall that protects the women of the family from the prying eyes of the street. Noor flings herself out of the vehicle before it has even come to a full stop and sprints into the house, pulling her *shayla* from her head and throwing it onto the rack of *abayas*.

Hind, following along behind, notices the rack is full. Someone, or many someones, is visiting.

"Noor, what in God's name..." Their brother Khalid emerges from the side of the living room, where a temporary internet area has been created for his electronic fixations.

"It's off," Noor says, panting.

"What?"

Hind enters the foyer slowly and, without meeting anyone's gaze, unwinds her *shayla* with precise movements.

"*Shinoo?*" Khalid repeats in dialect, when no one answers him. There is a smear of chocolate across his face.

Hind eyes him, her gaze lingering on his chocolate lips. Someone has come quietly into the room. It's their father, barefoot, the snap buttons of his starched collar undone. He looks on in mute shock.

"The wedding is off," Hind says, shrugging out of her mother's *abaya*. Lisa is there to take it from her and hang it on its white pearl-studded hanger. Hind rips her hair out of the bun she has worn it in to fit under her *shayla* and begins climbing the stairs to her room.

Her mother's voice rings out. "What is going on here?"

The kids freeze. Hind with her hand on the straight back of the banister, Khalid in his ascent after her, Noor collapsed at the foot of the stairs. Their mother whisks into the room in a burgundy floor-length skirt, a white blouse with lace cuffs setting off her fair skin. Her waist-length hair is braided down her back and swings with her movements. She peers fiercely at them all. Lisa gives her the same headshake Khalid received only a few seconds ago.

"The wedding is off, *Yuma*," Khalid says in a small voice. The youngest, he is always the breaker of bad news since, with his curls and dimples, no one can hold him responsible for long.

"Hind?"

Hind turns around and gazes at the sight of her mother, who wears diamonds at her ears, the thick rope bracelet, and the necklace with Allah's name just visible at the hollow of her neck. They are the most modest of her mother's jewels, given to her when her father was only a middle-class merchant.

"It's true, *Yuma*," she says in a steady voice.

Her siblings melt away as Hind descends the stairs, coming up to her mother, towering over her.

"How did this happen?"

"The bastard!" Noor bursts out, coming to stand at her sister's side. "He, he—"

Hind reaches for her sister's hand and squeezes it hard. "You don't want me to marry him, *Yuma*," she says.

Her mother peers at her quizzically, as if she has just said she wants to convert to Christianity.

"I don't? What are you saying? Your father chose that man for you."

Hind shakes her head, struggling not to show her heart cracking. "Abdulla is your father's favorite nephew." Hind swallows.

"He's gay."

Lisa ushers Khalid out of the room. Her father looks as though he has been struck by a flying object. Noor loses all power of speech and can only stare open-mouthed at Hind, unable to contradict her.

"There were rumors after Fatima's death," Saoud says, the first to speak. "No man has that much discipline to be away from women for so long."

Her mother starts reciting Qur'anic verses.

Hind closes her eyes; it is done. By tomorrow everyone in Qatar, half the UAE, as well as Saudi and Bahrain, and anyone with relatives abroad, will know she is not marrying Abdulla. Because her cousin prefers men. She keeps herself from thinking about the person who might be most affected in this scenario, because she doesn't know whether what she feels for him is pity or hatred. Or both.

After dinner in silence, her mother insists they must go to a friend's wedding reception, reasoning that in light of the recent news, Hind has to present herself publicly on her best form.

"But I don't feel like going out," Hind protests as the hairdresser arrives. Her mother and sister ignore her, one busy with her nails and the other taping on false eyelashes.

"The only excuse we have for not going is your wedding one day from now," her mother retorts. No one has to say, *"which isn't happening"*, though the thought races around the room.

"I have nothing to wear," Hind tries, after her hair has been curled into cascading waves down her back. Noor gives her a once-over and brings out all the dresses she thinks might fit.

"You've gotten fat," her mother comments, as Lisa tries vainly to pull up the zipper on a yellow chiffon number that can hardly be considered a dress, it is so short. *Why even bother responding*, Hind thinks, since "fat" is a word Arab women throw around indiscriminately.

"Student life," Hind says with a shrug, bending over and raising her arms so Lisa can yank the strapless yellow gown off over her head.

"Good thing you aren't getting married this weekend," Noor says.

For a second Hind catches her breath, as if a tiny dagger were twisting in her ribcage. She meets her mother's watchful gaze, and then forces a rueful smile for her sister.

"Yes, there are blessings in everything, *al-hamdu-lillah*," Hind says, praising God as she is supposed to do in everything. And isn't that what the failed engagement is, a blessing in disguise? But why does she feel such a growing knot in her stomach?

They finish their preparations, shooing Khalid away when he and their father wander in from the men's wedding party, which finishes before the women's has even started. Their *abayas* cover their Oscar-worthy glamour as the women leave Lisa alone for the night and climb into the car so Ramzan can drop them at the Sheraton.

As the car whizzes up the Corniche, past the water lapping in the manmade inlet, and her mother and Noor chat about who else is likely to be at this wedding, Hind tries to remember how she arrived at this moment. Her degree, her year in London, hasn't changed her life at all. In fact, the minute she set foot back in Doha it was as if she had never left. The social obligations, the family drama—all of it just as she left it. The only thing different is that now it is Hind who is the cause of the drama. And if anyone ever finds out the real cause of her failed engagement, even more tongues will be wagging.

Chapter 31

Sangita sleeps the rest of the day away, worn out from her confrontation with Hind and sensing that she probably won't miss much anyway for the next few hours. Evening, that's when Hind said Doha comes alive again during the summer.

The sunset call to prayer rouses her, the *adhan* ringing out from a webpage she left open while comparing Islamic practices in North Africa with those of the Gulf States. All of this research will go into her next blog post about the Arabian Gulf. After only a few days, the page has already received several hundred hits and comments from people interested in the Middle East, her target audience.

When she glances at the clock she realizes she's going to be late. Sangita showers and pulls on leggings and a light tank top. She has the heavily embroidered *abaya* to wear over both to dinner.

Abdulla is waiting for her at the bottom of the building. Outside, a blue Range Rover idles with an anxious-looking young woman in the passenger seat. Sangita crosses the marbled lobby, glad once again for the *abaya* that hides her from the prying eyes of the South Asian guards, who gawk at the sight of her greeting a Qatari man.

"Hi," she says.

"Hello," he says.

They pause for an awkward moment, aware of the camera in the lobby and the guards at the reception desk.

"I need to talk to you," he says.

She glances at the girl in the car, who she surmises is Abdulla's cousin, impatiently waiting for them.

"The blog," he says.

He has her full attention now.

"You're posting about Arabian women and dress," he says. "What am I supposed to do all day while you're at work?"

From the look on his face she can tell it came out more harshly than she intended.

Abdulla sighs.

"I knew this was a bad idea," she mutters. Standing in the lobby, covered from head to toe, she has never felt so exposed.

He takes her hand and the gesture in public surprises her.

"I know this is hard," he says. "But remember, if you're going to make a life here you don't want to make waves."

"I can't make a life here if I'm shut up in an apartment all day." He squeezes her hand.

"I've got to work on a few things to get you out of there," he says. "But in the mean time, at least Lulu can show you around."

"I can keep posting?"

"Under an alias," he says.

She feels buoyed by their resolving a disagreement, however small, with a compromise. Under the gaze of the guards, Sangita gets into the back seat of a car driven by a Qatari, which from their animated chatter she imagines will be gossip fodder for the rest of the evening. Luluwa, her face beaming with delight and triumph, takes Sangita by both hands, twisting around from the front seat, kissing her on both cheeks in rapid succession and squeezing her into an awkward hug.

"Why is that guy flashing us?"

Abdulla pulls the car into the next lane as a white SUV speeds past them.

"Everyone's always in a hurry," he mutters under his breath. "You could kill someone going that fast."

"People do."

They share a glance. Sangita remembers the night he told her about Fatima, the night that put everything in motion. As if he is also remembering, Abdulla squeezes her knee.

"This is so romantic," Luluwa whispers to Sangita when Abdulla takes a call on the car's speakers. "Abdulla has never done anything like this before."

"Tell me what he normally does," Sangita says. She feels like giggling in the presence of the younger girl, which comes as a relief after the tension of the day and the loneliness of the apartment.

"Oh, he's like a stone, this one," Luluwa replies.

"Luluwa," Abdulla says, his eyes meeting Sangita's in the rearview mirror. "Remember our terms for this dinner."

Luluwa sticks her tongue out at him before flipping down her mirror to give Sangita her own look.

"See what I mean?"

At a stoplight Sangita feels the weight of stares on her neck, as though of a crowd. She turns her head and finds a wall of eyes—men hunched in an out-of-date school bus, their dusty blue overalls identical to those she has seen on workers finishing a new tower at The Pearl. Thirty or so men crammed into what she would refer to as "the short bus" at home with her friends, and they are all Indian.

Thankfully the lights change and Luluwa asks her a question, giving her an excuse for turning away. They arrive at Chili's, a location that surprises and comforts Sangita. Like the McDonald's, Applebee's and Dairy Queen they have passed, it is a small piece of home, her other life in America.

"Lots of American chains," Sangita says as they pile out of the Range Rover. On the way in, they pass a family coming out, including a small boy who can't be more than six years old, basically waddling along in his child's version of a *thobe*.

Sangita pushes another tortilla chip into her mouth as Luluwa tells her about the big fight she's having with Noor.

"She just doesn't get that you're so much better for him," Luluwa says intensely, patting Sangita on the hand.

Great, so I'm the corrupter of all Qataris' lives, not just Abdulla's, Sangita thinks, remembering the look of rage on Hind's sister's face. She is starting to understand all the articles she's read where people rail against observers upsetting the environments in which they work. First Hind runs off to India, and now Abdulla breaks off their engagement. Sangita can't really explain to herself why she didn't try harder with her friend to explain the rush of emotions that led to her being here. Or whether she would give Abdulla up if Hind said that's what she wanted. But one thing is clear: Hind forfeited her fiancé when she left him for her "adventure." That would be the same in any culture.

"I love Bollywood," Luluwa is saying as Abdulla joins them at the table. "Have you ever met anyone famous?"

"Well, no, I grew up mostly in the U.S.," Sangita explains, despite herself. "But my parents wanted us to remember we were Indian, so we watched movies all the time. What's your favorite?" She feels her heart warming to the girl, thinking how they could teach each other about their respective cultures, these feelings warring with Ravi's reminders to be cautious. Gratefully, she is taken in by Luluwa, who strikes her as delightful. She bubbles with the artless enthusiasm of a girl on the brink of becoming a woman.

"You are not such a rebel," Luluwa says, pointing a French fry in Abdulla's direction. "*Yadd* Jassim would be happy she's Indian."

"Luluwa," he warns in exasperation. "We're supposed to be showing her the city."

"He would agree, that's all I'm saying."

"Agree to what?" Sangita looks from one to the other, but after another look from Abdulla Luluwa shakes her head.

Abdulla keeps eating, but Sangita enjoys the banter between siblings and tries not to think of Ravi. If she goes through with this thing, either Ravi or her father will have to sign the agreement on her behalf. They will have to come here. She starts to flush, remembering her mother's shock as she tried to explain the events of the past two weeks in a Skype call to her parents.

෧

Two days later, as the fog of jet lag lifts, Sangita finds herself on a girls' afternoon out with Luluwa and one of her friends. The teenagers, much more sophisticated in their fashion sense than most of the adult women Sangita knows, chat about hairstyles, colors of makeup, and shoes, adjusting their clothes and double-checking their lipstick in the car with Luluwa's driver Narin as he takes them all to the salon. Arabs, like Asians, never do anything alone, and for once Sangita is grateful for the company as she enters the imposing salon, drifting behind the girls past the *Ladies Only* sign at the entrance. She has been scribbling notes to herself about the love of all things designer. From their shoes, to handbags, to earrings, these girls are decked out in a way that makes Sangita realize Hind toned down for life in London. The comparison brings her the title of her next blog post, something about locals abroad and at home. She writes furiously, trying to keep track of all her ideas, wondering if there is a book somewhere in all of this material.

Inside, the *abayas* come off and are draped onto hangers. Yards and yards of hair are shaken out from underneath the *shaylas*. Sangita tries not to gape at these statuesque young women who, underneath their modest robes, are wearing only halter tops and micro minis. Luluwa and her friend move on into the salon itself as Sangita takes in the other female clients, women whom she may have passed in cars on the way here, though she wouldn't have recognized them wearing their *abayas* and *shaylas*. Filipino women in white uniforms are seating

Luluwa and her friend in black leather swiveling chairs.

In the waiting room, a row of women in various colored uniforms and headscarves sit with arms folded, looking straight ahead, several of them minding very small children. Sangita remembers conversations with Hind about the never-ending service in Qatar, much of it South Asian, as she's already seen from Luluwa's driver.

Everyone at the desk turns to her, and a Lebanese woman with dyed blonde hair and fake nose (Hind warned her about the noses)

eyes her with suspicion. Luluwa hovers at Sangita's side to ensure she receives proper care thereafter, but the woman's *assumption (Nanny? Maid?)* and then double-take lodge in Sangita's mind. The girls fan out in one corner of the salon, chatting easily about Qatari life so as to prepare Sangita for the gauntlet of female family members she may run that evening if Abdulla's talk with his mother goes well.

"What should I know?" Sangita asks as the Lebanese hairdresser starts combing out her hair.

"Stand up every time someone comes into the room," Dana says, as the woman working on her begins brushing out her hair. "And don't touch any men, not even his uncles."

Sangita pauses from taking notes as the hairdresser jerks her head backward to reach the crown of her scalp. Tears come to her eyes from the action.

"Dana, that's not true," Luluwa says, squinting at her friend. "Greeting the uncles is fine. But why would they be there?"

Dana leans over to confer with Sangita, her legs outstretched as a Filipino woman gives her a pedicure. Sangita leans back, taking in everything Dana has to say, ignoring the *tsking* sound of the Lebanese hairdresser, who is blow-drying her newly-cut hair into waves around her face.

"In India, if you're on your period you can't touch anyone," she confides. "That is, if you haven't had a bath." The girls break out in giggles.

Her mother's family being very traditional, Sangita had to sleep on the floor and be the first to rise on those mornings, first washing the clothes she had slept in, then her body, before anyone else could see her. When he was a boy, Ravi didn't understand why he wasn't allowed to sleep near Sangita certain nights during their summer visits to India. One morning, as she went outside to throw away her used pads, she ran into her uncle on the way back into the house. The thought that he knew what she had been up to and the reason for her being up so early made her blush furiously.

"What kind of job do you think I could get here?" Sangita asks when it is her turn for a pedicure. "I was thinking about AlJazeera English."

"You're going to work?" Dana says, glancing at Luluwa. Luluwa is looking at Sangita with interest.

"Well, what else would I do?"

"Have babies," both girls say simultaneously.

Sangita can't help breaking into laughter and apologizes to the Filipino woman who is trying to cut her toenails. She realizes that Dana and Luluwa aren't joining in. Have babies. They are in earnest.

"But I have a master's degree," she says.

"There aren't that many female-only offices left," Dana says with a sigh. "Only in the government, and those go mainly to Qataris, not foreigners."

"Dana," Luluwa warns. She's about to say more when the plump Indian technician indicates it is her turn to have her eyebrows threaded.

"Even AlJazeera is under Qatarization," Dana says, as if in contemplation.

"An office with only women?" Sangita says, pulling a notebook out of the designer handbag Luluwa gave her that morning so that she wouldn't "embarrass herself".

"What's Qatarization?"

"Getting more Qataris into the workforce to balance all the foreigners," Dana says.

"What color would you like on your toes?" Luluwa asks Sangita, while shooting her friend a look.

Scribbling notes to herself about the whole exchange with Dana, the girl's tone and her warnings, Sangita notices the designer bags on the tables in front of the other customers. The various shades and styles of leather explain why Luluwa thought Sangita might like to carry another purse in place of the *Bitch* magazine tote bag she had slung over her shoulder earlier that morning.

"They're domesticating me," Luluwa said, passing Sangita a red number in leather with a small smile. "I didn't think I'd pass on the favor."

"You've got to tell me about everything," Sangita said, returning the smile. "I've no idea what I'm doing."

The confession, even if only to a teenager, felt like a weight off her shoulders.

"Your life here will not be easy," Dana says, leaning over Luluwa's seat, pressing Sangita's forearm. "His family may not accept you; they will disown him. There will be no money."

Sangita is unnerved by the intense look on the girl's face, all sense of playfulness gone in the downward turn of her mouth, as though underlining her point.

"I'm not here for money," she stammers, and breaks eye contact with them. Sangita tries to ignore the nagging idea that this is what Abdulla's family might think.

"My father owns a hotel chain," Sangita says, raising her chin. "I paid for my own ticket here."

"Then why do you need a job?"

"What?" Sangita is speechless.

Dana settles back against her chair as the stylist begins teasing her hair into a fashionable bun.

"If you get homesick, will you try to take your kids with you?"

Sangita can't form an intelligible reply, simply because thoughts that far in the future haven't yet occurred to her. The idea of not working, of staying at home and having babies, is one thing she and Abdulla haven't discussed, one on a long list of things Ravi would probably say she was foolish for not thinking about. But a country where women don't work because they don't have to? Can she really see herself here?

"All done!" Luluwa says, returning to the main room, her perfectly arched brows showing no sign of enhancement. Her phone begins blaring a Justin Bieber ringtone, which she catches just before the chorus. Rapid-fire Arabic in dialect, and she is squirming in her seat.

"We're going," she says, sliding the phone closed with a click. Dana and Sangita exchange glances.

"Who?" Dana asks, as if speaking to a child.

"Abdulla says we'll go over in his car and wait for his call to go into the house."

Sangita draws in a deep breath. Of course this is a necessary step if their relationship is going to be official, the only way they can have any relationship at all in Qatar. But if they are all like grown-up Danas... Sangita hopes Luluwa is more representative of the women in Abdulla's family.

"If someone offers you something to drink, take it, even if you aren't thirsty," Luluwa says, launching a litany of advice that lets Sangita know she is nervous for her. Sangita is glad of the girl's presence. She was skeptical when Abdulla said that they could count on Luluwa. But thus far the girl has kept her opinions on their plans to herself and been the soul of Arab hospitality, sharing clothes, *abayas* and company.

Until now, Sangita has been relying on the commonalities of Arab and South Asian culture. Being raised South Asian, she knows without having to be told, for instance, that the hostess is always offended if you don't clear your plate and ask for at least seconds, if not thirds. It almost seems that life as an Indian has prepared Sangita for entry into Qatari society. Other than the fact that women cover their hair and pray five times a day, she can't make out any visceral differences.

Many of her cousins have had to do the same kind of sneaking around she is doing with Abdulla to make their parents think the boy they've met in college is the best bridegroom around, dropping hints about his family or likely high position after graduation to pique parental interest. What is the difference between a marriage arranged by matchmakers and one introduced by fate?

"Is this what your women's liberation is about?" her mother was always asking her as Sangita and her college friends came home for Thanksgiving break, their stories of the semester full of who was seeing whom and when a ring was expected. "We want love too, Ma," she would say, as the girls passed around photos of the latest sorority ball.

"You want everything," her mother would say, but not angrily, and she would take a look at the photos when they reached her.

Sangita never had more than a semester's flirtation with anyone. Ravi often accused her of going through men like he went through gym shoes for his various sports. There never seemed to be anyone, Indian or American, who could keep up with her quest for adventure and travel and interest in other cultures. Never, that is, until she met Abdulla, the modern religious Muslim. He wasn't secular like her brother or all the other men she knew at university. Certainly not casual about love like the Brits, who would just as soon ask you to leave as stay after a night together. Here was someone who wanted a family and a profession and a partner who would build a life with him in the most unlikely of circumstances. And he also wanted real love.

She hasn't told Ravi any of this in their recent flurry of emails and phone calls. He has had issues enough with Qataris expecting people to convert in order to share their lives together.

The truth is, right now the hard stares of people as she eats with two Qataris at a restaurant, or exits the hair salon with women clad in *abayas*, is a reality Sangita isn't sure she can live with day in, day out. This culture is like an onion, she observes. Every time she thinks she understands, there is yet another layer.

Then, as if in a blink, she is in the car, on the family compound, waiting to be summoned into the sitting room with the overstuffed gilt-edged furniture Luluwa has described, to meet Abdulla's mother, and for everyone to know the news. Sangita doesn't know which is worse, the idea that she has chosen for herself the very fate her parents made sure she would never face—a prospective bride-viewing—or the fact that she actually enjoyed being fussed over at the salon in readiness for this moment.

"Don't worry, they're always late," Luluwa says before slipping out of the car. "I'll come back as soon as I can."

Sangita bites her tongue instead of replying, the spark of pain a reminder that women all over the world have to deal with mothers-in-law. If she wanted a modern romance, she should never have gotten on the plane at Heathrow.

She clasps and unclasps her hands, wearing so much makeup it is a toss-up whether she is going to an Indian wedding or a drag show. She tries not to tangle herself in the purple satin *jellabiya* Abdulla brought by the apartment this morning before going to work. She twists the heavy gold braid of the *jellabiya* sleeve and resists the temptation to bolt from the scene. Her mother would be aghast if she knew that her daughter, the proud, independent one who insisted on moving away from the family holding of hotels and making her own name in languages, was docilely sitting and waiting to be judged by a parade of Arab women.

Focus, Sangita reminds herself. *You've got to get through this first.*

Chapter 32

Anita brings in a tray laden with tiny cups for Arabic coffee, and serves first Abdulla's mother then Luluwa and her friends. Each takes a small demitasse that looks like an enlarged thimble. Luluwa follows with a serving canister not unlike the kind that keeps tea hot in India. Bending slightly, she pours the yellowish cardamom-smelling liquid, stopping just below half-way in each woman's cup. The Arabic coffee is slightly bitter, and hot, but gives her something to do with her hands, for which she is extremely grateful.

"Al salaam alaikum."

Luluwa stands up again as a gaggle of women, her aunts Wadha and Hessa and sister Noor among them, troop into the room. They stop first at Abdulla's mother, Maryam, the eldest in the family, and greet her, showing the required respect for her place in the family, then proceed down the line. Many of the women strip off their *abayas* and *shaylas*, filling the room with the scent of their oils and the sight of their waist-length black hair.

Voices of children playing and singing outside in the courtyard reach Luluwa's ears, and she hopes her new friend isn't too lonely in the car.

"Ah, for children in our own house," Abdulla's mother says loudly to no one in particular.

Luluwa studiously avoids murmuring in agreement. As the hubbub from the kids dies down, in totters a shrunken figure wearing a gold mask, the *batoola,* across her face.

Each of the women in the room goes to the shrouded figure, the grandmother, and kisses her on the head. Luluwa is next to last.

"They came to your grandfather today and said Abdulla's marriage is off. The girl called it off because he is gay and will not be a good husband."

"Gay?" his mother strangles out.

Luluwa laughs, startling everyone. She lightly pinches Noor and Dana, who flank her on each side and force wide-eyed laughs as well.

"Luluwa, it's true," Noor says.

Luluwa tosses a long lock of hair over her shoulder and shrugs, as if a rumor of homosexual deviance in the family isn't going to devastate Abdulla and the family's reputation, not to mention affect her own chance at marriage.

"People will say anything, *Yuma,* as you've always told us." Luluwa smooths a furrow out of her black linen skirt. "Abdulla changed his mind. It's his right."

"How can you say that?" Noor retorts. "My sister—"

"Don't pretend," Luluwa replies, putting a hand on her cousin's wrist and pulling her down onto the sofa. Noor tries to resist but Luluwa is insistent.

"You know as well as I do they don't want to marry each other," Luluwa hisses.

Noor throws off her grasp.

"Then he should have never said yes, instead of bringing this woman here."

The grandmother waddles towards the sofa and sits down between them. The girls straighten, neither of them looking at the other. Anita, who has been lurking in the doorway, returns with the tray of Arabic coffee. Another girl, a few years younger than Anita and dressed in a similar pink housecoat, brings out another tray, this time laden with different colored juices. Luluwa takes drinks to give to her grandmother, the echoes of her grandfather's stories in her ears. She tries again to reconcile his tale of interrupted love with the look of pride her grandmother gives to all the women in her family assembled in the room.

Everyone sits in contemplation of the various ramifications of the broken engagement. Luluwa feels her ears flaming as she lets herself think of the horrible scene at Carrefour Sangita described to her. She hadn't thought ahead to what it would be like for Noor seeing Abdulla with another woman, someone other than her sister, just as Noor had put on blinders when insisting her sister was excited about the wedding.

But to tell people he's gay? Luluwa fights the urge to curse under her breath, any curse words, even in English, or to dig her nails into Noor and ask her what on earth her sister was thinking.

Abdulla has told her to keep quiet about the roommate connection between Sangita and Hind. The only people who know they were living together, Noor and a few of Hind's other female relatives, are unlikely to come forward with that information, since it would make Hind even more the outsider for rooming not with a family member but with a complete stranger. And a non-believer at that.

The aunties each take up a glass of juice as though it were made of something stronger. Luluwa selects a blue tumbler edged with gold filigree and filled to the rim, unlike the servings of Arabic coffee, with apple juice. She swallows a big gulp, her mind racing, wondering if Noor has really come to hate her that much for supporting Abdulla and Sangita. The aunties are murmuring amongst themselves now, truly distressed, because such a rumor has ramifications for the entire family.

In the midst of all this growing chatter, Luluwa feels her constricted chest ease as she hears the familiar stride of long steps in the foyer.

"*Al salaam alaikum,*" Abdulla says.

Despite the various stages of conversation in progress, the women pause as he takes off his *na'al*, discarding the open-toed sandals at the carpet's edge, and strides to greet his mother. They clasp hands and he looks into her eyes. Luluwa can clearly see the origins of his proud, feline gaze in her facial structure.

"What is going on, son?" his mother asks with a sigh.

"*Assif, Yuma,*" Abdulla apologizes, squeezing his mother's hand, "but I have someone I would like you to meet."

He gestures to Luluwa to go outside and she rises, holding her breath. She can't hide a small, delighted grin as she heads outside.

"It's time," she squeals.

Sangita nods; she has been watching the cars arrive into the compound. She slides down from the car and follows Luluwa, who is trying her best not to break into a run. Once inside the house there is no hiding from anyone, as the sitting room has a clear sightline to the front door. This is the moment, the moment they have tried to prepare her for. Sangita walks across the room under the gaze of the aunties, their eyes roaming over the folds of her *jellabiya.*

"This is Sangita Patel," Abdulla says, "and she will be my wife."

Sangita tries not to show the shock she feels, or the thrill at the sound of these words, though the gasp from Luluwa lets her know she's not the only one who is surprised.

His mother starts to fan herself and turns away. Abdulla squeezes Sangita's arm, leaving her standing near the sofas, and follows his mother deeper into the room.

"I hear you are gay," his mother says, looking at him.

Abdulla curses under his breath. "My cousin is upset that I refused her."

His mother sits down and gestures for Anita to bring her juice from the glass serving cart. She sips her orange juice and regards him over the rim of the glass.

"Are you sure that's all?"

"Look at her," Abdulla says, gesturing toward Sangita. "She would be wasted on a gay man."

Sangita laughs with the rest of the room, but shakily, and mostly to herself. Arabs rarely mince words, and she's not pleased to be put on display. It's much worse than she imagined.

Maryam takes another sip of juice, indicating he should sit next to her. He sighs and obliges.

"Why would the girl tell this rumor?"

Abdulla massages his face with his fingertips.

"I know you don't have any, but you're not unaware of the wiles of women."

"And this one, what did she use to hook you?"

Abdulla's reaction is swift and fierce.

"I see, I want to marry a foreigner, so I must be either gay or immoral." He throws up his hands. "This country is unbelievable."

"It is your country, too," Maryam says.

His mother tries to pat his leg, but he fends her off with a sound that is part growl and part cough. She drains the remainder of her orange juice and hands the empty glass back to the hovering Anita. "She won't know our traditions," Maryam says finally. "Think of your children—our grandchildren. Will they speak Arabic? Who will show them how to behave in the *majlis*?"

Abdulla snorts again, unable to help himself even in front of his mother.

"Traditions. You sit around, drink *gahwa*, listen to lewd stories, and share some of your own. What's so complicated?" He shrugs.

"You, the eldest," she reproaches him. "You should have more regard for your mother. You're supposed to take my side, not force an *ajnabiya* daughter-in-law on me."

Abdulla squeezes the scar at his wrist instead of replying. He sits back and takes in his mother, her yellow *jellabiya*, see- through fabric over a close fitting white sheath underneath. The artfully applied makeup, the hair pulled back from her face, all say she has come prepared for this moment, to lay on the guilt that he doesn't feel. Not for reaching for this chance for adventure, mystery, maybe even love.

Across the room, Luluwa has been trying to keep Sangita occupied with samples of Arabic music on her iPhone. Sangita pretends to listen but, like everyone else present, she is hanging on every word being spoken across the room. Whatever is passing between mother and son, she is thankful her knowledge of Qatari dialect hasn't progressed enough for her to follow it.

"These things you mention," Abdulla says. "They are more important than my happiness?"

His mother stands.

"Stop being a woman," she says. "You've been watching too many movies."

Abdulla rises, taking her hand. "I want this one, *Yuma*."

She moves closer to him, her first-born, brushing imaginary lint from his shoulder, straightening his *ghutra*, caressing his cheek.

"It isn't like acquiring a toy, my darling. Who is this girl? Her family? Who could be better than your cousin?"

Abdulla scratches the back of his neck and tries to pull away. "I won't take her into my house," his mother says.

"Fine," he says at last, willing to give her the full drama he senses brimming behind her words. "I'm a grown man. I don't need anyone's permission. And I have my own roof."

Luluwa tries to jump in. "'*Ameti*, she's a really nice girl and I think—"

"Child, be still," Abdulla's mother barks, eyes trained on Abdulla.

He warns Luluwa with a shake of his head.

"I'm going to speak to your father." It is an announcement, loud enough for everyone in the room to hear. "You're trying to ruin the bloodline with even the first grandchild."

"Really, *Yuma*?" Abdulla replies acidly. "As though the diabetes and blindness in the other tribes isn't a warning. Don't talk to me about our purity."

He waits for a rejoinder and, when there is none, shrugs as if to say *be my guest, talk to anyone about it, everyone*. He moves toward Sangita, who is suddenly looking very fragile against the patterned furniture. She may not know exactly what they were saying, but it doesn't take a genius.

"I will not see her again," his mother warns, her voice following him across the room. "I swear to God, she won't be allowed in this house again."

"Let's go," he says to Sangita, seeing the glassy look in her eyes. Once his mother sees it, that will be all she needs to move in for the kill. Then it won't matter what language anybody uses; the conflict between his mother and his future wife will be sprawled out in the open for the entire world to see.

Hastily, they leave the sitting room and keep going, Abdulla's hand at the small of her back guiding her through the house, Luluwa trailing behind them. Sangita looks back at the doorway and sees her young ally's rigid shoulders framing her lone figure as they climb into the Range Rover.

Chapter 33

Finishing another driving lesson with Luluwa, Abdulla avoids jumping the curb, even though cars much smaller than the Range Rover are taking to the sidewalk to avoid the backup from an accident at the light. Another accident. *This country really is the pits as far as traffic is concerned*, he reflects, drumming his fingers on the dashboard.

"How do you think it went with the aunties?" he asks. "*Yuma* aside, do you think she'll grow on them?"

Luluwa casts a doleful eye on him, then pulls down the visor and pretends to fuss with her makeup.

"That bad?"

"Do you really want to do this?" she says. "The fact that they *lost your application*"—she emphasizes the phrase with air quotes—"means the council is going to deny your request to marry a non-Qatari." Abdulla is silent, knowing she's right. What is he, some kind of fool for love? Wrenching the wheel, he abandons the disciplined driving practices he learned in Europe and the more cautious approach he's taken since Fatima's accident, and takes to the curb along with the rest.

He inches the Range Rover through the intersection and they ride in silence, broken only by the melodies of Nancy Ajram,

Luluwa's favorite Lebanese singer. *Enta omri*, Nancy sings, *You are my life…*

"Everybody wants to talk about love but nobody believes in it," Abdulla says.

Luluwa adjusts her headscarf in the mirror.

"I'm doing this for you too," he says.

She laughs. "I will never be allowed to do anything like this," she says.

He pauses for a moment because, again, he knows she's right. And anyway, for now, they're focused on him. Her marriage is still a few years away.

"You don't even like Hind. She wouldn't make me laugh, remember?"

Luluwa pauses as they pull into the family compound. He will go alone on his next errand.

"This will be a hard life, Abdulla. For you and for her. Then the children. Are you sure you aren't just angry about something?"

He reaches across to throw open her door for her as she gets down.

"Life is hard, *habibti*," he says, "no matter who your parents are. You know that."

He wheels the car around and drives back into the city, through the streets, and then makes a right into a dirt parking lot in front of a tan ministry building. *Council on Marrying Foreigners* says a sign in Arabic.

He walks into the main foyer alone, wishing Luluwa was at his right elbow. Men drinking tea and thumbing newspapers exchange *salaam alaikums* with Abdulla. An assistant appears and escorts Abdulla into the manager's office, where he offers him water, tea, coffee or juice. Abdulla waves the man away, and fitfully scrolls through his email, not retaining anything he reads.

"Where is the sheikh?" he asks the tea boy when he returns. He has been sitting in the manager's office for nearly thirty minutes.

The tea boy has no clue, so Abdulla ventures into the hallway. Another tea server appears, this one in matching brown shirt and pants, and indicates with his head that Abdulla should follow him through a crisscross of hallways.

Abdulla goes over again what he will say, not implicating Hind or himself, yet still getting the result he wants: permission to marry Sangita. His first promise to Sangita, at her insistence, was not to do any harm to his cousin, her friend. His immediate reaction was to wonder why he should have to make such a promise. Of course he will do no harm. And yet everyone thinks he is destroying the family by bringing in a foreigner.

It is supposed to be easier for him as a man, since he doesn't have to give up his nationality and can still pass it on to his children. At the thought of children the hair on his neck prickles. Children are serious. They can drastically hurt or disappoint.

Perhaps Luluwa is right; he is being too hasty and all this is a delusion. But he can't know that for sure without trying. Why aren't they all just happy he's decided to marry again, like they so desperately wanted?

Will his family ever accept Sangita? Will her parents really be as supportive as she is sure they will be? Is his entire life going to be a fraud?

"Come in, come in," his Uncle Saoud is saying.

Abdulla releases his pent-up breath and forces a smile. Once he takes the first step into his uncle's office, there will be no turning back. Facing Hind's father is going to be the hardest thing he has done since boarding the plane in secret to see her.

"*Marhaba*," Abdulla says.

"*Eshlonak? Shakhbarak?*" his uncle answers. They exchange greetings, bumping each other on the nose as they are required to as close relatives.

"*Tabi shai? Gahwa?*"

Abdulla declines both tea and coffee but is served them anyway by the man who showed him into the office.

They chat for a few minutes about his family and Saoud asks about work.

"I'm here to apply to marry an *ajnabiya*," Abdulla bursts out, exhausted by the pretense.

They eye each other.

Saoud, Hind's father, who has been flipping a Montblanc pen idly through his fingers, is suddenly still.

"There's no one in your family?" he asks. This is the standard question; they both know that. It gives no indication of how the rest of the conversation will go.

"I was engaged," Abdulla says, "to someone in the family." Uncle Saoud puts the pen down and splays his fingers across the heavy teak table. The carved legs give away its origin as Indian.

"And what happened?"

This is the moment Abdulla has dreaded. No one else in the family has bothered asking him because they know him to be bullheaded and private. He hasn't even told Luluwa. "We aren't suited," he says carefully.

"Because she's a woman?"

Abdulla gives his uncle a blank stare.

"My daughter tells me that you—"

Abdulla stands up. That bitch has destroyed his name in order to save her own, and now he's hearing it from her father. His pulse thuds in his ears. He knows he could ruin the rest of Hind's life and reputation by simply stating the truth of her Indian escapade. No more study abroad, or even going out of the house without a chaperone. Her father would have no choice.

"I'm trying to avert a divorce like so many of my friends. I'm doing us all a favor."

They size each other up; silence reigns.

"You have hurt her," Saoud says finally, uncapping his pen and pulling a government form towards him. "Any damage you are trying to avoid has already been done."

They stand silently as he signs the piece of paper that will start Abdulla on his journey to being Sangita's husband.

The assistant who served the tea comes back into the room. Ceremoniously he receives the completed form from Saoud and hands it to Abdulla.

"Go with Rajesh," his uncle says, rubbing his forehead. "He'll show you where the typist is."

Abdulla waits, finding his throat full of feeling but empty of words.

"Go," his uncle says, shooing him as he would a stray cat. "It is God's will."

"*Mashkoor.*" Abdulla thanks him, and follows the worker to initiate the first in a series of Byzantine documents.

⌒

Hind is watching *Toy Story 3* for the umpteenth time with Khalid when they hear the sound of their father's truck in the courtyard.

"Baba's home," Khalid yells to no one in particular.

"*Al salaam alaikum,*" Saoud says to the room at large.

"*Alaikum al salaam,*" Hind and Khalid answer.

Saoud sits next to Hind. She pauses the movie, surprised by this familiarity.

"You need anything, *Yuba*?" she asks, wondering what favor she needs to do for Noor at school this time. Since her return, even with her master's degree, this trivia is all the family seems to think she's useful for.

"Khalid, let me and your sister talk."

Khalid spins off in a huff, muttering how no one in the house ever wants to treat him like an adult. The maid, Dina, brings red tea and juice on a tray, setting it on the low table before them.

"Hind," he says, and pauses, as though searching for words. "You don't love your father?"

Hind spits out her tea and stares at him in disbelief. "Why, Baba? What are you saying?"

"Isn't it my responsibility to find you a good man and get you settled?"

Without replying, Hind focuses on placing the teacup on its saucer.

"I know everything," Saoud says with a heavy sigh.

Hind's mind races. The gay story had been a risk, but she had counted on... what, exactly, she can't name. Abdulla's goodness? Sangita's influence? She can't think of her friend without a grimace.

Can he have found out about India?

"I'm your father, Hind. If there was a problem with the boy, you should have come and told me. I would have done something."

Hind chews her lip. Of course her father knows everything, even that Abdulla is marrying again, and to a foreigner. She has been away too long, forgetting how all roads are connected in Qatar.

"He's obviously not gay," her father is saying.

Hind contemplates her options in the growing silence.

"I know everything," he repeats. "You might as well tell me why. I didn't force you into this marriage."

"No one ever really said there were other options."

"What?"

"He just seemed the best. The best of the worst."

"So the family's reputation pays the price?"

He is now standing directly over her, looking for the first time in her life as though he might lay hands on her.

"I wasn't sure I wanted to marry him," she whispers. "I didn't mean to hurt anyone. Just take a chance at my own life."

Her father has produced a set of yellow prayer beads that click as they pass through his fingers. It is the only sound between them.

"Well, he's marrying someone else. So you won't have to worry about him any more." Hind doesn't know whether to laugh or to scream. Her throat closes at the look in her father's eyes, as if she is a stranger who has wandered into his house.

"I want to be happy," she manages, sobs rolling through her. She starts to shake convulsively, part in horror, part in relief that her secret is out.

"This is not how we solve our problems, habibti."

She makes to leave the room, but his bulk blocks her in the arched entry. As she tries to pass, tears stream unchecked down her face.

Her father reaches an arm out, not to slap or pull her by her hair, as is his right, but to fold her into his side. With one hand, he brushes first one, then another tear from her cheek. The other grips her wrist. They are eye to eye, she in her heels, he meeting her gaze unflinching.

"You may not find what you are looking for," he says softly. "I don't know what is on this path you are on."

He releases her then, and opens his muscular arms to her like so many days in her childhood when he willed her to tell him of how she came to have scraped knees or rips in her clothing. Sobbing, she clambers into his embrace, knowing that unlike then, now there are many things she can never tell him.

Chapter 34

Sangita presses against her window, forehead on glass, looking down at the manmade ring of islands that unfurl around her seventeen stories below. Cranes jut into the air and men in blue overalls clamber over the high-rise scaffolds of The Pearl, the perennially unfinished luxury compound where Abdulla has ensconced her like a secret concubine. Since coming to Qatar nearly a month ago, she has seen Abdulla only in snatches, or talked on the phone late into the evening. They spend time together, but always in the presence of someone else, Luluwa, or strangers when in public. She can hear the fatigue in his voice when he comes back after his tenth trip to the Ministry of Interior to submit her papers.

"You look amazing, *masha'Allah*."

Sangita turns from the window to see Luluwa in the apartment's entryway. She had forgotten that the girl has her own key and is used to coming and going from this place, as it used to be her sister's apartment.

She smiles faintly. This is not how she had pictured getting married—alone, in a foreign country, waiting for her in-laws to come and get her. *Is it worth it?* The fluttering in her stomach when she thinks of him, the urge to wish the day gone so that he will come to her with news, with comfort?

Two days ago, on the phone with her parents, she tried to tune out the predictable semi-hysteria in her mother's voice.

"What do you know about these people?"

"Ma," she sighed. The irony wasn't lost on her that Abdulla's mother asked virtually the same thing.

"Your mother asks a very good question," her father intoned from the line in the kitchen. She pictured them facing each other, one on the cordless, one on the wall phone, gaping at each other in confusion. It was Ravi these phone conferences had previously focused on. Ravi was the one that everyone wanted to restrain from his wild adventures, yearning to climb Everest or spend a year doing yoga at the foot of the Hindu Kush mountains.

"They're tied to one of biggest real estate companies in Qatar," Sangita said, just as she had practiced it with Abdulla. "Qatari Diar. They have projects all over the world."

"Qatari Diar?" Her father. "We've got one of their contracts in Mauritania. It's backed by the government."

Sangita crossed both her fingers. If her father weighed in on her side, her mother was sure to follow.

"So they have money," her father said.

"Yes. Yes."

"But," her mother hesitated, "but they…"

"They're Muslim," Sangita said. "But so what?" she ventured, hoping to strike home quickly at the issue. "You're not even religious. Who cares that he's a Muslim? I was raised a Hindu. Do you really care?"

"I'm coming there," her mother wailed. "I'm coming out on the first flight I can get."

"Ma, I'm almost twenty-five years old," Sangita shot back, playing her wild card. "I thought you'd be glad that I'm getting married to anyone."

"How can you say that!" Her mother burst into tears.

"It's our responsibility to find you a good husband," her father said, and Sangita could tell from the diminished sound of the sobbing that he had grabbed the phone away from her mother. "We have failed you."

"But Dad, it's the same principle you raised me with," she pleaded, trying to soothe them. "Abdulla's a good man, from a good family. We're committed to each other."

"I've got an exploratory meeting about a new hotel for the World Cup," her father said. "It was to be a video conference, but I'm going to insist they bring me out there. Don't sign anything until I get there."

"I'm going to convert and marry him."

After that Sangita clicked off the phone and flopped back onto the bed.

Since then she has been snatched up in a whirlwind of preparations—first a quick tour of the city that is to be her home, then endless beauty treatments to get ready for the engagement.

She won't have to worry about the party. That's his family's responsibility, so he'll basically do the entire thing. Occasionally there are snatches of progress. The flowers will be red, because Abdulla knows that it's not only her favorite color but also important to Indian brides. The tablecloth will be gold, a proper contrasting color and worthy of Bollywood.

Luluwa supervises all her personal preparations, which necessitate a trip through all six of the country's malls to find the perfect dress. From sequins to satin, Sangita is thrown back to her high school prom and the search for *the* gown. Finally they decide on a red sari that Abdulla's aunt, who owns a tailor shop, will have altered into a strapless dress.

She wishes she had someone a little older to ask advice of, but having run off to England she missed all her close friends' weddings. She stands now, facing Luluwa, her hands at her sides.

"You are radiant," Luluwa says, clasping her hands to her chest. Her *abaya* hangs open and Sangita can see the low-cut black dress her future in-law is sporting.

Suddenly, from the half-open apartment door: "Yes, you are, *masha'Allah.*" Both women whirl around at the sound of Hind's voice. Sangita's instinctive reaction is a squeal of delight, which she instantly stifles, reminding herself that this is the very same woman who spread deadly rumors about her soon-to-be fiancé.

"Hind?" Luluwa says, as though she can't believe her eyes. Hind crosses into the room.

"Can you give us a minute?"

Luluwa looks uncertainly between the two until Sangita smiles to reassure her. Reluctantly, she walks out, but not before looking back at them twice. Sangita knows she will be on the cellphone to Abdulla even before her feet touch the hallway carpet.

"Hello." Sangita moves to her as if it is the most natural thing in the world that they are meeting in this apartment, in Hind's country, even though they haven't spoken in weeks.

"Sangita," Hind says, and they embrace in the way of Qatari women, kissing several times on the right cheek only.

After this formal intimacy they stand staring at each other without anything to say.

"You're really going through with this?" Hind says after a moment.

Sangita nods. "I've never known anyone like him," she says, knowing she's speaking of her friend's former fiancé. "And we have as a good a chance as anyone."

Hind wanders over to the window, now taking in the view that a moment ago was Sangita's.

"I was angry," she admits. "But I don't envy you this life. It will be hard. Harder than mine, even as a reluctant wife."

Sangita sinks into the sofa. "What is it you want, Hind?" she asks, watching her friend, who now seems so different.

Yes, something about her has changed, Sangita thinks. She seems transformed by the darkness of her *abaya,* contained and shaped, far removed from the free spirit who ran off to India a month ago and set their lives on this mad course. Her face seems older, although there are no lines showing. There is a stillness about her, and Sangita realizes it is because the smile, Hind's ever-present smile, is nowhere in sight.

"I want what you want," Hind says.

"No. If you wanted him, you had him," Sangita says.

As Hind turns from the window, Sangita thinks she almost sees a spark of the old Hind: loud, feisty, full-volume if angry. She braces for whatever might come next— cold fury, hot rage- but instead of turning on her, Hind sinks down onto the sofa next to her.

"No," Hind replies. "I want to be happy," she says softly, tracing designs on the suede surface.

Sangita takes in her friend's downcast eyes; this close she can see the veins underneath her eyes and the bent corners of her mouth.

"And what is that?" Sangita asks, leaning her head against Hind's arm. They are talking again, just like before in their tiny London flat.

Hind sighs, and Sangita can feel the weight of her friend's sadness so keenly that tears come to her own eyes. She reaches out and takes Hind's hand. It feels cold and brittle in her own. "I'm a woman," Hind says, looking past her onto the view of The Pearl. "So they won't give me an overseas posting."

The two women regard each other, the months of conversations in London, speculation-filled chats about what their lives would be like after graduation, filling the air.

"And I won't get married," she says.

The irony of the reversal of their situations means they allow each other a tiny smile.

"I'll do what I can," Sangita says, squeezing her friend's hand, hoping they will eventually return to the closeness they once shared.

Yet even as she says it, she has no idea what she can do, outsider that she is in a society so similar to her own and yet so different. She has no influence to get Hind the job she covets or to rehabilitate her reputation. But all her instincts tell her that if she is to have any chance at all at happiness with Abdulla, she must make sure her friend has her chance at happiness too.

Hind leaves her alone with her thoughts and quietly withdraws.

Sangita tries to think of the most persuasive strategy to try with Abdulla, aware of how little she knows about her soon-to- be husband. *Make him think it's his idea,* her mother used to tell her when Sangita was a teenager and wanted her father's permission for an overnight school field trip. There is very little chance of that happening in this case, Sangita knows.

"Sangita, it's time to go."

Luluwa is back, with Abdulla behind her. If she was surprised earlier at seeing Hind in the apartment she gives no indication, nor does she mention their unexpected visitor. Sangita shakes her head slightly so that Luluwa will keep her distance.

"I need to talk to Abdulla alone."

He pauses from adjusting his *ghutra* in the entryway mirror. "It's good to see you," he says softly, caressing her with his eyes instead of his hands.

Her breath catches at this hard-won praise, and suddenly all the hours at the salon, weeks of examining fashion magazines and deliberations at the tailors are made worthwhile.

"I'm sorry, the traffic was terrible," Abdulla says, striding into the room. He straightens his cuff links. "I got here as soon as I could."

To have him here in front of her, resplendent in white, smelling of Hermes and talking about something as mundane as the traffic, makes the room right itself again.

"You should never rush," she replies. The knowledge of Fatima hangs between them. Just to hear his voice, her pulse steadies. She smiles, knowing her smile is trembling at the edges, showing all her teeth, despite Luluwa's admonishments that she shouldn't appear too happy and court the evil eye.

"We need to hurry, *habibti*," he says. "They are waiting for us."

From his casual manner, Sangita can't help but be painfully aware that this is in fact the third time he has done all of this. He takes his hand in hers, and a current runs from the tips of her fingers to warm her sternum. But for the bobbing of his Adam's apple, she would have thought he was entirely calm as he tilts his head towards her. She clasps her hands together to steady the trembling in her arms.

"One final thing we should discuss," she says.

"We can look for another apartment if you want," Abdulla says. "This place depresses me too."

"It's not that at all," Sangita replies with a shaky laugh. "What I want doesn't cost anything."

He arches an eyebrow.

"This should be good," he says. "You're definitely not like other women."

She lets out a nervous giggle. Maybe lighthearted is the way to go.

"I can't be happy unless I know she's also happy," she says. His gaze sharpens, his lips going from a soft smile into a straight line.

She raises her eyes, aware of the flattering effect of the false eyelashes because she has stared at her own reflection for three hours as they curled her hair. Maybe the trick is to maximize the glow of the honeymoon period. She gives his hands, entangled with hers by the fingers, a squeeze.

"What kind of life can she have here after this?" he murmurs. Neither of them needs to say who "she" is. "Your life here is what I'm worried about."

She loosens her grip on his palms.

"I'll be fine. She won't. Can't she work at an overseas embassy?"

Abdulla lets go of her completely.

"Last I heard, she thought you were a whore."

Sangita winces.

"She's still my friend," she says. "I'm the one who betrayed her trust." He snorts. At her unblinking gaze he throws up his hands in frustration. "Only the minister gives out assignments." "You could try," Sangita says. "It doesn't hurt to ask. Luluwa says you have *wasta*." He slices a hand through the air as if to stop the words as they leave her mouth. "Luluwa is a child."

"She's becoming a woman," Sangita retorts, "if you haven't noticed."

"I would lose any influence I have the minute I got involved in such a thing."

"We need to give her this," she insists, reaching for his hand again, "otherwise we won't be in the right."

He holds her hand and a shudder courses the length of his frame, either from anger or from some other emotion, she can't be sure.

"What she does with her life is no concern of mine." The flatness in his voice makes him a stranger.

"Consider it my *mahar*," she says. "Replace it with the entire dowry in my contract. The divorce settlement, even."

In response to his silence, she presses his arm.

"I don't have enough influence to do this," he says. "I would have to ask Uncle Ahmed for help. Then I would owe him."

His left hand grips her fingers where they rest on his right sleeve. His palm curls so tightly around hers she wants to cry out.

"Ask me for something else."

She takes a breath. What else does she have to bargain with? "I'm giving up everything," she says in a measured tone. The sting of the tears she is holding back makes her throat raspy.

"I'm not asking for much."

"I can't," he says. "Everyone will think it strange if I even bring her name up."

"And having an Indian wife isn't strange?" He drops her hand and paces the room, the movement familiar to her from his periods of internal debate in London.

The swish of his *thobe* punctuates his abbreviated steps, his strides limited by how far it will allow his feet to travel.

Sangita feels her heartbeat slow as tears fill her eyes. Life with an inflexible man is not what she has in mind, not when she is choosing him over everything else. Everyone else.

"Luluwa, call Narin to pick you both up."

He is gone before anyone can say another word.

Chapter 35

The smell of *bukhoor* fills the house, and to Sangita's rapidly adjusting senses it is not unpleasant.

Maryam doesn't say anything when she sees Luluwa welcoming Sangita back into the house. She hovers in the hallway muttering into her mobile as Sangita submits to the incense burner being passed around her. Sangita doesn't bother telling her soon-to-be-mother-in-law that this ritual is very similar to the *arathi* that her parents perform if they want to bless anyone or anything, a sacred light taken from the temple or puja room fire and circled around a person. She stands still as Luluwa finishes; she wills herself to stop sweating. She didn't let on in the car the source of her argument with Abdulla, though she is fairly sure Luluwa was eavesdropping.

She can't help sneaking a glance at the girl in the red brocade dress in the mirror, trying to remember that it is indeed her, she of the endless black leggings and t-shirts, staring back at herself. Sangita suppresses a shudder, a combination of longing and a twinge of fear that Abdulla will choose to be stubborn rather than secure their happiness. Yet instead of diminishing her feelings for him, the intervening hours and possibility of never seeing him again has made the longing grow.

Now she stands in his mother's house waiting to profess her faith, waiting for the moment their life together will begin.

The same as her own mother during the first meeting with her father, she can't help but remember. As the story goes, her mother's sister chastised her for looking up and smiling when entering the room. This is the reason her mother doesn't beam with happiness in the black and white wedding album, but rather looks to the side as if in silent appraisal of the man who is now her husband.

Sangita takes a deep breath and steadies herself for the moment when she will see Abdulla on this night, the night their contract will be signed. Legally, after this they will be considered married. She isn't sure how to explain this idea to anyone, and so has left most of her friends in the graduate program in the dark. Ravi is supposed to be here as the stand-in for her father, but uncharacteristically he has been incommunicado. The last flight out of New York should have brought him here by now, but in the whirl of the beauty salon and yet another round of endless preparations she hasn't had two seconds to herself. Hind showing up this afternoon after another emotionally draining conversation with her parents hasn't made her head any clearer.

"This way," Luluwa says, and takes her by the arm. "The sheikh is here."

Sangita smiles, but none of the muscles in her face moves. She glances at her watch, but in its place is a stack of gold bangles, on loan from various female members of the family. She has no way of knowing if Abdulla is late or if Luluwa is jittery in the presence of her fuming aunt.

"Alone?" Sangita's voice cracks, revealing how tense she is internally.

"He's coming," Luluwa says, and flips out her BlackBerry, typing into the BBM. Where she has room to hide the small device in her pleated red satin gown, Sangita has no idea.

Although she wasn't there, Sangita feels an odd sense of déjà vu, remembering the photos Hind showed her from her own engagement evening. Hind was radiant, even if her foundation was a few shades lighter than her skin. This is a trick all the women her mother's age also try to pull off at Indian weddings, but for tonight Sangita has insisted with the MAC makeup girl on a foundation that is true to her skin tone. If she is really going to make her life here, there is no point in pretending that she is anything other than the non-milk-white beauty that she is.

"*Ta'ghatu rajal!*"

A shriek from Maryam as a man, resplendent in a black suit with a purple shirt, strides into the sitting room. His gleaming black eyes scan the room.

"Ravi!" Sangita says, standing up despite the *tsking* from Luluwa, who has been arranging her hair for the umpteenth time. Her brother strides to her and they hug, more fiercely than she can ever remember.

"I got here fast as I could," he murmurs into her forehead, "You alright?"

She nods, and feels the lump in her throat for the first time. She squeezes his hand as he surveys the hair piled on top of her head and the three inches of gold necklaces covering her collarbone all the way to the sari border which begins the top of her dress.

"Sangita, this man shouldn't be here," Luluwa says carefully, taking care to avoid looking Ravi in the eye. She has whipped a *shayla* over her hair and as much of the upper part of her body as possible.

"This is my brother," Sangita says with a shaky laugh. How like Ravi to have upset the gender balance in the house by charging in to see if she needs rescuing.

Luluwa and her aunt relax visibly after hearing this news. "Then he should wait for the sheikh," Maryam says, indicating that Anita should show him out.

The maid's eyes climb over Sangita and her brother with such naked curiosity that she feels herself blush.

Sangita involuntarily clutches his arm. He has arrived only to be sent away from her again. He turns to her and searches her face, unsatisfied by what he sees, but she wills herself to let go and pats the place on his sleeve she has just a second ago been clutching.

"You need to talk to the sheikh," she says to him, knowing this might be the only reason he would leave her. "The papers are all waiting."

He looks down between the two of them, and then stares down the brunt of Anita's inquisitive glances before pressing a kiss on each of Sangita's cheeks. As he comes in close he whispers to her.

"You're giving up everything."

She feels her throat tighten at the fear in his eyes and the echoes of her own words to Abdulla earlier in the day.

"You'll be here, far away from your family and friends."

"I'm getting what I want," she says. She strokes the fisted hand nearest to her. He clutches her fingers in return.

"I'm just in the other room," he says. "To sign papers, or if you change your mind." This last under his breath, only to her.

She fights the lump that rises in her throat again as he leaves. Her hands hang limply at her sides now that she has lost the anchor of his solid presence next to her. Her brother, her broken-hearted brother, has come all the way to stand for her and her marriage. She reminds herself to breathe and keep her knees soft, as Abdulla told her that time soon after they first met. In the quiet of that moment she feels the heaviness of the years before, alone, a stranger in this land. Her eyes well with tears, even as she knows she can't back down now, not to hear *I told you so* from everyone in the family. There's a rustle of movement in the doorway.

"Where is Abdulla?"

For the first time, she sees his father, notices the resemblance in the angular planes of his face, the slope of his nose. Sangita opens her mouth to answer and realizes she doesn't know.

"Yuba?" Abdulla enters, close on his heels. "Come into the other room."

Abdulla stiffens. "Whatever you have to say, let's say it here."

His father's eyes flick toward Sangita and then back. "I'm sure, *Yuba*. Don't you want me to get married?"

"Don't do this to hurt us." Mohammed leans in, lowering his voice. "This is serious."

"She's not as good as a Qatari woman?" Abdulla hears Sangita's swift intake of breath.

His father looks between them, clearly embarrassed, since now they are speaking in English.

"She understands Arabic, even," Abdulla switches back. "Call my grandfather," he says.

"Son, son…" His mother now, coming between the two men, linking them with her arms. "No one disputes your right to choose."

Abdulla shakes his head impatiently. "Either you can throw me out of the family right now, or you can accept my choice," he says. "It's up to *Yaddi*."

The trio turn so they are looking at Sangita, who has settled on the teal chaise lounge. He is simultaneously relieved at her uncharacteristic silence– that she hasn't launched into one of her speeches and frustrated with himself that he can't do more to stand up for her.

"You have chosen well," *Yadd* Jassim says, his shaky frame entering the room. Mohammed helps his father to a large, padded sofa. "I wish you the happiness I never had."

"But—"

"My grandson has chosen," his grandfather says, and gives Abdulla a pinch on the cheek. He takes a much-folded piece of paper with a grainy black and white image and slips it into the breast pocket of Abdulla's *thobe*. Abdulla knows it at once as the duplicate of the one he has carried for over three years.

So his wife hadn't been able to wait, after all, to share her joy with the one person who would be even more excited than she was. Even without looking at it he knows, somehow, his grandfather has a copy of the one sonogram Fatima had of the unborn baby.

The one he found when the hospital returned her personal effects after declaring her dead. The one he has carried around for years, until now. Not a week has gone by without him taking it out from his wallet and looking at it. The last time was…some time before leaving for London, he realizes now with a shock. Nearly two months ago. His grandfather gives him a wink as Abdulla kisses the elder man's forehead.

"Your happiness," Jassim says, catching Abdulla's arm, "does not allow you to disrespect your family."

Abdulla kisses his forehead again. He turns to where Sangita sits in the room, waiting.

"Have you thought about things?" she asks, keeping her eyes trained on her hands, as aware as he is of their audience.

In the yawning silence she tries not to clutch the gilt arm of the sofa in panic. "I can't go through with this otherwise," she says.

"I don't take well to ultimatums," he replies.

"Don't punish her for wanting what we have," she says. "This is about fairness, not power."

He ducks his head and exhales forcefully.

"Your grandfather stood up for you," she says, her voice rising despite the listening ears. "How can you withhold good from someone else?"

He paces the room, avoiding her gaze. The silence between them grows into a living thing, filled with their harsh breathing.

"I'm going home," she says. "Enjoy being alone."

She stands, wondering how she can get to the door without Luluwa's help in the six-inch heels the girl insisted she wear. With the shoes, she is almost his height and returns his gaze.

"You can't leave," he says.

"Give me a reason to stay," she replies. "And it's not the conservative I fell in love with."

"I forgot about your one-liners."

He stands in the doorway, keeping her from exiting. His jaw clenches and unclenches.

"You'll get a lifetime of them if you agree," she says softly, recognizing a glimmer of the openness she saw in London.

"Promise me it will be a lifetime," he says. "Nothing less."

"I promise," she says without hesitation.

They share a shaky laugh.

"For you," he says. "Because no one negotiates like you."

"For us," she whispers. "For the future we're going to have."

They walk into the other room to seal their fate.

Chapter 36

The heavy cream envelope that Lisa brings to her at the breakfast table gives Hind pause, because it has the seal of the Emiri Diwan across the front. She carefully lays down the spoon with which she has been absentmindedly shoveling *foul* into her mouth, thinking about Noor's current obsession with what she should pack for the start of school in a few weeks. Hind has toyed with the idea of asking her father to send her as a chaperone for Noor or one of their cousins studying in the UK, but hasn't had enough courage to face him.

For the past few weeks he has come home from the office in the blackest mood, not speaking to anyone, and ignoring the servants completely, which is puzzling to the entire household. Even if he is upset with one of the children, he almost always has a nice word for Lisa or Ramzan, both of whom he regards as being among the adults of the house. No, her father has been avoiding them all, and Hind can't help feeling that it has something to do with her but he isn't ready to talk about it just yet. Or maybe ever, if it has to do with her failed alliance with Abdulla's family.

"Well, open it," Khalid says, coming through the dining room and scooping some hummus onto a slice of pita bread. Hind rolls her eyes at him.

The thing about being at home is that you are never alone. This means you have no secrets. She wistfully thinks of her days in London, which seem such a distant memory now, although it has been less than two months. If she didn't have the framed diploma hanging on her bedroom wall, just to the right of her vanity mirror, she wouldn't believe herself that she was once a girl free to come and go as she pleased.

That's why I ran away to India, she thinks to herself, avoiding eye contact with her siblings. *Because I knew I was returning to a lifetime of this.* She restrains herself from sighing or screaming at the thought of a hundred days exactly like this one rolling out before her. Sooner or later her family will ask her to consider another groom – one who will undergo even more scrutiny than the last. Or will Noor be next? She contemplates her sister, just as Noor joins them all in the dining room, rubbing sleep from her eyes.

"What's this?" she asks, her gaze going straight to the heavy cream envelope.

"A letter for the sheikha," Khalid says, coming around her and snatching up the letter.

Limply, Hind tries to swat him and get the letter back. His height, plus the fact he is already standing, puts him out of her reach.

"*Salaam alaikum*, peace be upon you... *ketha, ketha, ketha*," Noor intones, skipping the flowery Arabic introduction.

"His Excellency the Deputy Foreign Minister asks that with God's help you will serve in the position of– "

Hind is torn between interest and despair. A job for the government means sitting on the ladies' side of buildings, using only certain elevators, and getting less pay than the men. But a job would mean fewer hours at home after Noor returns to school and leaves her the only girl in the house, a prospect Hind is avoiding thinking about for any length of time.

The letter flutters from Noor's hand as she clasps Hind's shoulders.

"Position of what?" Khalid screeches, jumping up to finish the letter-reading.

"Assistant Secretary to the Qatari Ambassador in India!"

Hind feels ringing in her ears, as Khalid takes his turn to look at the letter and mutters to himself in grade school Arabic, reaching the same conclusion.

"Can I come and visit you?"

"Good luck getting *Yuba's* permission," Noor says, creating another swath in the hummus. "What can they be thinking, offering this to an unmarried girl?"

Hind's head snaps up and she regards her sister, her hip propped against the table as she chews thoughtfully.

"That's horrible," Khalid says huffily. "Hanoodie's just as qualified as anyone else in that office. She actually has a degree."

"No family would let their daughter go alone to India."

The sharp pain in her sternum agrees with Noor. Having returned from a year away, Hind doesn't think her father is likely to let her leave again.

"She could get married, then," Khalid says. "Her husband could go with her."

Hind's breath eases. Her brother has come up with the only feasible scenario to which her parents might agree. Another wedding. Another groom.

"What?" he says, as Noor stares at him blankly. "It's true. She can go anywhere with her husband."

Hind takes the letter from Noor and rises from the table, her mind whirring. What can have brought her to the minister's attention?

Her family is well known, but her father prefers to stay and serve his country from within Qatar. And Noor is right, loath as she is to admit it. They have never named a female diplomat before, much less a divorced one.

Why the sudden grace, the sudden drastic change of attitude from reputedly one of the most misogynist offices in the country? An image of Sangita comes to mind. Hind thinks of her friend, of their meeting on the night of her profession of faith. She was gorgeous. And firm.

She takes the letter upstairs to her room and presses the creases out at her vanity table. Suitcases. She will need twice the number of suitcases if she is moving abroad.

Glossary of cultural terms and Arabic phrases

Abaya: Black robe-like covering for women, worn loose to cover their bodies in front of men in public.

Adhan: The call to prayer.

'Agal: A black coiled circle of wool or cloth, used to keep a man's ghutra (worn over the head) from moving.

Ajnabiya: Foreigner (female)

Ajnabi: Foreigner (male).

Al salaam alaikum: Peace be upon you.

Allah yerhamha: May God have mercy on her, praying for mercy after a woman has died. (Allah yerhamu for a male.)

'Ameti: My (paternal) auntie.

'Ammi: My (paternal) uncle.

'Azaa: Consolation visits by close friends and relatives after a funeral.

Baba (or Yuba): Name used to refer to one's father.

Bukhoor: Small wooden pieces of incense which produce scent when placed over charcoal in the midkhan.

Darb: Warning to Qatari women to cover their hair if a non- relative male is nearby or about to enter the room.

Eid al Fitr: Holiday to celebrate the end of Ramadan (the word "Eid" is used for holidays in general).

Emir: The title used for the ruler of a country in the Arabian Gulf.

Emiri Diwan: The ruler's palace.

Gahfieh: A cap made of wool or cotton worn under the ghutra.

Garinga'o: A special night midway through the month of Ramadan during which children of the Arabian Gulf sing cultural songs, dress in traditional outfits and gather nuts and sweets from their neighbors.

Ghutra: A piece of white cotton cloth used by men to cover their heads.

Habibti: My darling (female)

Habibi: My darling (male).

Hayach: Word used to welcome someone (female)

Hayak: Word used to welcome someone (male)

Hijab: A square head-covering worn by Muslim women; also refers to the Islamic practice by which a woman covers her hair, arms, neck and hips.

Hukoomi: Relating to governmental services.

Iftar: The meal used to break the fast during Ramadan.

Insha'Allah: If/when God wills; God willing.

Insha'Allah kheir: A phrase that's said when hoping for good (kheir means good).

Inti ba'ad: Literally means "you too" or "not you as well".

Jellabiya: The traditional dress worn by Arab women at home.

Kaffan: Shroud, white grave cloth.

Khalas: Literally means that something is finished.

Khutouba: The Muslim engagement ceremony after which a couple is considered legally married.

Maghreb adhan: The sunset call to prayer.

Mahar: The dowry given to the bride by the groom.

Majlis: A place where Arab men gather, usually outside the house with a separate entrance.

Masha'Allah: Used to indicate that something is a blessing from God.

Midkhan: A traditional object used for burning incense and scenting an area.

Milcha: The day on which the marital contract is concluded between bride and groom.

Misbah: A large string of beads, usually the size of a palm, used to count prayers.

Na'al: Open-toed sandals worn by men.

Na'am: Literal meaning is "yes". Used to respond when someone calls you.

Niqab: A piece of black cloth used by Muslim women to cover their faces.

Ramadan: The holy month of fasting that is one of the five pillars of Islam.

Shayla: A rectangular head covering (usually black) used by Muslim women to cover their hair and worn in the Arabian Gulf along with the abaya.

Sheikh: Title of respect for an important person, leader or religious figure (used in Qatar in place of mulla). Can also indicate a person is royalty or closely related to royalty. (Sheikha for females.)

Souq: Shopping area or market.

Sura: A chapter of the Qur'an.

Thobe: Formal white dress with long sleeves, for men from the Arabian Gulf.

Ubooy: My father.

Ummi: My mother.

Wallah: I swear to God.

Wasta: The amount of influence a person may have.

Ya waldi/Ya benti: An expression of endearment, meaning "Oh my son/Oh my daughter".

Yaddi: My grandfather.

Yadd: Grandfather.

Yalla: A slang word meaning "Let's go" or "Come on".

Yuma: Name used to refer to one's mother.

Yuba (or Baba): Name used to refer to one's father.

Zamzam: Sacred water from Mecca.

Qatari Names

Abdulla

Ahmed

Amal

Dana

Fatima

Haya

Hessa

Hind

Jassim

Khalid

Luluwa

Maryam

Mohammed

Noor

Nouf

Saad

Saoud

Wadha

About the Author

Mohanalakshmi Rajakumar is a South Asian American who has lived in Qatar since 2005. Moving to the Arabian Desert was fortuitous in many ways since this is where she met her husband, had a baby, and made the transition from writing as a hobby to a full time passion. She has since published eight e-books including a mom-ior for first time mothers, Mommy But Still Me, a guide for aspiring writers, So You Want to Sell a Million Copies, a short story collection, Coloured and Other Stories, and a novel about women's friendships, Saving Peace.

Her recent books have focused on various aspects of life in Qatar. From Dunes to Dior, named as a Best Indie book in 2013, is a collection of essays related to her experiences as a female South Asian American living in the Arabian Gulf. Love Comes Later was the winner of the Best Indie Book Award for Romance in 2013 and is a literary romance set in Qatar and London. The Dohmestics is an inside look into compound life, the day to day dynamics between housemaids and their employers.

After she joined the e-book revolution, Mohana dreams in plotlines.

Learn more about her work on her website at
www.mohanalakshmi.com or
follow her latest on Twitter: @moha_doha.

www.ingramcontent.com/pod-product-compliance
Lightning Source LLC
Chambersburg PA
CBHW031315170626
46807CB00001B/431